AND OTHER MISTAKES

ERIKA TURNER

FEIWEL AND FRIENDS
NEW YORK

To my love, for always encouraging me to move forward.
And, to AJR: We got through it, y'all.

This story is a work of fiction. However, it deals with many real issues, including depression, homophobia, self-harm, alcoholic and abusive parent, suicide ideation, and references to non-consensual outting.

A Feiwel and Friends Book
An imprint of Macmillan Publishing Group, LLC
120 Broadway, New York, NY 10271 • fiercereads.com

Our books may be purchased in bulk for promotional, educational, or business use. Please contact your local bookseller or the Macmillan Corporate and Premium Sales Department at (800) 221-7945 ext. 5442 or by email at MacmillanSpecialMarkets@macmillan.com.

Library of Congress Cataloging-in-Publication Data is available.

First edition, 2023
Book design by Angela Jun
Feiwel and Friends logo designed by Filomena Tuosto
Printed in the United States of America

ISBN 978-1-250-83484-3 (hardcover)
1 3 5 7 9 10 8 6 4 2

"If I don't get out of this town,
I just might be the one
to finally burn it down."
—"Caution" by The Killers

WELCOME
TO FABULOUS
LAS VEGAS

CHAPTER 1

This Bug is dying, and hideous, and should've been sold for parts years ago. That's why the damn thing is stalled for the hundredth time at a green light fifteen minutes from school—but I keep my mouth shut. One word (again), and Marissa will definitely make me walk to practice. Instead, I throw my feet on the dash and wait while she curses back at the six cars that honk and drive around us. I have no idea how manual cars work, but after some magic with the clutch and gear shifts, the engine roars to life and the whole Bug finally lurches forward.

"Heeey!" she cheers, and I brace myself against the seat.

"Marissa. You know the speed limit is forty, right?"

"Do you want to be late, dude? No, I didn't think so." She sticks her tongue out at me, but her face, covered with thick black sunglasses, is toward the road, so her tongue flies to the side like a puppy's. With the windows down, her fire-hydrant-red hair whips around the Bug, hitting me in the face. I should mind, but it only makes me smile.

We've only been friends for, like, four months, but it feels like it's been an eternity. Our chemistry teacher paired us up for a class project last semester, and when we exchanged numbers, I explained that my house was off-limits because my dad is a drunken rage-monster. Then she explained that her mom would either be "too hungover to bother us or sober enough to be fucking her boyfriend in Summerlin."

We've been inseparable ever since.

Now it's June, and our junior year has *finally* ended . . . which means today is the start of our new training season. I lean out the window, away from her wild mane, and she puts her hand on my leg. Even with the rush of the wind from the window and the ever-present hum of her engine, she can probably hear the loud thud of my heart. It's been eight months since I ran cross-country. Eight months since I felt the sun sear into my skin and I raced with the wind. Now we're on our way to the school's field and I'm about to face my teammates for the first time since Coach stripped me of my title as captain last November.

Yaaay.

We pass the casino by our school in five minutes when it should've taken ten and veer left onto Las Vegas Boulevard. Since it's a Saturday in June, the parking lot is mostly empty, except for the cars that I assume belong to our fellow runners. When Marissa puts the car in park, I take a deep breath and give her my best serious look. "So. You sure you want to do this?"

She scoffs. That was not the question she was expecting to hear. "What do you mean?" She lifts her sunglasses off her head and shakes out her hair, so that it settles into less of a mane and more of a cascade of very loose curls. Her natural hair is a much lighter strawberry blond, but the deep red reminds her of Batwoman and pisses off her mom, so she's been rocking that look since May. She tried to convince me to dye my hair something shocking—like electric blue—to celebrate the end of the year, but my mom would've been far more than pissed. Then again, it's been months since Mom and I have had any kind of argument. Now, she just sort of glares at me occasionally. A snippy word here or there. I don't know if she doesn't care anymore, or if she's just tired. I guess I put her through a lot last year.

Which is fine. She put me through a lot, too.

I shrug, careful not to smile. "I just mean that cross-country is intense. It takes a lot of stamina, and it's going to be a lot different than—"

"Yeah, Aali, I know." Marissa waves me away. "Cross-country is for hard-core badasses, and track is for thrill-seeking pussies. I get it. I'm still totally in. Like I've said a million times already: If I don't do something after school this semester, my mom is gonna make me work part-time as some stupid promotional model on the Strip. Again." Then she fixes me with a cool stare, her eyebrow raised. "And what about you?"

"What about me?" I keep my voice level, annoyed that my attempt at diversion didn't work.

"Are you ready to kick ass this year?" Her voice is kind, but her words make my lungs want to seize. Am I ready? The last thing Coach said to me was, "I know you can do better." That was only two months ago, when Marissa dragged me to see him after her track season ended. I'd mumbled something akin to "I'd like to join cross-country again," although I had been thinking more along the lines of "I'm sorry I'm a useless, heartbroken disaster of a queer who can't get her shit together."

He'd only grinned his typical toothy smile, put his hand on my shoulder, and said, "Absolutely, Aaliyah. We miss you, and I know you can do better."

Of course, he doesn't really know what went down last year. No one on the team does, except Naomi, whose role as new team captain makes her the keeper of all team secrets. I do wish there was a way to explain myself quickly, though. Like, *Sorry I bailed on you guys last year. Mom grounded me for six months for liking girls, and I was too busy planning methods of self-harm to show up and give a real shit about running.* But I'd rather not have to relive that fresh trauma so soon.

Marissa squeezes my leg, still waiting for a response. I give her a tight smile that I know she can see right through. "Don't worry about me, dude. I will run circles around your slow ass." With that, I hop out of the car and speed-walk toward the field, my heart in my throat as I think about the team I failed last year that is now lined up in a neat little row.

I recognize basically everyone except for a few freshmen, but one girl sticks out to me. She doesn't look like a freshman, so maybe she's new. She's also Black, like me, which brings the total count of Black kids on the team up to three. Our school is like 50 percent white kids, including Naomi and Marissa, with the other 50 percent a mix of Vietnamese, Filipino, and Mexican, with a handful of other Black and brown kids thrown in.

Even if there were another ten of us on the team, though, I'd still notice this girl. She has a mix of green and white braids piled on top of her head, and she's wearing a shirt that says THE BIGGEST LITTLE CITY IN THE WORLD, over short black shorts that reveal incredibly long, toned legs. Legs that announce she's definitely not new to running.

Not that I'm staring or anything.

"Aaliyah!" someone calls. I look past the girl to see Naomi standing especially close to Curtis, the captain of the boys' team and the only other Black person on the field. Like a few of the other kids here, they're both wearing last year's team shirts, the logo of a white gold miner in a blue outfit grinning beneath the words HENDERSON HIGH SCHOOL. Our school is on the outermost edge of the city of Henderson—one mile farther and we'd be in greater Las Vegas. But having Henderson in our name means we get cred for being in a rich district—even if a lot of us don't come from that kind of money. And by a lot of us, I mean me.

I'm happy to see Naomi, since she's part of the reason I even thought of coming back. But I haven't seen Curtis in months. I ran away every time he tried to talk to me in the hallways at school last semester. We've never been close, but it was supposed to be us this season—we were supposed to be the leaders of this little running gang, two Black kids excelling at a high school sport other than football and basketball. And I let him down.

I think he'd understand, if I told him everything that happened—Curtis is and always has been a good guy. But. I don't want to talk about it. At least, I shouldn't have to. Straight kids don't have to deal with this stuff—this whole coming-out-to-your-parents thing, as if you've been an alien all along, body-snatching the normal kid they thought they'd been raising. They don't have to deal with the fear that they might wake up one day and have a parent who looks at them like they don't know who they are.

Like the kid they loved is gone.

Anyway, Curtis probably isn't too bothered about the whole being-stranded-as-captain thing. Looking at the way he moves just a little closer when Naomi tries to get his attention, his hand hovering just above the small of her back, I'm thinking he's probably thrilled by the replacement. Interesting.

Naomi mutters something in his ear, and then he looks up, finding me near the track entrance. Together, they wave me over.

Ugh. I'd hoped I could just blend in with the gate, but it seems my cloaking abilities have failed me.

"You got this," Marissa whispers, her breath tickling my ear. She places a kiss on my cheek, pushes me forward, and walks away.

"Where are you going?" I hiss.

She turns around and begins walking backward. "Booty calls!"

Double ugh.

I watch as she makes a beeline to Coach's son, Emmanuel. He's standing next to Curtis and Naomi, trying—and failing—to not look too eager as Marissa approaches. Even though it feels like a funeral song is sound-tracking my steps, I surge into a jog toward them, a big smile plastered on my lips.

"Hey, guys," I say. Without warning, Curtis grasps my hand and pulls me into a tight hug against his white tank top.

"Good to have you back, Champ," he says.

"Agreed," Naomi says from behind Curtis's shoulder. He lets me go, and I grin at the both of them—genuinely this time.

It's a warmer welcome than I expected—certainly more than I deserve. Still, it gives me a boost of confidence. Like, maybe I do have this.

I'd been beating myself up all spring semester for how I screwed up at the end of last season. Cross-country was my one escape out of the house of horrors—away from Dad's tirades, and Mom's tears, and my little sister Trinity's sad eyes—and I fucked it up because I couldn't deal with a little motherly rage and disappointment. But I'm here now, and the earth hasn't swallowed me whole. No one's come over and cursed me out, although a few girls on the team are giving me the side-eye. Like Radhika, who I've never liked anyway. Still, I feel the muscles in my chest unclench just the tiniest bit.

I glance back toward Marissa, who is now standing so close to Emmanuel that his hand has slipped to her bare thigh. Apparently, Naomi notices, too, because she rolls her eyes at the same time that I pretend to gag. That makes her snort, which makes me laugh, and then we both turn to each other in quiet hysterics until Coach Carter jogs up. Per usual, he's got a wide grin on his young, tan face. It's like the guy's never seen a rainy day in his life. Which, I guess, is probably true, unless you count the occasional summer flash flood. He's already drenched in sweat, so I bet he's coming from a prepractice run. The adrenaline drips from his pores.

"Hello, hello, Henderson recruits and returnees!" He makes

a point to smile at each and every one of us, but he pauses when he looks at me. Then he gives a quick thumbs-up, and for the first time since I woke up this morning, I feel like I can breathe. This is what I've been waiting for since the season ended last year.

A chance to start again.

CHAPTER 2

Distance running isn't about brute strength, or any particular skill. It's not even really about beating the other person. It's just about you, and how willing you are to just keep going.

See, Marissa is used to going hard and fast—pounding flesh against dirt for a brutal sixty seconds or less for an immediate payoff. It's not even enough time to think; just to act. It's the kind of reward system that keeps you cocky, and easy to please. That's why, during our very first practice two weeks ago, she had a shit-eating grin on her face after only a mile into the team's three-mile trek. She was too proud to admit she was out of breath, so she didn't even try to speak, but the look on her face said, "*See? I told you I can do this.*"

And she wasn't wrong. One mile? That was easy.

But after another few laps, her legs started to stiffen, her shoulders started to hunch, and then she started to trail behind me. When I passed her on our last lap, she could barely manage a *fuck-you*.

But even then, I was too focused to gloat.

Sure, I've gotten a couple of good teasing sessions in after practice, but when we're running, all I see is track ahead of me, and all I hear is the wind in my ears. I can feel the sweat dripping down my armpits and my feet hitting the path again and again, a steady rhythm just like my heart. This is my church, my heaven. I pray to the god of movement, and she tells me I can fly.

It's been a while since I've gone to my mom's church, but these last few weeks, I've finally returned to mine.

Last semester, I had this *ache* every time I watched Naomi and Marissa run during track season, but I ignored it. Figured I could get by hiding from my mom in my room and crying myself to sleep, or walking circles around the neighborhood if my parents were fighting and the cops hadn't come yet. I stopped running. Stopped caring. Just watched TV with Trinity and let the days roll by.

But now . . . ? Now, I'm back where I belong: steady breath and moving feet. A hymn only I can hear.

Today, I don't know where Marissa or anyone else is and I don't care, either. It's just me and the wind testing each other's breaking point. Yeah, Naomi's the girls' team captain now but I've always kept the best time.

Everyone knows that.

Just as I approach the last lap, footsteps fall in tempo with mine. It's probably Naomi. I don't even consider turning my head, but I don't have to because soon she's in front of me: a girl just my height with braids streaked with white and dark green piled on top of her head. The new girl. *Tessa.*

I almost pause—for once, I nearly consider slowing down. I'm not sure why—we've barely exchanged words these last few weeks. Still, a thousand questions burn in my throat, like, *How long have you been running?* and *Where are you from?* and *Are you possibly single and gay?* Or maybe that's the lack of oxygen from all the running. But she makes the first mistake: a small smile. As if to welcome us both to this space. This moment. And she's got a lovely smile, but she's wrong. There are some things you just don't share.

I don't return her smile, or even acknowledge that I've noticed. I just dip my head and pump my legs faster, harder. This is the final lap, and I won't stop.

Not for anyone.

By the time we return to our checkpoint, my throat is hoarse and my arms and legs are slick with sweat. My hair, gelled back this morning, is embarrassingly frizzy yet again, but I try to be used to it after all these years. If Mom had her way, I'd just straighten it all the time—that way, I'd look more "respectable," like her. But then I'd have to worry about sweating it out, and that's more work than I care to do. She also won't let me relax it, because the upkeep is expensive and doing it from a home kit could mean frying it permanently (aka, she tried to perm it once when I was five and all my hair burned off; she prayed for, like, three months until it started growing back again). So I keep it long, like she likes it, and I keep it pulled back, like I like it. Well, I don't like it. But I don't really know what else to do with it, so here we are.

I try not to strain my neck looking for Tessa to come down from the hill. Unlike me, she kept her shirt on for this run, but even before we started, I got a peek at the dark brown skin just beneath her gray sports bra and the white tee she'd been wearing. I could tell by the jaggedness of her shirt's sides that she cut the sleeves off herself, and that only made her look that much sexier. I actually had to catch my breath when I first saw her. It was the kind of outfit you'd see girls wearing on gay Tumblr fashion blogs, not in real life, with real people. I mean, I still don't know if Tessa's gay—we've barely talked, and that's a weird thing to ask someone right out the gate. Right? I don't know, I'm new at this kind of thing. Still, I think it's okay to look every now and then.

While I wait for the team to regroup, I knock back several gulps of water that's been kept freezing in my thermos. Curtis waits patiently behind Naomi as she fills up her water at the drinking fountain several feet away from the playground. When she finishes, he leans down to say something into her ear and I swear I can see the faintest hint of red touch her cheeks.

The others trickle in. Coach jogs in first—he almost always goes on the long runs with us. Then Tessa and Emmanuel round down the slope of the last hill together. Tessa's now got her T-shirt tucked into her shorts, and her braids are tied up again, piled atop her head. She smiles at me but heads straight to the water fountain, and I ignore the swarm of butterflies in my stomach as the sweat glistens off her stomach. Marissa follows shortly behind; her white legs—tan again after these weeks of training—have reddened with the efforts of her muscles, and her faded gray Siouxsie and the Banshees T-shirt is draped around her shoulders, revealing a purple sports bra. She looks tired but happy—like she's won some epic battle.

She slows to a light jog when she sees us and then stops in front of me with her hands on her knees, breathing deeply. Without a word, she grabs my thermos and gulps down my water.

"You're welcome," I say.

She plants a kiss on my cheek and otherwise ignores me, walking to the semicircle our team has begun to make in the grass beside the playground. She takes the thermos with her. I take this as my cue to follow, sitting as she all but collapses, a dramatic show of fatigue. Tessa, who is sitting across from us, tries hard not to laugh, but I hold on to the sound that escapes anyway. She was watching us, like I was watching her . . . I don't want to make a big deal or anything, but it gives me hope. For what, though, I'm not sure.

As the team slowly re-forms, Coach asks if anyone wants to lead the stretch. For the first time since practices began, Tessa volunteers. She moves to the center of the circle and lifts her left arm above her head, revealing the taut muscles of her abs. I can't believe she's only a runner—she must do some other kind of workout on her own. I've never seen a girl that ripped and lithe at the same time. Not that I'm complaining. Not at all.

When our stretches end, I start to stand, but Marissa stops me with a hand on my knee. "Hey," she says, her voice oddly small. Almost timid. Something's wrong. Marissa doesn't talk this way—not ever. I sit back on the grass and lean closer to her, minutely surprised to realize that she's been wearing makeup this whole time—her green eyes are etched in black, now smudged from the sweat and exertion of the last thirty-five minutes. They make her look a little like an owl, wide-eyed and curious.

"Uh," I say, "yes?"

"So . . ." Her tone is so slow and cautious that my palms start to sweat, as if already anticipating disaster. "I'm thinking about doing theater for my elective this year."

The statement hangs in the air.

Oh.

Marissa in theater means Marissa in theater with Yasmin

and . . . that's enough to make my stomach churn. Enough to make me grip the grass so hard I might rip up the earth beneath it, until all I feel is wet soil lodged in my fingernails.

"I don't *have* to do it," Marissa says. I nod, not listening. And then I nod again, because I realize it's important to be a good friend and not an asshole.

"It's cool, dude," I say, even though it's obviously not. But what else do I say?

Marissa gives me a look, and I force myself to relax. "Really, Mar. It's cool. But also . . . why?"

Marissa has never struck me as a theater girl. A thrash-around-the-stage-and-scream-at-the-top-of-her-lungs-in-a-tutu-and-leather-jacket girl? Sure. But since last year, she's been shit out of luck with performing.

Ah. Right. Performing.

Her band, Light Pollution, dissolved suddenly at around the same time Mom entered her antigay frenzy. Cosmically, it worked out for me, I guess. I'm not just a face in the crowd anymore. But I know Marissa misses it.

She confirms my suspicions, reaching for my hand and leaning her head on my shoulder. It's a heady combination of sweat and lavender shampoo. "I just need to be onstage again, babe."

By now, most of the team has dispersed, but Tessa and Radhika are still ambling away, caught up in conversation. Yay for

Tessa making friends with the team, but I *really* hope Radhika hasn't sullied my name already. The two walk toward their cars together and pass Emmanuel, who, I notice, is still lurking by awkwardly. He sits on the lower yellow step of the playground's minifortress with his phone in his palms. He's pretending to listen to Coach, who's leaning on one knee, still stretching while he chats away. He's probably talking about upcoming competitions, or whatever his wife, Emmanuel's mom, has planned for lunch today. I can tell Emmanuel's not actually listening, though, because he's sneaking furtive glasses at Marissa, clearly waiting for her to join him.

"You're not gonna ditch me for Yasmin?" I ask. I know the answer, but I still want to hear her say it.

Marissa scoffs and disentangles herself from me. Immediately, I feel colder. Then she stands, as if I've offended her so much that she has no choice but to vacate the premises. "She's lucky I don't punch her in the eye, Aali. I'm gonna try out for a play or two this year, just to keep my ass out of my sad, empty house. I'm not going anywhere, I promise."

"Uh-huh," I say as she helps me to my feet. "Your boyfriend is waiting."

She flips me the bird as she turns around, and Emmanuel bolts to his feet so fast that his phone nearly falls out of his hand. She glances back at me, but I blow her a kiss—my blessing to do as she pleases. Not that she needs it.

I watch as she and Emmanuel walk hand in hand off the field, probably to her car. I don't want to think about what they're planning to do, so I find a bench and watch the sky instead, the shapes of the clouds changing with time.

Marissa in theater with Yasmin. Okay. That's not a crazy thought. So maybe they'll do some plays together. That's fine. And Marissa hates Yasmin—probably more than is necessary, if I'm honest, but I appreciate the loyalty.

In truth, they barely know each other. Even though Yasmin and I used to rock out to Light Pollution together, the magic wore off when she and Marissa actually met.

It was right before the end of classes when this crazy-rich girl from history class, Susannah May, begged Marissa to sing at her house party. Being the Savvy Broke I know and love, Marissa agreed for a fee and dragged me along.

That night, Marissa enchanted her audience with a guitar Susannah had rented for her, swaying and jumping around in Susannah's majestic, hotel-like living room, complete with a fucking *chandelier*. I stood in the back, nursing an ice-cold can of refreshing, nonalcoholic Sprite.

Like a ghost, Yasmin appeared at my shoulder, a red cup in her hand. "Aali," she said, and I jumped five feet in the air. Without any classes together, we hadn't spoken in months. Neither of us had tried. And now here she was, wearing some crazy gold-and-sparkle dress that clung to her frame, snagging on her curves. Her black eyes were outlined in kohl, and her lips were a dark, deep red. I, on the other hand, was wearing black jeans I'd rummaged for in Goodwill and a blue tank top I'd picked up off the floor earlier that morning. It was probably clean, but who can be sure? "What are you doing here?" she asked me.

Not an unusual question. Why would I be at a party without her? Who could I know? I swallowed and pointed at Marissa with my soda can. Yaz nodded, taking a sip from her cup. It was definitely not Sprite.

"Cool, right? I was wondering when she'd start performing again. I miss Light Pollution."

I nodded. "Totally."

We stood there for another moment, Yaz watching Marissa perform, and me feeling like I needed to take several showers to clean off the stench of my stupid blue floor shirt. For a moment, I thought that maybe she was here to apologize—to make amends, somehow. Say something that would help me understand how she could kiss me one night, and then ignore me the next. We'd been best friends since we were kids. But the longer I stood there, the more it became clear that she wasn't going to say anything. And yet she also didn't show any signs of moving, as if us standing together like this was still totally normal. Totally fine.

I didn't move, either. I couldn't. To be so close to her like this again, her bare shoulder brushing against mine as she bobbed gently, side to side to the music. How could I possibly function, thinking of her pale brown skin, the fullness of her curves, her soft red lips, and that fucking dress; thinking of that night we'd kissed, just before the winter break, my back pressed against her mattress and her mouth on mine, closer than this, closer than I'd ever been with anyone before.

For days after that kiss, I'd been stuck in a dream, the fairy tale of having Yasmin—not just popular and gorgeous Yaz, the girl everyone adored in theater, but *my* Yaz, the person I loved and trusted most in the world besides my family, in fact *more* than my family at that point—want me as something more than just her friend. I felt special. Desired. Loved.

Except that I didn't hear from her for a few days after that. Then another few days. And another.

It was two weeks before she returned any of my messages. Her text said, Hi! Sorry I've been MIA. I met someone!

The song ended. Marissa thanked her adoring fans, looking more flushed and freer than she had since we'd met. She pushed through the throng of people, promising another song, another time, maybe later that night. When she saw me, her lips split into a wide grin and she nearly toppled me over with wide arms wrapped around me.

"Ahhhh!" she screamed into my ear. "That was AMAZING! Ah! I haven't done that in months! MONTHS, Aali!" She nuzzled her face into my hair, which I had tried to finger-comb into submission earlier in the day, but she seemed unbothered with fuzzing up my greasy curls.

"Hi," Yasmin murmured from beside me. She cocked an eyebrow at me, smiling, as if a little surprised. A little impressed. "I take it you two are friends?"

Marissa draped an arm around my shoulder, pulling me close to her and still buzzing from her performance high. "Absolutely."

"I'm Yasmin," Yaz said, sticking her hand out.

Immediately, Marissa straightened, her arm tightening on my shoulder, a frown pulling on her lips. She knew about Yaz. It was one of the first things I'd told her about, when we'd bonded over our unstable households and Lost Friendships of Junior Year.

"Cool. So you're the shitty friend who fucked Aaliyah over."

Oh, for the love of fuck. I cleared my throat and moved squarely between them. "Mar, you were awesome! Just like old times. Good, old times. Do you need water? Let's get water." Then I slipped past them both, tugging on Marissa's arm so that she would walk with me. She acquiesced, but kept turning back, glaring at Yasmin, who stayed where she was. I don't know if Yaz was shocked, or angry. Secretly, I hoped a part of her felt at least a little guilty.

Or maybe a little jealous.

An hour later, she huddled in a group of friends I didn't

recognize, laughing and smiling next to a girl in suspenders and a white button-down blouse with frills down the front. She was an Asian girl with dyed blond hair, a piercing in her eyebrow *and* her lip, and a sleeve of tattoos down her right arm. I couldn't really make out the details from where I was standing, but I noted the upside-down pink triangle. The symbol Nazis had used in World War II to identify gay people, the way they made Jewish people wear yellow stars.

Now, like the rainbow flag, it's used by some as a symbol of pride and defiance—something I learned in one of the queer history books Yaz bought me last summer, right after my mom went on her Jesus train. It's definitely not something I would've learned in school. I doubt this girl did, either, and she didn't look much older than us, meaning that she was not only super attractive, but well read, too. Deep. And she probably smelled her clothes before she wore them.

While I watched her and Yaz talk, Marissa shooed off would-be suitors and old fans, her energy from earlier rapidly depleting. She wasn't the lead singer of Light Pollution anymore. Just Marissa, surly and annoyed with the classmates who kept asking for her goddamn autograph.

"Ugh," she muttered after she managed to disentangle herself from a group of freshmen who tried to show her their band's music on YouTube. She hopped onto the kitchen counter I was leaning against. We hadn't left the area, partly because I was too cowardly to venture closer to Yasmin and her girlfriend, but that served Marissa's desire to be antisocial for the rest of the night. "I'm so ready to go now."

"Mhm," I muttered, gaze still locked on the tatted-up girlfriend. What an aesthetic. How did one even learn how to look like that? Pinterest?

God. No wonder Yasmin bailed.

"Dude," Marissa said, a little too loudly. "Stop staring."

"It's not like I kissed her first," I said, apropos of nothing. Marissa sighed, because she'd heard this mantra before. "This whole drama could've been avoided if she'd kept her hands to herself."

"Yeah, well." Marissa stretched her arms above her head. "Now you know that she sucks."

Maybe. But it didn't make it hurt any less. Ten years of friendship is hard to let go of. I kept staring for a few more minutes, miserably plucking at my dingy shirt and flat frizzy hair until Marissa gently shook my shoulder. "Hey. Look," she said, turning me toward her. "I have an idea."

I struggled to drag my eyes back to her. "What's that?"

"You could kiss me. And then you can have a much better memory to dwell on."

I choked on my spit. Then I looked at her—let my eyes distract me from the sudden rush of anger that pounded at my lungs and ears. She was wearing a pale blue shirt that hung off her right shoulder, tight black jeans, and beat-up Chucks. Her hair—still blond at the time—was mussed, mostly from the performance earlier, and her eyes were edged in their usual thick black liner. Marissa, like Yasmin, was gorgeous and beloved by many. And Marissa, like Yasmin, was fucking with me. It was the only explanation.

"Whatever, dude," I said, turning away from her to grab another can of Sprite on the other side of the sink. "Not cool. Even if you are drunk."

"I'm not," Marissa said. She hopped back off the counter to follow me. Then she reached around me and grabbed a can of Sprite, popping the tab and pouring it into her red cup. She lifted it to my eye level and sloshed it around. "See? I gotta drive you home, babe."

I shrugged, reaching for my own can. "Okay, so you're just being cruel for no reason."

"I'm *not*."

There was laughter in her voice, as if she couldn't see the tears pricking at my eyes. It was irrational how furious I felt, but this wasn't supposed to happen—not again. When Yasmin and I had kissed, I'd thought things would change for the better—that the best friend I'd grown up with could somehow magically also be my knight in shining armor, come to whisk me away from my prison. I thought I'd finally get to experience that thing in movies when sparks fly and the world falls into place, and all the butterflies would ascend into rainbow letters that said CONGRATS ON YOUR FIRST GIRLFRIEND!

But that didn't happen. I didn't gain a girlfriend; I lost my best friend. And for what? A few minutes of heavy petting, which is apparently all she'd wanted. Awesome. Even now, it makes me seethe.

So, no, I wasn't interested in playing this game again. I was ready to say exactly that to Marissa, but then she touched the side of my face, her thumb trailing over a tear that had fallen to my lips. "I'm not," she whispered again. Somehow, her arm had found my waist, and already she was pulling me closer. "I promise." Her eyes dropped toward my mouth as if in question, and her hand pressed firmly against my back. I could feel her breath against mine as she dipped her head, and my heart doubled, tripled, every nerve on my skin on fire.

Then I broke away, nearly crushing myself against the sink as I backed up. Our lips had touched, but barely. Another meaningless kiss between friends.

"Okay, Mar." I steadied my breath and put on a wobbly smile. "Point made. There are girls other than Yasmin." I gestured toward the front of the house, where our exit would be. "You ready to go?"

She wavered, like she hadn't quite registered that I had moved. Then she righted herself and ran a hand through her hair. For a brief moment, it stayed, loose waves of hair bunched just at the top of her head. She looked like maybe she'd say something else, but what was there to say? She knocked back her cup like a shot and then tossed it into the sink.

"Yeah, let's go." And she took me home.

When I think about it now, it still makes me angry—hurt, I guess. I get that she was playing around, but I don't understand that. With her, or Yasmin. Fuck around with some groupie in the audience, then, not me. Not your friend. And if it had been any other night, that would've been the end of it, but I was running high on emotions. I was feeling angry and a little excited—a little self-righteous. After all, if this is how the game is played, why shouldn't I get something in return?

It was late when we got home that night, and my mom had left the light on in the porch, so what I did next was incredibly stupid, but I wasn't thinking straight anyway—pun 1,000 percent intended. I asked Marissa to walk me to my door, and, this time, I kissed her. I pushed her against the door, and she didn't hesitate, letting her fingers find my hips as mine dragged against the skin beneath her shirt and her teeth pulled against my bottom lip. It was frenzied, and fast, both of us pressing ever closer as if the fabric between us and the fact that we were both beneath the porch light in clear view of the rest of the neighborhood was the only thing keeping us from going further. It felt just like when Yasmin and I had kissed, except this time, I had no silly notions about love and romance. It was nothing but teen lust and intrigue. And if Marissa wanted to fulfill her curiosity, why shouldn't I? Straight girls weren't the only ones who could experiment.

Yasmin taught me that.

★ ★ ★

Anyway, that's all in the past. Yasmin and I don't talk, and Marissa and I know where we stand. I mean, we haven't really talked about it—she tried to ask me how I was feeling a few days later, right before our chemistry class started, but I didn't want to make a big deal about it. Didn't want to do to us what I'd done to me and Yasmin, and lose yet another friend. So I told her we were good, and we are. We're great.

So, probably, it'll be fine if they're in class together. I'm fine with it—really. And in any case, it's starting to get hot now that the sun is higher in the sky. The concrete bench beneath my ass is starting to burn. If I wait any longer, I'll be sweaty again by the time I walk to work, so I close my eyes and do what Coach says before every competition: Breathe, and don't look back.

CHAPTER 3

My boss greets me with a crinkled nose and raised eyebrow.
"Heeey, Dee," I say. She's standing next to a tall person with dreadlocks and an easy smile. I think I recognize them, but . . .

"Hi, Aaliyah." Deneisha eyes my running clothes. "Did you walk here?"

"Nope." I give her my most charming smile, and she rightly ignores it.

"Next time, you shower. You hear me?" She gives a little huff and then points to the person next to her. "Lonnie, this is Aaliyah Marshall. Aaliyah, this is Lonnie Martinez. They'll be taking over your shift once the summer ends, so you'll be training them for the next few weeks."

My heart sinks into my feet. So this *wasn't* just a post-run-inspired hallucination. Lonnie Martinez, the former drummer of Light Pollution, is really and truly standing here beside me. Awesome.

"Nice to meet you," I say. It comes out halfway between a squeak and a growl.

They give me an awkward smile and then follow Deneisha toward the employee break room while I wonder which god I have to appease to stop fucking me over with these weird surprises. The truth is, I don't know anything about Lonnie or any of Marissa's other band members. All I know is that they broke up, and Marissa doesn't talk about them. Out of the unspoken code of friend solidarity, I have to assume the worst.

I still have to do my job, though, so when Lonnie returns from what I assume is a short employee orientation, I take them through the boring steps of superstore etiquette. They seem pretty quiet, which is wild for me, seeing them up close. In the *before* times, when I watched Marissa sing her heart out with the band, the person standing next to me now—tall, dark, and, I admit it, *handsome*—was a lunatic on the drums. Onstage, they were literally bursting with energy, sweat dripping down their face, dreadlocks swinging all over the place. It was unreal.

I mean, everyone had a crush on Marissa, naturally, but Lonnie came in a close second on the local band scoreboard.

And now, here they are. In the flesh.

Stocking cans on aisle nine!

Okay, so maybe I'm geeking out just a little. But I can't let them know that. Marissa would be horrified, I'm sure.

"Those are kidney beans, not black beans," I say when they accidentally mix in a stray can. "They should go to your left."

"Oh. My bad," Lonnie says.

Damn straight.

After we're finished with Cans 101, I take them back to my cash register to teach them the ins and outs of ringing up groceries. We've gone through some customers together when a few cans of sparkling flavored water and two bags of trail mix float toward me. "Hey, Aaliyah," the customer says, "I didn't know you worked here."

My heart declares war against my ribs. I don't even have to look up to know that it's Tessa, but I do anyway, because I was raised with manners, no matter what my mom says. Tessa's wearing a green plaid flannel shirt open over a black tank top, and her braids are still up, but this time she has a pair of sunglasses perched on top of them. I'm a little surprised that she's already changed out of her workout gear, but then I remember that she has a car. She probably drove home, showered, and changed in the time it took for me to walk here and start my shift. And here I am, still sweaty and gross. I mean, I'm in my Greg's gear now, but still. Deneisha was right; I should've showered first.

Tessa's eyebrows furrow, and I realize I haven't responded to her yet. "Oh! Yeah. Uh, I'm a, uh, worker. You, uh—you been here before? To . . . here?"

I hear Lonnie stifle a small giggle behind me. Jerk.

Tessa smiles, revealing straight white teeth except for a little gap in the front. It only makes her cuter. "Yes, I've been here before. I live nearby."

I nod too long. "Cool. That's. Awesome."

"I guess. You do, too?"

"I do what?"

"Live near here."

Lonnie snorts out a laugh, and I turn to them with wide, angry eyes. "Lonnie, want to bag this?"

"Uh-huh," they say, still chuckling to themselves.

My ears burn as I ring up Tessa's groceries. This time, I don't dare look at her face, as I'm sure she's now convinced that I'm a fool. And who knows what the rest of my teammates have said to her. I mean, no one's said anything to me yet, but Radhika has barely managed not to knock me over during practice runs. If I wasn't faster than her, I'm sure she would've mowed me down by now.

"Here you are," Lonnie says, handing Tessa's bag of groceries back to her.

"See you at practice?" I say as she thanks Lonnie. It's a stupid question—of course I'm going to see her at practice. Still, she considers me. Maybe I'm imagining it, but I'm pretty sure her eyes dart up and down, taking me in—but that would be weird. I'm just wearing an employee-standard yellow polo, and the rest of me is hidden behind the cash register But if she *was* checking me out . . . The thought makes my lungs constrict a little more. Then she fixes me with another smile, pulled to the side.

"Wouldn't miss it. See you soon." And then she's gone, walking past the cash register in short, ripped jeans that reveal smooth, dark legs. I've seen her legs during practice, of course—we all wear shorts every day. And yet, every time, it takes a lifetime to pull my eyes away from hers.

"Yooo," Lonnie says, waving a hand in front of me. "What the hell was that?"

I clear my throat and return to the important business of rearranging random items at my station. I think this pack of gum needs to go back—there, yup. Looks good. Tidy.

"Dude," Lonnie says again.

"*What.*"

"'See you soon,'" they repeat, in a perfect imitation of Minnie Mouse, giggling exaggeratedly with their hands over their mouth.

"Shut up," I mutter, though without any sort of force. Honestly, it's kind of nice to get this kind of reaction to my obvious, er . . . crush? Is it a crush? Let's call it a recognition of attractiveness. I haven't been able to talk about a girl I like in ages, to anyone. I mean, I guess I like her. I mean, I don't *not* like her. I don't even know her. She's just impossibly gorgeous. That's all. Lots of girls are, probably, to someone.

Lonnie smiles, but doesn't push the issue. It's respectful, which I appreciate, but I realize suddenly that I like the teasing.

Mom would rather I was a nun, my dad's an ass, and Marissa . . . well, I guess I could tell Marissa. Maybe later.

Lonnie and I don't talk too much for the rest of the shift, but what had been a weird and awkward silence between us becomes easy. Comfortable even. I don't have to be best friends with Lonnie—friendship solidarity with Marissa and all that—but . . . it's nice to know other queer people. Especially another Black queer person. It was nice to be teased about liking a girl. It felt . . . normal.

I need normal.

When I get home later that evening, Dad is at the kitchen counter, chopping up vegetables for what I assume is tonight's dinner. He's always been a big cook, but he makes his most special meals in the days following a recent fuckup. Apology meals, as Trinity and I call them. Mom, too, when she's feeling feisty. It's been weeks since there was a major blowup that I'm aware of, so I can only assume something happened in the few hours I've been gone.

Mom's at the sink, washing dishes while still wearing her sea-green scrubs. She must not have had an opportunity to change when she got home. Clue number two.

"How was cross-country?" Mom asks when I come in. I shrug and grab a piece of raw carrot from Dad's chopping board.

If this were last year, Mom would be simmering with passive-aggressive rage over the idea of me spending hours on end with sweaty, scantily clad girls. But that was when she was still trying to pray the gay away—though she was discreet enough to keep it from the rest of our church, on the off chance I could be cured and they'd never have to know. She's good at keeping secrets like that—that's why they still don't know that Dad's a drunk. *Oh, Melinda, he's visiting family right now. What bruise? This? Oh, girl, I tripped down a stair and Terry tried to catch me. You know we both ended up falling! Ha ha ha.*

Last year, Mom and I had a routine. I'd wake up; go to school (aka sleep through class); go to practice (aka slump around the track and stare at the ground); and then come home and read scripture (aka scream at each other until we're blue in the face).

If Mom and Dad were already screaming at each other, then Mom and I would reschedule for another time.

Mom: Shove an ex-gay brochure in your face at ten?

Me: Sure. Let me pencil that in right after I contemplate flinging myself from a window.

But then, I don't know, I guess she got over it. Maybe it's because she finally saw how badly I was handling everything. My failed competitions, my abysmal grades, my missing friends. I've always been thin, but I got to the point that I was full-on skeletal. Maybe she was worried about me. I mean, after all, I'm still her kid, right? Or maybe, she just gave up.

So we don't fight about it anymore, but I don't know if the space she gives me now is a good thing.

"Proud of my girl," Dad says once he's done chopping. "Running in that hot sun like a champion!" He wipes his hands on the apron he's wearing, and I wince, just for a second, but I can already hear Mom's voice in my head. *Don't make it worse.* So I let him hug me, plant a wet kiss on my cheek, and indulge his questions about practice. His being hypersweet could be clue number three to a recent transgression, but Dad is mercurial. When he cares, he actually seems to care. It's not at all infuriating.

"Honey"—Dad turns to Mom—"thank you for doing all them dishes. You know I appreciate it." He wraps his arms around her torso, his lips falling to her ear. Mom is stiff against his embrace, but she doesn't say anything. She just stands there, her eyes on the plate she's been scrubbing for five minutes.

I leave to find Trinity, knowing she's probably holed up in her room. Compared to a lot of my classmates, we don't have a big house, but Trinity and I both have our own rooms, and Mom and Dad's bedroom is downstairs. As expected, Trinity's upstairs, eyes glued to the television as she sits cross-legged on her princess canopy bed, her arms in her lap.

"*Arrow*, huh?" Final clue—Dad definitely did something fucked up.

Trinity nods absently, putting her hands out for a perfunctory hug without turning her head. I wrap my arm around her small frame. "I missed you," I say.

She doesn't respond—just tightens her little arms.

"How was Dad today?" I venture to ask.

"Fine," she says, her mouth muffled against my shirt. That's a surprise. "We watched *The Avengers* today, and he bought me ice cream and Spider-Man headphones while you and Mom were at work."

With what money? I want to ask, but I kiss her hair instead. "That's great, Trini."

She shrugs. "He feels guilty for calling me the b-word and throwing my chair across the room this morning." I cringe. There we go. Classic Dad.

I don't know if he was like this when he and Mom married, but I know he's been like this since as long as I can remember. Sweet when sober; a monster when not.

Trinity and I hold each other for a moment, lingering, perhaps, in this moment of relative safety and quiet. Then we settle into the pillows on top of her bed and turn our attention back to the TV. She's apparently been watching reruns of *Arrow* season one, where Oliver Queen hasn't grown a conscience yet and is seriously spiraling from untreated PTSD. He shoots an unarmed man in the chest with an arrow. "Isn't this too violent for you, Trini?"

This time she looks at me, irritated at first, then sad, until a little smile breaks out on her face. "He only kills bad guys." I smile back. Justice served is justice served—however ill-gotten.

After dinner, I retreat to my room and sink into my sheets as I shore up the courage to pull out my phone. Tessa's Instagram profile isn't hard to find—she's apparently already friends with a few of our teammates. It's set to private, though, so I have to request an invite.

I don't know if that would be too obvious, or forward. Obvious about what, though? It's not like I'm asking her on a date or something. It's not like I *would* ask her on a date. I'm just being friendly. A good teammate.

I swallow down the pit of fear that swarms in my chest. Okay, I'm just going to do it— One. Two.

Fuck. Okay. Request sent.

I keep the phone in my hand for a few seconds longer. I could text Marissa—she'd probably want to know the details. Maybe she'd laugh at how silly I was being, or gush about how hot Tessa is, too. Not that she'd think Tessa was hot. Which is the other problem. Without Yasmin, I'm down another queer friend. I don't know if Marissa would understand. And anyway, it's not exactly like she texted me about Emmanuel when they started doing whatever it is they do now.

Besides, the idea of texting Marissa is making me want to text Yaz and that's a colossally stupid idea. Instead, I throw my phone as far away from me as I can so that I don't check it every fifteen seconds for Tessa's response. Then I open the laptop Mom bought for me during last year's Black Friday sale and spend ten minutes trying to connect to the neighbor's Wi-Fi.

When the signal finally steadies, I find an email waiting in my in-box.

Dear Student,

Congratulations on reaching the final year of your K–12 education. All of us at Henderson High School are thrilled about your achievements, in years past and those to come. As you know, due to unfortunate circumstances, your junior year ended with academic probation. To ensure an academically successful senior year, you have been paired with myself and a peer adviser, Naomi Pratt, for mentorship. Please report to my office before your first class this coming Monday.

Thank you, and I look forward to our collaboration this year.

Well wishes,

Claire Eccleston, M.S.W.

Senior Year Counselor

Henderson High School

PS: A copy of this notice has been forwarded to your on-file guardian.

So it's official, then. My senior year of high school has begun.

CHAPTER 4

The next morning, instead of hitching a ride with Marissa as usu-ally planned, I decide to take my chances with Dad. He's jolly today, and, I don't know, I guess I could use some cheer. He's humming to an old Musiq Soulchild jam on the radio, and he's leaned back in his seat with one hand on the wheel. A cigarette falls to the side of his lips, and his hair is gelled back with blue Eco Styler, making his trim black curls glisten in the sunlight. "Anyway," he says after the song ends, "I got this gig coming up. The church needs someone to see about some of the plumbing around the building. Your mom told them I'd do it. It's cool and all, but it's like, damn, can't I get two seconds since I got back to get situated?"

I glance at him, to demonstrate I've heard him, but I'm not in a talking mood. That's mostly why I avoided Marissa's ten text messages this morning, confirming our usual joint ride to practice. Sure, Dad is exhausting, but I'm used to that exhaustion. I don't have the energy to think about Marissa and Yasmin hamming it up in theater class, or deal with the fact that the person who replaced me as captain of the cross-country team is the same person tasked with making sure I don't flunk out of high school.

In other words, I'd rather deal with old irritants than new ones.

Since practice is at school today, Dad rolls up to a spot just in front of the track. "Bye, hon!" he says as I jump out of the car. As I jog toward the field, I see Naomi step out of her car, her nose in a hefty-looking book. I could run past, pretend I'm in some kind of hurry, but I might as well get this over with. I stop a few feet in front of her.

"*Heart of Darkness*?" I groan by way of greeting.

She stops and smiles a little. "I know. It's racist. We still have to read it before AP English starts."

"Have to? I'm one thousand percent sure that email said it was a *suggested* summer assignment. For the most 'eager' among us."

"I am that," Naomi says. She drops the book to her side, fingers still holding her place, and faces me full-on. Straight tendrils of brown hair fall into her eyes as she waits for me to speak, and suddenly my throat feels like it's filled with desert sand.

"So . . . ," I say, feeling very much like a preschooler. "You're my adviser."

"Peer adviser."

"And my captain."

"We're still friends," she says, and I roll my eyes so hard I see stars. "Aaliyah . . . ," she starts.

"I know. It just feels like salt in the wound."

Naomi's lips pull to the side, and it's an adorable gesture that makes me feel a little less small. "I can advise someone else," she offers.

I consider it. It would feel maybe a tad less humiliating. Then again, if anyone could make me feel as unhumiliated as possible in this situation, it's probably Naomi. Despite the super saiyan–level bullshit I experienced last year, she never once showed an ounce of judgment.

Not when I blew off nearly two weeks of practice last fall and a semiregional competition.

Not when I showed up to a team dinner two hours late and told her to fuck off when she asked me why.

Not when she pulled me into her car when I came in dead last during our final competition of the season and forced me to tell her what the hell was wrong with me. (Well, she asked, "What is wrong with you?" Cursing's not really her thing.) And I did tell her.

And other than Marissa, she's the only one who knows. I can trust her.

"It's cool," I say, finally. "You're probably the best peer adviser a kid could ask for."

She gives a half smile. "I will try my best."

We begin walking together toward the track, but as the team comes into focus, anxiety seizes my heart. Tessa offers a quick wave, but she's pulled aside by Radhika, who tugs her to the other side of the girls' warm-up line. Before I can feel the sharp sting of rejection, though, fiery green eyes and a thrust of bright red hair force themselves between us.

"What the entire fuck?" Marissa's face and body appear before me like an apparition. Naomi, clearly recognizing drama, mouths a "see you later," and hurries on ahead of me. I don't need to ask why Marissa's pissed, and whatever bullshit excuse I had for ignoring her many morning texts and calls dies on my lips.

"I'm sorry, Mar. I don't know what my problem is."

"I do," she says. She crosses her arms and takes a step back. "Yasmin."

"I don't want to talk about her."

"Neither the fuck do I. But apparently, we need to so that you don't abandon me this semester."

I groan and brush past her onto the track, where the rest of the team is off on the far right side, doing their stretches before we set off on our warm-up jog. "I'm not abandoning you, Mar," I say as I continue walking toward the field. "I'm sorry. I just . . . was trying to feel it out, you know. I get you wanting to try out theater—seriously. Go for it. I just am not looking forward to having to see . . . her." And deal with the fact that she's part of the reason I need a goddamn peer adviser to begin with.

Marissa sighs. "You won't have to see her any more than you do in the hallways, dude."

"Yes, I will!" I stop walking and throw my hands up as if this is the most obvious thing in the world. "Marissa, I *know* theater. I basically lived it with Yasmin. And here's the thing *you* need to know: It's a cult, not a class, or an 'extracurricular.' There's no such thing as showing up and leaving. If you're gonna throw yourself into this thing, that means I'm gonna be thrown along with it—auditions, rehearsals, cast parties, the whole shebang."

"Oh, I see." Marissa crosses her arms. "So you're planning to be my understudy for the lead roles I'll obviously land."

"You know what I mean."

"I don't. You don't have to be part of everything I do."

"I—" I pause. I mean, true. I don't. I guess I never considered that before. With Yasmin, it just made sense that I would follow her like a puppy.

A sad, lovesick puppy.

Marissa must see me wilting because she wraps an arm around my shoulders and presses her forehead to mine. "Look, I'm not saying I don't want you by my side at all hours of the day. I kind of do. I'm just saying that you don't have to be."

I nod slowly, warmed by her words, and how close she is to me. Which is maybe exactly why she's telling me to back off. Of course. "Right," I say, taking a step back. "Just because theater is your thing, it doesn't have to be my thing."

"Except the audition," she clarifies. Her arm stays on my shoulders. "Please don't leave me to the wolves."

I scoff. "You can't be serious. You've been performing for years. When you were with Light Pollution—" I swallow my next words as Marissa's eyes fall. Right. Off-limits topic. "I just mean, you're going to be great, and you know it. You won't need me there." I give her a sly look. "Apparently, you don't need me at all. I'll just be running over here all on my lonesome, while my best friend and ex–best friend become each other's best friends."

"Oh my god." Marissa shoves me away gently as I begin to laugh, and we start walking again. "You're literally the worst."

We pull up short of the team so that we can continue our conversation. I stretch my arm out to the side as she lifts up a leg and pulls it to her chest. Emmanuel begins to walk over to us, but Marissa jerks her head slightly and he nods and rejoins the group. "Look," Marissa continues, switching legs, "it will be fine."

"I know," I sigh, twisting side to side. "I know. And I'm sorry for being shitty to you. I just get in my own head."

"I am well aware," Marissa mutters, but it doesn't sound like she meant for me to hear. Then she gets a wicked gleam in her eye. "And when cast parties roll around and you're forced to see

Yasmin with her girlfriend, which is what I know you're *actually* worried about"—she gives me a pointed look—"we'll make her jealous by making out again. No problem."

My eyes go wide just as Coach blows his whistle. "OKAY, TEAM," Coach shouts like the god of well-timed interventions. Marissa winks at me as Coach surveys the team, his hands on his hips. Then he jerks his thumb backward. "Let's go!" Marissa breaks into a jog with everyone else, and, for once, I struggle to catch up.

After the warm-up, Coach leads us in an hour of strength training that includes crunches, push-ups, sprints, and pretty much anything else that will guarantee we'll pass out by the time practice ends. Once it does, Marissa and I find a patch of grass to hang out on, and she picks up where we left off. "Next time you're anxious about something, try not to be an asshole," she says.

I nod awkwardly from my spot on the ground. "Noted." Then I turn toward her. "Guess what?"

"What," she asks, her eyes closed.

"Lonnie works at Greg's now."

Marissa's frown fades as she opens her eyes. "Oh yeah?"

"Yeah."

She makes a noncommittal sound and doesn't look at me.

Selfishly, I want to ask what the hell happened—not just between her and Lonnie, but the band itself. Why did they break up? Why won't she talk about it—especially with me? But she doesn't say anything more, and for a moment, we're both utterly quiet.

"Well," I say finally, "do I hate them, or do I deign to acknowledge their presence?"

Marissa's lips quirk up. "You can deign. I like the deigning."

Then she moves her hands behind her head and closes her eyes. I turn back toward the sky. Seconds pass, and then her hand finds mine. Our fingers grasp for each other's, and we continue to lie there, watching the clouds roll by as everything else fades away.

✦ ✦ ✦

It should be quiet when Marissa drops me off. Mom should be at work, Trini is at some overnight thing at the church, and it's been barely more than an hour since I've seen my dad. But I can hear music blasting as I approach the front door, and when I push it open, it's immediately clear that every damn light in the house is on—in Mom and Dad's bedroom, in the kitchen, in the living room, and apparently in the rooms upstairs, at least from what I can tell glancing up the hallway at the foot of the stairs. All of it will make for an outrageous electricity bill neither Mom nor I can afford.

The level of petty is breathtaking.

In the middle of the room, Dad is on his back, a cigarette stuck in his mouth like a toothpick while the stereo blares

Anthony Hamilton's *Comin' From Where I'm From.* His eyes are closed as if he's fallen asleep, but I know that he's drunk. I can see a half bottle of Jack Daniel's on the kitchen table at the far end of the house.

I take a deep breath and quietly shut the door behind me, reluctantly alerting him to my presence. He turns his head to the side and grins, his eyes taking on a sardonic squint. "Hey, baby girl."

My jaw and fists clench, but I stay rooted to the floor. I know he won't hit me—he's never hit me, or Trinity. Still, he has a bad habit of breaking other things in his proximity.

"What, you too good to talk to your old man?"

He turns onto his side and watches me. When I still don't respond, his lips slip into a snarl and he staggers to his feet. "Stuck-up bitch. Just like your mama." That's probably his favorite insult—the swipes about how Mom think she's better than him because she can hold down a job and he can't. Weird how he turns that back around on her.

He walks over to me, the stench of whiskey growing stronger with every step. "You ain't talk to me this morning, neither." Oh my God. That's what this is about? I was quiet most of our ride this morning, which I thought was neutral, and he's reacting like a fucking crybaby. He sticks his face into mine. "Cat gotcher tongue?" He stays there for a moment, breathing heavily, waiting for me to make a move.

I don't, though every muscle in my body has started to shake. My brain is used to this, but I guess my body didn't get the memo.

Finally, bored with our little standoff, he half-heartedly shoves my shoulder, the force of which makes him stumble past me against the door. "Go on upstairs," he mutters when he's able to stand up straight, then he walks to the stereo and collapses back onto the floor.

For once, my feet move faster than I want to, and I'm in my room within seconds, shutting off each of the lights as I go. On my bed, shrouded in darkness, I lie on my back and stare at the ceiling, counting the minutes until my heart learns how to beat normally again.

When it does, I reach for my phone and call Marissa. I don't say anything when she answers, because I can't. I'm too busy trying to breathe and hold back the tears that are clouding my eyes as she tells me it's okay, that she's coming back, that she'll be here soon. Then I text an SOS to Mom.

Five minutes later, Marissa's car stalls on the street. She doesn't say anything to me when I jump into her passenger seat, just nods and turns up the music as she backs out of my driveway.

"Thank you," I breathe. I lean back in the seat and close my eyes, sinking into the music. It's a band my mom used to listen to when I was really young—Linkin Park. She and I used to scream along to the lyrics after Dad had one of his episodes. We'd lie in bed together, and she'd wrap her arms around me, telling me it would be okay, and that if I needed to, I could just scream it out like Chester did. I told Marissa that once, when we were hanging around her apartment while her mom was out on a gambling fix. She's not really that into them—she prefers a little more soulfulness to her rock 'n' roll—so I know she's playing this for me. That's why we're friends.

"You want to run?" she asks as we leave my neighborhood.

"No, I . . . can we just drive around?"

"Of course. How many hours until your shift starts, babe?"

I shrug, ready to tell her that I'll ask Lonnie to cover my shift. Then I remember the electricity bill. "Four," I say.

She nods, and we lapse into silence, both of us just mouthing the lyrics we know as she drives deeper into the hills. She skips around the album before finally landing on a particularly scream-y song, and our depleted energy rises until we're both shouting, "Shut up! I'm about to break!" Then we break out into a fit of giggles. When Chester stops screaming, Marissa turns the music down and we're left with the hum of her janky Bug and the rush of wind from the crack at the top of her window. We're cruising down the street of a valley in some ritzy neighborhood, passing a park neither of us is familiar with, when I ask her if she believes in heaven.

"No," she says. Then: "I think that *I think* there's something.

After this. Something else. Not the heaven we learn about in church, but. I don't know. Something."

I nod quietly. Heaven, hell, purgatory. God. It's not that I don't believe. I had been going to church since kindergarten, and then spent years watching the babies in daycare while their parents were in worship services or teaching youth Bible studies classes. I've gone to church my whole life—until Mom found out I was gay. A year ago, this month.

In junior high, Yaz and I would talk about death an oddly frequent number of times. Yaz wondered if her mom had died, since she hadn't seen her since elementary school. She wondered what it might've felt like—if people felt anything at all. Most of the time, I just listened to her. I never really thought about death like that, although maybe I should've. Maybe it made sense for a kid like me with a dad like mine to wonder what it'd be like to disappear. But I didn't. Not then. But Yasmin was enthralled. She had books like *What Comes Next?* and *Connecting with the Afterlife*. She was always curious—one of those book-reading people, like Naomi. Research was her thing, so it didn't strike me as odd at the time. A little morbid, but nothing serious. We didn't know then that Yaz had the same kind of illness her mom had—the kind that makes you think that this life just isn't worth living. But when her dad saw the cut marks that started appearing on her arms, he took her to see a doctor. You'd think he'd pay more attention after that, but he just stayed away longer—always on one business trip or another. Yasmin had the best therapists money could pay for, and a mansion all to herself. But at least we had each other.

When Chester died a few years ago, there were a bunch of advisories floating around queer blogs about suicide ideation, reminding us all to be kind to one another and reach out to a hotline if we needed anything. I can still remember the number for the Trevor Project. After everything with Mom happened, I ended up calling all the time. Funny how that happens.

The screaming crescendos to a new song—one of their last. *Who cares if one more light goes out?* Chester sings. *Well I do.*

"You think he's there?" I don't have to tell Marissa who I'm talking about. She doesn't look at me. Just keeps her eyes straight ahead, one hand on the wheel and the other on my headrest. Then she turns the music back up until Chester's voice is the only thing we can hear.

CHAPTER 5

The sun is hot and high above us when we roll up to Roberto's, the vegan taco shop off Sunset Road. We've been driving around for the past hour, and neither one of us has eaten anything but a banana and Gatorade since practice this morning. When Marissa turns the engine off and we hop outside, the heat hits us like a wall. We speed into the shop, where we're met with sweet, cool air and the fresh scent of sizzling seitan and lime. I'm salivating in bliss until Marissa grabs my shoulder and drags me to the side of the entrance, away from the ordering line.

"Dude, what—" But she shuts me up with an aggressive nod toward the cash register. I know she's trying to get me to look at something, but I'm hungry and emotional, so I'm not prepared when I turn back toward the line and see none other than Yasmin Reyes. She's not facing us, but I would recognize that short wisp of black hair and her light brown skin anywhere. And right now, she's angled toward some curvy blond with multicolored highlights and a sleeve of tattoos.

Yaz looks our way just as I feel the wind rush from my

lungs. We haven't spoken since that night at Susannah's party. No texts, no awkward school run-ins. Once, I saw her walking from the theater with two big boxes stacked in her arms. Her girlfriend was beside her, holding another stack. They were looking at each other, lost in their own world, and Yasmin was smiling this huge, easy smile. Her eyes were bright, focused. She was the poster child for romantic bliss. I've never seen her look like that before—not since we were kids. Like she'd never been more comfortable. That's how I knew the girlfriend wasn't temporary, a fluke. Whatever Yaz had felt when she kissed me all those months ago—it didn't come close to this.

That hurt more than anything.

When she sees me, Yazmin gives a little wave. She hesitates for just a moment, then tugs the girlfriend along as she walks toward us. All I can think about is how much of a mess I am. I haven't showered since practice this morning, my hair is probably still frizzy and gross like a sweaty sunflower, and my eyes are probably puffy and red.

Shit, shit, shit is the only thing running through my brain when Marissa steps between us, her lip curled halfway between a smirk and a snarl.

Yaz sighs, like she's above all this unnecessary emotion. "Hi, Marissa," and it sounds a lot like "Fuck off, Marissa."

"Hi, Yasmin." Marissa's tone isn't any nicer.

The girlfriend and I nod at each other in an attempt at

civility. Then Yaz turns to me, her hand resting on her girlfriend's waist. "Aali," she says, and despite everything, it sounds a lot like nothing's changed, like we're still best friends, the best of friends, maybe even more than that, maybe . . . "This is Skye."

And I'm back to reality. Skye? *Skye.* Her real name is probably *Sarah*, or *Daisy* like in *Agents of S.H.I.E.L.D.* I clench my fists, aware that I'm seething for no rational reason, and, not for the first time, I take Daisy—or whatever—in: the tattoo on her wrist, the baggy black cargo pants, the super-short-and-spiky blond hair like she's freaking Cloud from *Final Fantasy*. I take a deep breath and smile despite the knife doing twists and turns in my stomach.

"Nice to meet you," I say, and it must sound genuine, because Daisy offers a real smile beneath her oh-so-cool tufts of hair. A few seconds pass as we stand around searching for things to say, until Yasmin speaks up again, her hand suddenly on my shoulder.

"Are you okay?" She must see how red my eyes are. Maybe I should be embarrassed, but part of me is relieved. She still knows me. And she still knows my dad. We have a lifetime of history between us, a lifetime of me running to her door and hiding out in her house. She would understand, if I told her. She would hold me, like she used to, and we'd pretend the rest of the world didn't exist. If I told her, maybe the universe would finally right itself and we'd be friends again.

For a second, I consider telling her the truth. That I'm far from okay. That I don't really know the last time I've been okay. But then I remember the weeks she left me hanging. The night she turned my life upside down so that she could—I don't even know. Fool around with someone? That's not what friends do. I need more than an "are you okay" to make that right again.

I shrug and look away. "I'm fine. Just hungry." Then Marissa puts her hand on the small of my back, and I resist the urge to move away. For some reason, I'm kind of irritated with her, too, now. Being around them both at the same time is making me feel all sorts of confused.

Yaz cocks her head at me, but I think the tension in the room is uncomfortable for everyone involved. Finally, she nods. "Okay. Well . . . it was good to see you, Aali. It's been a while. We should catch up sometime, before school starts. I'll call you?" And I nod, even though I'm sure she won't. Then she and Daisy walk between Marissa and me and out of the shop. I watch them go, my eyes trained on the blond girlfriend. Is Daisy *that* cool, or was I just *that* boring? Marissa gives me a knowing glance while I try to keep myself composed. I feel like I'm going to cry, and that makes me feel pathetic. Marissa drapes an arm around me and pushes us forward as the line moves.

When we finally get our food and sit down to eat, a dreadful thought has formed in my head and it's so distracting that I can barely eat my burrito.

"What is it?" Marissa asks.

I don't want to tell her, but I know she'll bug me until I do. "Do I look cool to you?" I say to my plate. I refuse to meet Marissa's eyes, which I know must be filled with righteous indignation.

"Don't even," she says, and I sigh, pushing my plate away.

"You don't get it."

"Don't get what?"

I touch the back of my neck, beneath the poof of hair that I have pulled back. I don't know how to explain *the look*. The kinds of aloof, artsy girls who get other girls. The magnetism that both Yasmin and Daisy—Skye, whatever—have, that draws people toward them, and them to each other. Hell, even Marissa has that look—the whole *I know who I am and what I want and I don't give a fuck about what you think* vibe. It's like lesbian catnip, and I don't know how to explain that girls like me, who look like me—brown skin, and frizzy hair, and old clothes from Goodwill—clearly have the opposite effect. So instead, I just pick at my tortilla in silence. Marissa doesn't push, except to tell me that she's going to eat whatever I don't. I roll my eyes and take a bite, my wheels turning.

CHAPTER 6

I've finally done it. When this is over, I will have driven my mother to murder.

I can feel the promise of my imminent death with each snip of Jackie's scissors, my curls succumbing to their own doom on the black mat beneath our feet.

My hair hasn't been this short since I was born. Now, it falls around my head like a bowl of pasta, and if I had a mustache, I'd look just like the rich boyfriend in *Coming to America*. My mother could probably live with that, but Jackie is taking a razor to the back of my head now, and with it, buzzing off the last of Mom's hopes and dreams.

Since our run-in with Yaz a couple days ago, I kept begging Marissa to take me to the salon. I knew damn well that Mom wouldn't, and it was too hot for me to walk the two hours it would've taken to get there. When Marissa finally acquiesced this morning, it took another thirty minutes for Miss Jackie to even *kind of* think about *maybe* considering my request.

In fact, up until twenty minutes ago, we'd been in a standoff.

I stood at the front of the store, pointing at my wild hair freshly loosed from the poof it was usually in and screaming about bodily autonomy. She stood stalwart at her station, lips pursed and fingers wrapped tightly around a comb as if it were a rosary. In the ten years I've been coming to her salon, neither I nor my mother has ever asked for anything more than the occasional blowout, because I had that "good hair." Why, she asked me, would I want to chop it all off? Her other customers, most of whom were regulars like me, nodded and mm-hmm'd, talking about "You don't know how good you have it." With my heart racing and my fingernails making half moons in my palms, I tried to calmly explain that it was just something I wanted to try. To experiment, like teenagers do! I even pulled out my phone and tried to show her an example of what I was looking for, swiping through pictures of my favorite band—twin sisters who had pixie cuts that framed their angular faces.

"These are *White Girls*," Jackie said, her Jamaican accent slowing on each word as if I were particularly thick headed. "Your hair don't look like this if I cut it."

"SO RELAX IT." I'd never raised my voice before to Jackie. Never had a reason to, of course. But everyone knows you don't talk back to grown folks, and here I was, acting a fool. I tried to compose myself while everyone in the salon stared at me with both contempt and pity. My shoulders slumped, and my anger faded. "It's just hair, Miss Jackie. I just want to see what it looks like. Please?"

Jackie looked at me evenly. "Does your mother know you want t'do dis ting?"

Of-fucking-course-not. And Miss Jackie knew that, so she refused, and I persisted, until finally I threatened to go home and shave it all off. That's when she relented, pushing me into a chair and promising me a cut that would grow out "quick and easy" and "without the creamy crack."

Now, she's running her fingers through my hair with a mix of sweet-smelling conditioner and some other kind of goop, a scowl permanently on her lips as she does so. I stare at myself in the mirror, at my new fro-hawk and the curls that fall just above my right eye. Do I look better than before, or just different? I can't tell. I try to smile, and it makes my face look pinched, unnatural. It's not quite how I thought it'd turn out, but it's new. Different.

I need different.

As I stare, Jackie moves to the side and crosses her arms yet again. "So do you like it, or no?" I nod and offer a smile she doesn't return. "Your mama better not call here asking what I did to your head," she says, and walks to the cash register.

Outside, I shiver at the breeze that brushes against my newly exposed neck as I walk to Marissa's car. My now useless hair tie is hanging loosely from my wrist, and I consider turning it into a tiny slingshot against the window to get Marissa's attention, since she's obviously too wrapped up in thrashing around to some song I can't hear to open the damn door. Instead, I tap once, twice, and then three more times in rapid succession until she finally turns to me with a scowl I know and love. "How kind of you to let me in," I say when I slide in next to her. She turns on the ignition.

"I know," she says. "So. You feel gayer?"

I let out a breathless laugh. "Are you serious?"

She shrugs and backs out of her parking spot. Then she turns onto the street, heading toward the grocery store so I can make my shift. "Just asking," she says. "I think you looked fine before."

"Yeah, well. So do I look like shit or halfway decent?"

"You look good, dude. Just . . ." She lets the words hang in the air until I realize she's not going to continue. Instead, we sit in silence for the ten minutes it's going to take until we get to Greg's.

Is it wild to get a haircut that looks maybe a little like your sort-of-ex-girlfriend's new girlfriend? Possibly.

Marissa is reading my thoughts as usual, because the only thing she says is "fuck Yasmin" before turning the music up to blast.

✴ ✴ ✴

I had hoped Mom would have a late shift tonight, but the hair gods considered my request and laughed. Instead, her janky green Toyota is in the driveway and my heart is in my throat.

When I walk through the front door, the house is appropriately lit and Dad is in the kitchen while Mom lounges on the couch. I've barely closed the door behind me when I hear the baritone in her voice, so deep it could be my father.

"What have you done to your head?"

Fuck.

"Hey, Mom!" I try to sound cheery. Dad stifles a laugh, and I ignore him. Evidently, he's sober enough today to be annoying as opposed to traumatizing.

"You're home!" I hear Trinity call from upstairs before she flies down the steps and latches onto my waist.

"Hey, kid." I pat her back, but Mom still wants my attention.

"Your hair," Mom says. "Where is it?"

"Whoa," Trinity says, now noticing the change. "Cool," she says.

"No, it is not cool!" Mom's baritone voice has suddenly become a soprano. "What in God's name have you done? Are you out of your mind?"

"It's just hair, Mom." I try to shuffle past Trinity into the living room. I don't want to admit it, but whatever Dad's got on the stove smells incredible and what I had for lunch hours ago isn't cutting it.

"What are you cooking, Dad?" I ask, because talking to him suddenly seems better than trying to calm Mom down.

Before I reach the kitchen, she grabs my arm so hard I feel like my circulation has stilled. "Listen to me when I talk to you. You are not the adult in this house."

"Yes, ma'am," I whisper, and the house goes still. For a moment, it feels exactly like the night I came home last July. The air feels poisonous, like if I breathe too hard, I'll start convulsing. My throat gets so tight I'm afraid someone somewhere will have to cut a hole into it. Between the two of my parents, Mom's the only one who's ever hit me. With her nails in my skin, the memory of the sting on my cheek blooms.

Before I was outed, things were so much easier between us. Yes, we fought about Dad, but we were good. Your typical mom-and-daughter. She complained about me doing my homework, and I complained about my part-time job, and then we'd both come home and relax together, watching old reruns of *Perry Mason* and new episodes of *Judge Judy*.

But now I'm the enemy. I'm the one capable of mischief and deception. And for most parents, maybe, this hair thing would be annoying. Frustrating. A go-to-your-room kind of thing. But I can see how dilated Mom's eyes are. I can feel her fingers tightening. Maybe this is it. The battle we've been waiting for. Maybe Mom feels like this is my final transformation: I've gone total alien and launched a full-scale invasion against her tidy, Christian home.

But then Dad eases in between us.

"Hey now," Dad says, touching Mom's arm. Of all the devilry the man brings into this house, his one saving grace is that he never, not once, gave a shit that I was gay. Somehow, when he found out, it was like water on a duck's back. He even congratulated me for being honest with myself about who I was. *You should be proud of her*, Dad said to my mom that night, pressing an ice pack to my cheek. *Some kids would go crazy with the lie.* He couldn't stop the daily Bible study sessions that Mom subjected me to—I don't even know if he disagreed with them, exactly, but he didn't encourage them, either.

"It doesn't look bad, baby! She looks just like her old man." Dad uses the same breezy tone he used then, reaching over and rubbing a hand into my newly short curls. I want to relish the approval, but it makes me feel angry, instead. Ill. Like maybe I am doing everything exactly wrong.

I look at Mom. Her nostrils are flaring in and out so fast that I'm afraid she'll hyperventilate.

"What's going on? Is it that little girl again?" she asks. I don't know if she's referring to Yasmin or the girl Miss Taylor caught me with the day she called to out me to my mom. I try not to think about that too much—it's mostly a blur anyway.

Lots of screaming and tears, and Trinity hiding in her room. The girl's name was Hayley, though. Hayley Gomez. She was nice. I wonder what happened to her. But that's not the question Mom wants answered.

"No, Mom," I say.

"Drugs?"

"What? No! God." Jesus, again with the drugs. She asked the same thing when I got outed. I pull away from her, and we both stumble backward, me accidentally knocking into Dad, but he steadies me with his hands. "Mom, I just cut my hair. I'm not suddenly flunking out of school and hanging with junkies."

She stares at me, but somehow the distance between us clears her eyes. She starts to breathe normally again.

"Still gay, though," Mom mutters, and that's it—that's the line between us. One wrong move and I could trip us into war. I could scream. I could throw things. I could be my dad.

Instead, I laugh. "Really, Mom?"

She glares at me, and I feel the string waiver, push, and pull.

"Yes, then. I cut my hair, and I'm still gay."

She takes a sharp breath, and lets it loose. Then she squares her shoulders and turns away from me. She goes into her room and shuts the door. The string goes slack, but I still struggle to breathe.

Later that night, when Trinity falls asleep after a couple of hours of watching Barry Allen and his distinctly quieter family on *The Flash*, I go back to my room. Tessa still hasn't accepted my friend request, and I don't want to stare at my phone all night, so I turn on my shitty Lenovo laptop instead. It's literally only good for writing essays for class and listening to music, but that's all I want right now anyway. I check my email perfunctorily and see a couple of welcome-back-to-school messages, including one from Naomi. I assume it's a required message, since the counselor is cc'd on the email. It's the end of July, so school doesn't actually start for another three weeks, but I guess they have to make sure the delinquents catch up. It's filled with suggested meeting dates, including a couple that include all three of us, and then a few college prep sessions.

Right. College. That's a thing people think about. I used to think about it, in the *before* times. Truth be told, though, it's barely crossed my mind since then. The email suggests I prepare a list of colleges to apply to, but I've barely accepted the fact that I'm back on the cross-country team. I haven't processed too much beyond that.

I turn on my Queer Lady playlist and type "colleges" into Google, scrolling idly as Hayley Kiyoko begins to sing.

A knock at the door interrupts my thoughts. I turn, and I'm only vaguely surprised to see Dad, leaning against an arm over his head in the doorway. By the hesitant smile on his lips, I can tell he's been there for a minute. Standing there, watching me, wanting to say something but not knowing what. He does that a lot.

"What?" I ask, trying to be neither aggressive nor welcoming. I hope my voice conveys the ambivalence.

"Oh, uh . . ." He moves the overhead arm to scratch his chin, as if he wasn't expecting my acknowledgment. "Sorry about your mom. You know she can get crazy sometimes."

Dude, seriously?

He scratches his chin again and points at my lap. "What are you looking at?"

"Colleges," I say, and then immediately regret it. I don't need any more people commenting on what I should or should not be planning for over the next twelve months.

Thankfully, since education isn't Dad's expertise, he only nods. "Can I come in?" he asks. I shrug and gesture toward my bed. He takes a seat on the edge, and I turn my chair so that we're facing each other.

"So," he says after a moment of silence. "How are things? I never know what's up with you anymore."

I try not to clench my jaw. If this becomes one of his waxing-nostalgic moments about how we used to build pillow forts together before I was old enough to maintain my well-deserved irritation with him, I will snap. Or, I would snap, if I wasn't so goddamn used to it by now. But he doesn't continue. Just lets the statement hang in the air.

I do, too.

"I like that." He tries again, and at first I don't know what he's talking about, but then he nods toward the Lenovo. "What's that song?"

"Oh." I forgot the music was on. "'Talia,' by this singer King Princess."

"She's cool." He nods along for a minute. "Yeah. Yeah, I like her sound."

"Yeah, me, too." I hesitate. "Yasmin showed her to me. She, uh, she made this playlist actually."

"For real?" Dad pauses to listen again. Then, he says, "She's got good taste. I'd like to listen to more. Does she—she has an album?"

"Oh—King Princess? Yeah, maybe. I don't have it, though."

"I'll look for it," Dad says, this time to himself. "I'll see if I can find it at Greg's or something later. Get it for you."

I look at him while he nods. Nods and listens and nods. Of everything he's done, this is always the worst, because I believe him—I do. I believe that in this moment, right now, he completely intends to do the thing he's promising to do.

I also believe that he won't.

Alcohol does funny things to your memory. To your promises. To your intentions.

"And, now, who's this?" I blink again, realizing the song has changed. "PVRIS," I say, pronouncing it like *Paris*.

His smile grows wide as he assesses me. "You like that rock music, huh? The, like—" He stops talking to bang his head around a little, and move his hands like a drummer. It makes me laugh, just a little, but it's enough to make his grin confident. "Yeah, yeah. You get that from your mom."

"Really?" And I ask the question not because I mean it—obviously, Mom and I have listened to her music collection once upon a time—but because I can't help it. Despite everything, I want him to keep talking. To keep being normal, being my dad, for just a few more minutes. I need at least one moment of normal parenting behavior.

"Yeah," Dad says, growing more animated. "Yeah, she liked that—what do you call it? That crazy stuff. That Linkin Park, AFI, Foo Fighters, all that kinda stuff. Took her to some concerts when we was kids. But, you know, I managed to convince her to let us name you after one of my favorites."

"I know, Dad." For once, I'm only pretending to be annoyed that he's repeated this story at least a dozen times to me throughout my life. About the R & B goddess Aaliyah and how God took her way too soon (amen and amen). But it makes me wonder. Maybe Mom would want to listen to this stuff as much as he seems to want to . . . but the name of the playlist literally includes "Queer Lady." Mom isn't ready for that yet. Clearly.

"You said Yasmin made you this?" he asks, and I nod again,

suddenly feeling a little smaller and then a little angry, because this time it's not his fault. "I haven't seen her around here lately."

He waits for me to respond, and for some reason, I feel like I owe him something. Or rather, it's that I don't know when this will happen again. This moment of father-daughter normal. "Yeah," I say. "We're not really talking right now. But she made this for me last year." Before Yasmin kissed me, but after Mom had declared our house a homo-free zone. When Yasmin was still my best friend, my chosen family. The last person, after Mom, who I thought would let me down.

But that's what you get for trusting people, I guess.

Of course, I don't say this to Dad. I just look away. Let the music play.

"It's good," Dad says, finally. "It's a good mix." I nod yet again, and after a while, he stands, stretches. "I'm gonna make a bowl of ice cream," he says. "Do you want some?" He waits for me to respond again, and when I don't, he walks to the door, touching my shoulder as he goes. Just before he leaves, though, he turns back to me and says, "I love you."

And that—that makes me so angry. Because what does that even mean? That he'll change? That he's sorry? No. If that were true, we wouldn't be in this situation to begin with. Mom wouldn't be miserable, and Trinity wouldn't be numb, and I wouldn't be . . . whatever I am. So what is love, exactly? If it's this—this house, and these people, full of anger, and heartbreak, and letdown after letdown after letdown—then fuck love. I'm over it.

When another loud, angsty PVRIS song comes on, I turn it up as high as it can go. I hope he hears it—and Mom, too. I want the house to hum with fury. With all the rage, and confusion, and hopelessness I've felt for the past seventeen years of my life.

How's that for love?

CHAPTER 7

I don't have practice the next day, and since it's my last week of summer employment so I can prep for school in a couple weeks (Mom's rules), I'm tasked with making sure Lonnie Martinez is a superstore employee before I go. We're in the back, sorting extra-firm tofu from medium-firm tofu when Lonnie suddenly looks up, squinting at my head.

"Your hair is gone."

Incredible powers of observation. "Yes."

"It's dope. I like it."

I try not to blush, but I'm betrayed by leftover fondness for Las Vegas's favorite teen drummer. "Thanks," I mutter.

"You talk to that girl yet?"

I nearly drop a container of tofu on my foot. "What girl?"

"The cute one."

"Because there can only be one?"

"Oh, are you a player, son? My bad."

I snort at the ridiculous suggestion that I could possibly manage more than one love interest. I have enough trouble managing anxiety, depression, and crippling self-doubt. "Ha ha. No, I haven't. I mean—I *have*. We run together, so I see her. Sometimes."

Lonnie nods thoughtfully. They don't say anything more, but I still haven't had anyone else to talk to about Tessa yet and . . . well, fuck it. "I *want* to talk to her."

"Mm-hmm?"

"But . . . I'm gay."

"Right, right."

"And . . . what if she's not gay?"

Lonnie bursts out laughing. "Ah! That ultimate fear!"

"I'm serious!"

"It's a serious thing!" Lonnie takes on a sage look and leans forward on the trolley they were holding. "Okay, say she's not gay."

"Okay."

"So you move on."

"Great."

"But I have eyes that see, and you have eyes that see, and regardless of her professed sexuality, she is very clearly into you."

"What? No. She . . . I mean . . ."

Lonnie gives me a hard side-eye. "Aaliyah. My dude."

I feel like my bones have gone slack. "I don't know! Girls are weird! I've thought *some* girls were into me who *weren't*, and now I don't know *what* to believe!"

"Classic queer anxiety." Lonnie nods to themself. "Listen. I don't know about these previous girls, but I will say from experience that any person who demonstrates interest, usually has interest, regardless of whether they either (a) act on that interest or (b) act on that interest and then pretend said action never took place."

"That is highly specific."

"Welcome to the gay experience, my friend. This is only the beginning."

My bones melt, and I become a puddle on the ground. Lonnie bends down and gently pats my shoulder in a there-there kind of way. We're being utterly dramatic and ridiculous, and I *love* it. My God, to be a queer among queers. It's an intoxicating feeling.

"Oh. Hey."

The new voice brings us back to reality. Marissa is standing in front of us, one hand gripping her phone so hard her knuckles turn white. I know I haven't done anything wrong, but I suddenly feel exposed, like I've been revealed to have some secret self that has aligned herself with Marissa's worst enemy. "Dee said I could come back here," she continues, "but, um . . . I'll meet you outside, Aali." She turns and walks away, and Lonnie stares after her, their mouth open in a small "o."

"Y'all are friends?" Lonnie says, still staring at the door that has closed behind Marissa.

"Yeah," I say. I don't know why I'm so quiet.

Lonnie laughs softly to themself. "Damn. That's a trip." I continue sitting there on the floor, staring at my feet like I've been scolded by a parent. "We used to be friends," Lonnie says then. "Her and I. We were in a band together."

"I know," I mumble. "I used to watch you perform."

"Ah." Lonnie nods. "So that's why you been so weird with me. You know all the 'ish." They go back to unpacking tofu, and I stand quickly.

"Actually, I don't. I don't know anything except that the band broke up."

Lonnie nods again but doesn't say anything. I know Marissa's waiting for me—my shift ended ten minutes ago—but I feel awkward leaving Lonnie like this. Like I've . . . betrayed them, or something. Or like I've messed up whatever possible queer bonding we had going.

"Um. I gotta go, but . . . I'll see you at our next shift?"

"Sure," they say. And that's that.

★ ★ ★

Outside, Marissa is leaned back in her seat, dark sunglasses covering her eyes as she props her legs up on the dash. I rap on the windshield with my free hand, the other one gripping a six-pack of Coke. Dad has apology meals; I have apology soda. And while I know I didn't do anything wrong, I still feel weirdly guilty.

Marissa lifts her sunglasses lazily. Then she reaches over to the passenger seat and unlocks the door. "About Lonnie," I say when I take my seat, but Marissa waves it off.

"Don't worry about it. You're coworkers."

"Yeah, but . . ."

"It's fine," she says, in a tone that indicates that the conversation is over. I could overrule her, but there's really no reason to. I sit back and wait for her to fuss around with the engine. It takes three or four tries for the car to start, but we get there eventually. "To our spot, right?" she says.

I hesitate, but there's no reason to dwell.

"Yes," I say. "Please."

Our spot is in Coronado Hills, a ritzy new neighborhood still in the midst of development. It's got several winding roads that lead to both dead ends and plots of land getting dug up, and we turn onto a familiar street dotted with lampposts. Marissa parks her car in front of a vast desert of sand and construction debris. When we first started coming here a few months ago, there was a lot more nothing, but it's slowly turning into a park or condominium or whatever right before our eyes.

Until that happens, though, we've still got the view. From here, you can see the entire city of Las Vegas, from the airplanes flying out of Reid airport to the stratosphere. And yet amid all the neon lights, the stars still shine at night.

It's beautiful. And it's ours.

Marissa pulls over, and we slam the doors shut together. Then we both climb onto the hood, me still holding on to the six-pack. Marissa grabs one from my hand and pops it open. Then she takes a long, loud gulp, finishing with a satisfied sigh.

"That good, huh?" I grab a can for myself as she leans over and burps into my ear. "Wooow, dude. Really?"

"You love me," she sings, and it's a real melody—not the fake intonation she uses to be annoying. It's a line from one of Light Pollution's old songs, a midtempo rock ballad that Marissa wrote:

You love me
I know you do
So let's let go of the past
And what it put us through

Watching her perform was like magic. Even now, as I'm looking at her, I can feel some of it. The light is reflecting off her sunglasses as she takes in the sunset, and her red hair blows gently in the wind. Sometimes, I remember that she used to be a real-life teen idol to me. A girl I used to daydream about in my classes. And now here she is next to me, sipping soda and humming to herself.

Sometimes, if I'm not careful enough, I let myself remember our kiss the night of Susannah's party. I replay the way she looked at me when we finally broke apart, lips swollen, eyes glazed. It was teen lust, sure. Just two gal pals having fun—nothing serious. But just when I thought neither of us would say anything—that we'd laugh it off, maybe, and call it a night—her eyes had fluttered closed and she pressed a kiss to my cheek, and then another to my ear. She held me there, and I let my head fall to her shoulder, burying my head just beneath her chin. For that instant, that *millisecond*, I let myself believe there was something between us. Something real.

And I swear I've learned my lesson, but it's still nice to pretend.

"I miss that song," I whisper, meaning that she should continue, keep us in the world of memory and fantasy. But as soon as I speak, she stops. The spell is broken.

I try to think of something else to say, but she beats me to it.

"So," she says. "Have you thought about what colleges you're applying to, yet, Miss Marshall?"

"Ew, gross," I groan, and she laughs, probably taking pleasure in her sweet and sudden revenge. "Why would you bring that up?"

She takes another sip of her Coke. "My mom asked me."

"Really?"

"Yeah, you know she's weird. Has her moments of interest in my life."

"Mm."

"So?"

"So what?"

"Soooo," she says, now using the annoying singsong tone. She leans against me so much that I nearly topple over. "Thoughts?"

"Fine," I say, pushing back against her so that she just has her head on my shoulder. "I'll probably apply to CSN."

"The community college?"

"Yeah. It's nearby so it'll be easy to get to."

"Is that where you *want* to go, though? Like, if you could go anywhere."

I think for a moment. "Last year . . . I had my sights set on this place in San Diego. Near the beach. I thought it seemed nice. Calm. And not too far from Trinity, once I get a car."

She waits for me to continue, but I don't. I don't want to talk about what I used to want. I guess she senses it because she finally just nods against my shoulder. "So when is the car thing happening?"

"Um." I rub my chin. "I haven't saved enough, but eventually. Maybe I'll convince Mom I can work next semester."

"And what do you want to study?"

"Mechanical engineering." She rolls her eyes and goes back to looking at the desert skyline. I smile. "I don't know yet. Haven't thought that far." I glance down at her red hair. "What about you?"

"Music, probably," she says. "If I study somewhere."

"You still think you'll take a year off?"

She shrugs beneath my chin. "Or more." I move to look at her, and she takes the opportunity to finish her can of Coke and grab a new one. "I don't know. I've thought about college," she says. "Berklee, maybe, in Boston, you know? But that's far from . . ." She clears her throat, and for a moment I would've sworn she was about to say "you." *But that's far from you.* "It's far. And cold," she continues, shuddering. "I'm thinking maybe if I can get a full-time job at the casino Mom works at after we graduate, I could make enough to get a new guitar. Start performing again. Like, really performing."

This would be the perfect time to pry. *What happened to the old guitar?* I could ask. *Why did you stop performing?* But I don't want to push her too far. Marissa rarely talks to me about this stuff—doesn't talk to anyone about it. Other than that night at the house party, she hasn't performed onstage, and even then, it's because Susannah was loaded and offered a crap ton of money. These days, she prefers to pretend like her life as a local legend never existed. Like it was a dream she's already forgotten, and I know all about that. But she's talking now, and I want to savor it. It may not happen again.

She settles back onto my shoulder, her fingers playing with the Coke can's metal tab. "One of these days, I'll do it," she whispers. "Get the band back together again. Or I'll form a new band. After school ends, and I can get out of Mom's house and do my own thing, I'm gonna make some real music. And get the fuck out of here."

"Where do you want to go?" I ask quietly.

"Maybe Los Angeles," she says. "Or something. What's the music scene like in San Diego?"

I try to quiet my chuckle, so that the vibration doesn't disturb her, make her shift. "When I find out, I'll let you know," I say.

She stays where she is, and holds on to my arm. "Please do," she sighs, and the words float on the wind, sounding almost like a song I want to play on repeat.

★ ★ ★

When dusk settles in, Marissa and I get ready to go, strapping ourselves back into our car, and just as I'm clicking the seat belt in, I get a text from Naomi.

"What is it?" Marissa asks, probably noticing the deep frown that has etched into my face.

I look up. "Oh. Uh. The team dinner. Naomi's making sure I'm coming." I've been getting along with the team cordially for the past two months, but I'm not exactly ready to break bread with them. It's one thing to run in someone's proximity and stretch in their general direction for ten minutes before and after. It's another to spend two hours sitting and talking and opening yourself up to memories of how much you were a shitty teammate the year before, especially since part of Coach's tradition is to take aside the parents of whoever is hosting that night's dinner and leave the rest of us to "bond."

"Of course you're coming!" Marissa cocks her head at me. "Aren't you?" Before I can answer her, my phone starts to buzz with a call. *Fuuuuck.*

"Sorry," I murmur. "Do you mind if I take this?"

Marissa waves a hand, and I click accept.

"Hi," Naomi says. "So are you coming to the team dinner tonight?"

Apparently, she's ignoring my noncommittal "Not sure" text. I rack my brain for a satisfying response and come up short. "I actually . . . kind of . . . thought that I'd skip it."

"You WHAT?" Marissa shouts at the same time Naomi says, "Absolutely not" with unnerving calm. Marissa stops the car just as we're about to hang a left at the intersection out of Coronado Hills, leaning in closer to make sure Naomi can hear my admonishment.

Reluctantly, I switch on the speakerphone.

"Aaliyah! You've been talking for the past three months about redeeming yourself. About being a better runner, about being a better teammate—"

"Exactly," Naomi cuts in. "You are absolutely not missing this."

"We won't let you."

Oh, my good lord. "Okay!" I shout at the both of them. "Okay, okay, fine. Yes, I'll be there tonight."

"Good," Marissa says, settling back into her seat and starting the car again.

"Glad that's settled," Naomi says, her voice displaying the height of perkiness. "See you both tonight."

"See you!" Marissa calls as I mutter a goodbye and click off the phone. Then she reaches over and touches my knee. "You're gonna be great. Promise."

I sigh and sink farther into my seat. Sometimes, having friends is overrated.

CHAPTER 8

If I could fast-forward through this dinner tonight, I would.

Unfortunately, Marissa and I can't get ready together. Her mom is home tonight—shock of all shocks—and she's helping Marissa get pretty, whether she likes it or not. I guess it's fun to play mommy-and-daughter as long as it's not full-time. So I'm on my own tonight, staring at my shorn curls in the bathroom mirror across the hall from my bedroom.

Cutting my hair seemed like a good idea at the time—after all, shorter hair is supposedly easier to deal with. But now that nearly a week has passed and I've slept off whatever goop Jackie put in my hair, my curls are just as flat and fuzzy as they've always been. They're just shorter and closer to my head. On top of that, everything about my outfit feels wrong—from my holey jeans to my plain white shirt. I was trying to go for my usual look—casual, but cool. Or I thought it was cool. Right now, it strikes me as lazy. Team dinners aren't necessarily formal affairs, but Coach does expect us to clean up nice. It is, after all, one of the only times we aren't all sweaty and dehydrated.

After another moment of staring catatonic in front of the mirror, I realize that it might be time for me to call in reinforcements. With Marissa out of commission, I only have one option left. I swallow my pride, knowing I'm going to regret it. "Mom!" I yell from my open door.

"What?!" she responds from downstairs.

I take a deep breath, almost 100 percent certain that I'm about to make a horrible mistake. "Can you help me?"

There's a moment of quiet, and then I hear Mom's voice more clearly than before. I realize she's probably moved to the bottom of the stairs. "With what?" she asks. I don't know why she doesn't just come up the stairs; everything is always just a *little* more difficult than it needs to be between us, isn't it? I let out another breath and walk to the top of the stairs, popping my head over the railing so that we can see each other. Mom is tapping her fingers against the staircase, waiting as if she has better things to do than whatever fresh hell I have in store for her. For a moment, I want to just shut my mouth and leave her be. Who cares if I look like I just rolled out of bed? At least I won't have to deal with another awkward and unpleasant conversation with Mother Dearest.

Then again . . . tonight is a big deal. Tessa's going to be there and, fuck it, for that matter, so will Radhika. I need to look like I give a damn. And since Mom is the whole reason I fell apart, she can damn well help me look put together. Even if it's just for a couple of hours. I swallow my pride and plaster on a smile.

"I'm not sure what to wear tonight. Can you help me?" It's my church-daughter voice, the one I've learned to cultivate with even more perfection over the past year. Quiet, clear, and polite. Nonthreatening. Mom looks down with an "oh," as if she was expecting a much more monumental ask. I don't know what that would be, but everything I do seems big to her now. Once I started kissing girls, every step I took could set off a land mine with her. I don't know if she realizes that's her fault, though. Not mine.

It's not mine.

Why did I ask for her help again? The question bounces around for a while as Mom nods to herself and then looks back up at me, her eyes a little less cloudy than they usually are when they're staring at me. Usually, she looks like she's trying to look at anything *but* me. A memory, perhaps, of the daughter she raised, and not the one she ended up with. She makes a move toward the stairs, and I back up rapidly, retreating to the bathroom, like each step she takes forward is a promise of malice, revenge for every disappointment I've managed to become.

That's what it used to be, not too long ago. Her steps up the stairs, clenched jaw, pursed lips, a clouded look of rage and disappointment. But when she finally reaches me, her touch is gentle. A light brush of fingers on my shoulder. "Let me look at you," she says.

I swallow the fear, the painful memories. I turn toward her, and take another step back. She nods again, looking at my outfit. "What about the dress you wore for Lawrence's baptism last year? The dark blue one?"

Of course she'd suggest a dress from church. To quote *Aladdin*, I think I might have a heart attack from that surprise. But it's not a terrible idea. The dress has a nice sweetheart neckline and flairs at my waist, falling just past my knees. Being barely six weeks old, Lawrence clearly didn't care what I wore that day, but my aunt and uncle approved.

"My niece is so beautiful!" Aunt Linda had said, pressing a kiss into my cheek before dashing to another relative, eyes bright with the joy of a child who wasn't yet old enough to disappoint her. This had been just two weeks before Mom found out about me being gay, so she didn't have reason to be disappointed with me, either. That day, I had been exactly who she thought I was—the dutiful Christian daughter, pretty and feminine in a perfect blue dress.

Now I want to rip the dress to shreds.

But even though she's trying to hide it, I see the flicker of hope in Mom's eyes. The memory is not lost on her, either. A time from *before*, when her smiles weren't quite so few and far between. And despite what Mom might think, I do want to make her smile.

I do want to make her proud.

Tonight, I want to make a lot of people proud.

So I keep my mouth shut again. I plaster on another smile. I return to my church-daughter voice. "That's a great idea, Mom!" I say, voice bright and chipper. And I walk to my closet and pull out the blue dress. She's still standing in the doorway of the bathroom when I return, and when I make my grand entrance, she smiles.

"There's my daughter," she says. And I want to scream, and I want to cry, but I smile back, and even do a little twirl.

"Good choice, Mom."

She keeps her smile and steps forward, taking my chin into her hand. I flinch out of reflex, but she's not hurting me. Just looking. Examining.

"Do you want to try some makeup?" she asks, and this time, the hope in her voice is barely concealed. I want to say no, but I don't know the last time she touched me without anger. I don't know the last time we were this close without a threat trailing behind. I don't know the last time I felt safe with my mother.

Like I was the one being cared for.

And it may not be the way I want, or the way I need, but I am willing to settle. I am willing to take whatever I can get. So

I swallow my pride, and the tears pricking the side of my face, and I smile, smile, smile. Keep her hopeful, keep her here.

"Yes, Mom," I hear myself say. "I would love that." And so she turns and hurries back down the steps to gather her makeup collection. She hurries like I might disappear at any second, might return to the alien who's taken residence in her home, and I watch her go, feeling smaller with each step she takes until I feel like maybe I will, finally, disappear.

✳ ✳ ✳

Curtis's house is a lot fancier than mine by a long shot. In his neighborhood, the mountains are basically in his backyard, and the house itself has a brick exterior in various shades of gray. Two rustic-style lampposts light the way down a pebble-stone path lined with different kinds of cacti, a few large boulders, and rosemary in full bloom. Grass landscaping isn't unusual in Las Vegas; there's just no point, unless you're willing to foot a massive water bill or go with fake grass. Most people just stick with gravel and call it a day, but Curtis's parents are clearly interested in style.

That's cool. My parents don't have style, but they also don't have money, so there's nothing I can do about that. I wave to my mom after she drops me off, with a pit burrowed into my stomach even as she keeps smiling, driving off into the night. I don't turn until the car disappears around the corner, desperate as I am to hold on to the extended moment of normalcy. Maybe the moment has no room for the real me, but the peace and calm might be worth that.

In my other hand, I'm holding two small boxes of vegan chocolate cupcakes. We had to rush to Whole Foods for them after Naomi sent a text reminding me that dinner tonight was a potluck. God knows what I would do without that girl. It was an extravagant expense, but I have a lot to make up for tonight.

Another car shows up just as I begin walking toward Curtis's driveway—a new-looking silver car that I've come to recognize over the past two months. Tessa steps out, and tonight her long braids are pulled into one large braid and swept over her right shoulder, revealing three gemstone studs in her left ear. She doesn't usually wear earrings during practice. She's wearing black wedges and a flowy purple dress, not too short but short enough to show off the muscles in her legs. I can't tell if she's wearing makeup from here, but God knows she doesn't need it.

She smiles when she sees me, and we fall in step together.

"I like the hair," she says as we approach Curtis's door.

I swallow and try to smile, the pit in my stomach suddenly filled with a swarm of butterflies. "Thanks."

For a second, there's that look again—that quick up-and-down like maybe she looks at me the way I look at her. But I don't dare hope. After all, she still hasn't accepted my Instagram request—not that that matters. Who even notices that kind of thing? Not me. And honestly, with Mom's shred of decency tonight, there's a part of me that doesn't even want to entertain the thought. Wouldn't it be nice if I were exactly the daughter she wanted—a straight, feminine girl excited to see one of the boys? Curtis, maybe?

But then Tessa reaches out and knocks on the door, her shoulder brushing mine and sending my lungs into overdrive. Yeah, there's no use. I'm as gay as Elton John's husband.

Coach is the one who opens the door. Immediately, his face pulls into an exaggerated look of shock and awe. I can feel my heart rate speed into double-time. Maybe it's the makeup, or the fact that I bothered to show up this time, but in this moment, I'm almost 100 percent sure it's my new short haircut.

I brace myself for a joking comparison to the Dora Milaje from *Black Panther*, or something equally related to Coach's limited repertoire of Black pop cultural trivia that will undoubtedly—though accidentally—come off as racist. But before he can say anything, Curtis bursts forward with a broad grin splitting across his lips. "Yo," he says, clapping me on the shoulder and bringing me farther into his entryway. It quickly opens up into a big living room and a spacious kitchen, where most of the team has already begun unpacking their dinner items. Curtis gestures toward Tessa, who follows in after us. "Aali looks good, right?" he says to her. "I gotta step up my hair game!"

Tessa smiles as she walks past us to put her dish on the

kitchen island. "She looks amazing." At that, my eyes dart toward her, but she's looking at Curtis now. "And you're right. We're out here changing things up, and you're still rocking that same old look."

This garners a couple of chuckles from the team, and Curtis pats his head for effect. Then a few compliments are thrown my way, and Emmanuel appears from somewhere to distract his dad and pull him off to the side, ostensibly to ask about whatever it is they brought for the potluck. Coach may be a white man from Minnesota, but Emmanuel's mom is from Lima, in Peru. Most people can't tell by looking at him that he's half brown, but he's showing 100 percent brown-kid solidarity. I adore him for it.

Curtis wraps his arm around me in a half hug, indicating to the team that they're dismissed. Then he takes out his phone and pulls up his photos, scrolling through the album until he lands on a picture of his older sister, Sharice, who graduated two years ago. "She got her hair done like yours when she went natural last year. Dope, right? She ain't even grow it out since then."

"Thanks, Curtis." I give him a half hug back, and he squeezes my shoulder, letting go only when the doorbell rings again. I walk to the island to take out my cupcakes, acutely aware that neither Naomi nor Marissa has arrived yet. Tessa has moved to a group of the girls—Radhika, of course, along with Jaslene and

Tracey. I consider joining them, but I feel rooted to the ground beneath my feet.

I was never close to the three of them last year—outside of cross-country, we had different classes, different interests. They talked about boys, and I talked about . . . well, not that. I felt awkward around them, as if there were a code of heterosexuality that I was still puzzling out. I don't mind if they know I'm gay; I'm sure a few people could guess. It just hasn't really come up.

They probably wouldn't care. Last year's homecoming queen and the captain of the dance team are both trans—which is to say that our so-called popular groups at school are seemingly teeming with queers, so I have a vague sense of safety myself when I walk the halls. But after everything that happened last year, I'm feeling generally uncomfortable with making nice. I can't even trust my own friends and family to have my back—who has time to figure out new people?

I fiddle with the cupcake box more and then spin around slowly, looking for a recycling bin. I don't find one. Instead, there's a growing pile of discarded grocery bags next to the side of the island. I drop my box there. Then I reach for the open bottle of sparkling apple cider and pour myself a glass, sipping until Coach finds me again.

"Aaliyah," he says as he leans against the counter, one arm crossed over the other. "I just wanted to say that I'm really proud of you. You've really been kicking butt this summer, doing some great practice runs. Seeing your motivation really keeps the team on point and focused."

I nod mutely, but my palms are starting to sweat. This is exactly what I want to hear, but praise after failure also has a funny way of making you remember everything you should be guilty for. Coach grasps my shoulder lightly and gently shakes me. "You're gonna kill it tomorrow. I know it."

This time, I try to smile. "Thanks, Coach." He smiles back and moves to probably offer a rallying speech to another teammate, but then he doubles back, his index finger in the air. "One other thing: *love* the short hair." He touches his own smooth, clean-shaven head. "It'll make getting ready for practice so much faster!" Then he departs, and I pretend not to notice Emmanuel giving his dad the thumbs-up from the mix of varsity boys and JV kids he's sitting with on the sofa.

"What are you chuckling at, lady?" I hear Marissa's voice from behind.

"Dude, finally!" I set my cup down on the island and fling my arms around her neck. "I thought I was going to be abandoned and alone tonight."

Marissa reaches around me to place whatever she brought onto the island. Then she wraps both her arms around my waist and lifts me up a few inches off the ground. I shouldn't be so surprised at her strength, given her muscular build, but I still lose my breath for the briefest of moments. "Don't be silly," she says. "I would never abandon you." She sets me back on the ground. "Mom was just having a little too much fun tonight."

I take the invitation to give her a good look—she's wearing fake lashes, bright red lipstick, and smoky eye shadow. "I mean, you look good. Not sure it's the occasion, but—"

"Shut up," she says, shoving me aside gently to put a box of Coke on the island.

"You know I love you," I singsong to her.

"I am aware," she says. Then she gives me a once-over. "Although you're one to talk. What happened to you?"

I blanch. "I look stupid, huh?"

"No! No. You look. I mean." She chuckles a little. "You look good. You *always* look good. Just a little different, that's all. I like the look."

I shrug. "Sure."

"I do! It's a little churchy—"

"My mom picked the outfit."

"—and that explains it. But you could never look bad, babe." She drapes an arm around me, and I let myself fall into her. Together we lean back against the counter and take in the territory. Tessa and the rest of the varsity girls team are standing off to the right, next to the dining table and the door that leads to Curtis's patio—I can see a sparkling pool outside, lit up by night lights. Emmanuel and most of the varsity boys are sitting on the couch ahead of us, in front of the fireplace and Curtis's big-screen TV mounted above it. I nod toward Emmanuel. "You want to join him?"

"No," Marissa says lightly. "I'll see him later. I'm good here."

She doesn't need to say that she's staying for me. We go back to scoping out the room in silence. Curtis and Coach are still standing in the hallway, with Curtis's dad, Mr. Barker. He's a tall, thin man in a dark jean button-down and black slacks, wearing expensive-looking loafers and what I imagine a Rolex probably looks like. Unlike Curtis, he has short, soft curls, like my dad— and me, now, I guess—and a diamond stud in each ear.

The man is the definition of fly. I see where Curtis gets his style, given his own red dress shirt and designer jeans. It's clear Curtis just got another haircut from the fresh fade on the side of his hair, framing his short locs perfectly. His shirt is unbuttoned, revealing a bright white crew cut tee underneath.

I study the two of them, standing so close together, a parent and child looking like they've never been more comfortable with another human being. Both of them are smiling with a level of ease I couldn't fake if I tried. If they've ever fought with each other, no one would know it. I've seen Curtis with his mom, too, and they look just like he and his dad do now. Tonight, she's probably working late on another case for the DA's office. Maybe that's something his parents fight about. There has to be something, right?

Curtis stops grinning with his dad long enough to look at his phone. A second later, the doorbell rings and Curtis speeds over before anyone else has a chance to react. When he flings open the door, Naomi is standing there, a massive bowl in her hands. Curtis grabs it without question, and Naomi turns around back toward her car, announcing that she has more food to bring.

"She must've texted him," someone near Tessa mutters from behind us, as Curtis places the bowl on the island.

"You sure he didn't just sense that she was nearby?" I hear Radhika snicker.

I turn toward them in time to see Tessa roll her eyes, but I can tell she's trying not to smile. "I'm gonna go help her," she says. She puts the bottle of water she's holding down between us, apologizing quickly before hurrying out the open door. Curtis follows close behind.

Marissa nudges me. "Should we help?"

I shrug. "I would, but I think the three of them have it covered."

A few minutes later, they reappear, carrying bags of disposable plates and utensils, a salad bowl, and several more bottles of water. Evidently, Naomi didn't trust most of us to bring the essentials. Judging from the chips, cupcakes, and trays of vegetable platters, she wasn't wrong. Marissa, Emmanuel, and I use this opportunity to be helpful and start to unpack the items she just brought in.

"Hey," Emmanuel says to me, holding up a can of Inca Kola—the most delicious soft drink known to mankind. Emmanuel's mom often brings him back snacks and other things from her visits to see their family in Lima.

"DUDE." I nearly tear off his hand trying to get to the can. Then I pop open the tab and inhale three gulps. "This is literal heaven, Manuel. Like, the literal drink of gods. Thank you." I don't know whether to hug him or shake his hand, so I go for a combination of both.

"Yeah, of course," Emmanuel says as he pulls away. "I know it's your favorite, so I made sure Dad didn't forget."

I blink. He brought it for me?

"I'm sure Dad and Naomi have already said something," he continues, "but I just want you to know that we're glad to have you back." He doesn't wait for me to respond, just goes back to helping Naomi and Curtis rearrange dishes on the kitchen island.

Sometimes, the idea of him and Marissa together makes my stomach curl—but it's not because Emmanuel is a bad guy. No, he's probably one of the most decent humans on the planet.

We dated for approximately eleven seconds in sixth grade. Mostly because that's what our classmates said we should do, since we hung out a little back then—and by hung out, I mean we sat together at lunch with Yasmin and a few other kids. But our classmates said we should do a lot of things that eleven-year-olds aren't ready for, and Emmanuel was the sweetest gentleman a girl could ask for. Once, he punched a kid in the nose because the kid kept demanding we kiss to prove we were together. We were in the middle of the cafeteria, and the boy kept chanting that I should "put out" because that's what Black girls do. He left with two bloody tissues stuck up his nose.

I always remembered Emmanuel for being a sweet guy. Apparently, that hasn't changed.

When the food is all set up, we begin piling food onto our paper plates and finding seats at the dining table. I sit between Naomi and Marissa, and Curtis sits next to his dad and Emmanuel. Once we're all settled in, Coach lightly taps his Coke can with a plastic fork.

"Okay, team, okay! Listen up." He clears his throat. "As we all know, tomorrow is our very first meet of the season." He pauses as some of our teammates clap and whoop. "Now, there are three things you're all supposed to remember tonight. Right?" He puts three fingers in the air. "What are they?"

"Eat well. Stretch right. Sleep." The whole table, even Mr. Barker, recites Coach's three rules back to him as he ticks them off each finger.

"Exactly! Good. And the last thing for tomorrow: It's not about speed, right, but endurance. If you jet through the first mile, you'll be dead on your feet by the last one. So take your time, and ramp up. Visualize one step at a time. Okay?"

We each murmur a different version of assent. He nods. "Fantastic. Now let's dig in!" A few of the kids, including most of the girls except me and Marissa, take a moment to bow their heads, eyes closed as they say grace before their meal. I don't do either of those things, but old habits die hard. I say a quick prayer in my head—*Thank you, God, for this meal we are about to receive and for blessing us with friends and family to receive it with*—and dive in. Then Coach nods to Mr. Barker, and they retreat to the outside patio.

Immediately, the table explodes into conversation—about school starting next week. About college applications coming up. About tomorrow's meet. I try to keep up, not saying much, but laughing at the right jokes and commenting where appropriate. Naomi, Marissa, and a few kids who ran track last season start in with one another about which is better—cross-country or track. Marissa, to my horror, is Pro-Track; Naomi is Pro-Cross-Country. A debate erupts that nearly launches us into a food fight when someone—probably Jason on the JV team—jokingly throws a cupcake across the table. Well, he lightly tosses it and it lands three inches away from his plate, frosting down.

"Hey, man," Curtis says, grabbing a napkin and furiously rubbing at the frosting mark. "Watch the furniture. This ain't a house party!" But he's laughing, and so are we. Then Cody, another boy on the varsity team, makes a prediction that we'll make state tournament this year, now that Tessa's joined.

"I'll try to make you proud," Tessa says, a laugh in her voice.

"If Aaliyah can keep up," Radhika mutters to Tracey. They're sitting beside each other on my side of the table, but it's not like she whispered. We all heard her. A hush of "ooooh" settles over the table as my stomach plummets to my knees, and I suddenly feel like I'm going to puke. I see Tessa staring at me, and I stare down at my plate. If this had been before last season, I would've said something—a snarky comment about my running time to put Radhika back in her place. But I deserve her frustration. If it hadn't been for me, we probably would've made state last year. Apparently, I was a bad daughter, a boring friend, and a useless teammate. I deserve every shitty thing said to me.

Every word.

Beneath the table, I feel Marissa's hand find mine just as Emmanuel clears his throat.

"Rad," he says, taking a big bite of Naomi's spaghetti. He covers his mouth for a minute as he chews, as if he's trying to find the right words. Then he swallows and sticks a finger in his mouth like he's picking out the leftover pieces. Finally, he puts both elbows on the table and leans forward. "You know." He pauses, looks at Radhika. "And I know." He looks at the rest of the team. "That if Aaliyah were to literally fall asleep on the track, her ass would *still* run faster than you."

"Dayummm." Cody covers his mouth as the others try to hold back their laughter. I peek my head up in time to see Naomi's face struggle to stay composed.

"Whatever, Manny," Tracey says, glaring at him. "Just because you're *hooking up* with Aaliyah's girlfriend doesn't mean you get to be an ass." I blush at Tracey's implication and stare harder at my plate. I don't know if Marissa ever told Emmanuel about our kiss, even though it happened like the week before they started fooling around. Still, it's the last thing I want to think about right now, especially with Tessa sitting right across from us. I don't want her to get the wrong impression. That is, if she *had* been checking me out earlier. Then again, that could've been all in my head.

"Oh my gosh, I'm so lucky," Marissa says, releasing my hand long enough to let it fly to her chest. "I have not one but *two* lovers on the team?"

"I mean, we are all very attractive people," Emmanuel says.

"Yup," Curtis cuts in as a few people snicker and Radhika's ears go red. "A very attractive *team*. And as a *team*, we have each other's back. Right?"

"Right," Naomi says. Her voice is firm as she leans across the table, giving Tracey and Radhika a firm glare. Big sister of eight, everyone. One word, and suddenly the two girls are chastened little sisters.

For a few seconds, no one really talks. Then someone makes a comment that we're all hotter than the track team, and the argument continues anew. I feel Marissa's fingers brush the top of my hand, and even though she's not looking at me, engulfed as she is in defending the track team's honor, she keeps her hand in mine for the rest of the conversation.

Once everyone has become distracted enough, I quietly excuse myself to the bathroom. I shut the door behind me and then lean against it, my eyes closed as Radhika's words drive through me again. I don't want to be angry at her—she doesn't know why I fucked up. She doesn't know anything about me. Maybe I deserve to curse her out for exactly that reason, but I get it—I do. I understand feeling like someone you trust, like your team captain, has let you down in spectacular fashion.

Still, I can't get my heart under control, or my hands, which are shaking so bad that I have to put them behind me just to keep them still. I'm not angry, but I think I deserve just one minute. To remember that I really do fucking deserve this second chance; that I am worth more than anyone's disappointment, and anyone's expectations about who they thought I was, or should be.

I've spent almost a year trying to convince myself of that. And I deserve at least one minute more.

CHAPTER 9

I'm getting what I want today.

Last night, Mom got her perfect church-girl daughter, and my teammates got to tell me exactly what they thought of me. Good for them. But today? Today is all about what I want, and what I want—no, what I'm going to do—is leave Every. Single. Person. *In. The. Dust.*

We go through our stretches. Coach sends us on our warm-up run. And then I line up beside Marissa, Naomi, and the rest of the girls on the starting line, with Radhika and Tracey as far from me as they can be. Good. They're about to be even farther.

Marissa reaches over and squeezes my hand just before some man in the distance yells for us to ready ourselves. When the whistle blows, we're off.

Unlike last year, I start steady, keeping an even pace. I don't pick up until halfway through the second lap, and I sustain that speed just until the third mile. I'm not paying attention to the other runners, or to my team. You're only as good as your last run, and my run at the last meet was a shit show, so I know I'm better than that. I stay focused, passing each runner until I'm leading the pack. I don't even need to sprint by the time we near the finish line, but I do it anyway, because I need to make good time. Because I need to start out strong, and make sure that by the time this season ends, I can only ever say that I've done my best.

Coach is red in the face when I cross the line, and I realize that he's been cheering for me for the last lap and a half, probably jumping up and down and wearing himself out. He crushes me in a bear hug and then pushes me toward the water station, where a smiling volunteer hands me a paper cup filled with ice-cold water.

Ah. Sweet, sweet victory.

As I wait for the other runners to finish, I sit in the shade of our school's white tent, branded with our logo, with my earbuds in. The next finisher is Naomi, then a girl from the other school. Marissa comes through five minutes after her, and almost every girl from either team comes after that, including Radhika, then Tracey.

Tessa isn't dead last, but by the look on her face, she may as well be. She doesn't say anything to us when she crosses the line, just grabs a cup of water from a volunteer and stalks to an empty field to cool down.

"That sucks," Marissa says, one of my earbuds in her ear.

She's sitting next to me on the grass, her team jersey drenched in water and draped across her head. "She's normally so good at practice."

I mutter an *mm-hmm*, but I'm too busy watching Tessa. Something had to be up to run that badly. I would know.

"Hello?" Marissa says suddenly, speaking directly into my earbudless ear.

"Huh?" I turn back to her.

"I said, 'I kind of sucked, too.' Don't you think?"

"Oh." I lean back on my elbows, still watching Tessa. "No, I mean. I told you cross-county was hard. It's easy to keep focus during practice, but there's a lot more pressure when you've got a hundred people screaming at you and people you've never met crowding your running space. You'll do better next time."

"You think so?" she says, but I'm already standing and wiping off my legs. I hand her my remaining earbud and walk over to Tessa's field, ignoring Marissa when she asks where I'm going.

I don't really know what I can say to Tessa. I try to remember at least one of Coach's more rousing speeches about staying focused and keeping strong when your legs fail you, but when I get closer, I'm staring way too hard at how her body moves when she bends down to stretch, one arm over her head with the fingers of the other touching the ground. She stops her stretches when she sees me, and a smile replaces the scowl that had been on her face since the race ended.

"Hey," I say as she looks up. "You did really well."

She releases a breathy laugh and resumes stretching an arm above her head. "I did not."

I can't disagree with that, so I shrug and drop down next to her. "I mean. No." She laughs again. "But I know you can do better. And you know you can do better. And that's good to hold on to, right?"

She smiles at me, and something in my chest begins to piece itself back together. A horn goes off, and I glance back to see the boys start their run. My gaze sweeps over to our tent, and I see Marissa standing, her hands cupped around her mouth, probably cheering for Emmanuel. She glances my way and waves me back over. "Go on, cheer on the boys," Tessa says. "I probably should, too, actually."

She seems surprised when I offer her my hand, but doesn't hesitate to grab it so I can help her to her feet.

I count five seconds before she finally lets go.

★ ★ ★

When I get home, Mom's feet are propped on the coffee table and she's bent forward with what I assume is her signature red nail polish. In front of her, *Of Course the Husband Did It* or whatever is blinking across the faded color of our RCA big screen, which she still refers to as "new," even though it's older than I am.

I drop my bag by the shoes and lean against the staircase,

pretending to be interested in whatever fame-seeking detective is droning on about crimes of passion.

"So," I say when the show turns to the tearstained faces of the deceased's family. "I won."

Mom hesitates, the polish applicator held lightly between her fingers. Her nails are already expertly painted. After a second, she lets out a long, arduous sigh and sets the polish aside. She rises as if with great effort and turns to me, her arms open.

I hesitate. Is this . . . a hug? Seems suspect. But she squares her shoulders like she's preparing for war and then wraps her arms around me. It feels stiff and awkward, but it's . . . something. "Good job," she says. Then she plops back down on the seat. "Not that it'll make that hair grow any faster."

I bite down the frustration and proceed with a smile. "Thanks, Mom," I say, heavy on the sarcasm.

"I'm picking up Trini from her friend's house in a few minutes," she calls as I walk up the stairs.

In my room, I sit on the edge of my bed and flip through the channels until I find a rerun of some ninja fitness challenge that I've already seen. I should probably be stretching, like Coach always demands, but I'm feeling restless. When I hear the garage door open below, I decide to wander into Trini's empty room and riffle through the DVDs Mom bought her at the thrift store a few months ago.

Should I be ashamed of what I'm looking for? Absolutely

not. I pop her copy of *Sailor Moon R: The Promise of the Rose* into my PS4, the most expensive thing in my room, and maybe this house. Dad bought it for me years ago, the day after he kicked a hole through my wall. I don't remember why.

I settle onto the bed, satisfied. Marissa would laugh her ass off if she saw me watching this old and corny-ass anime, but Marissa doesn't have to know that it's one of my favorites. Marissa and I share almost everything, but this is too nerdy, even for her. I used to watch this with Yasmin all the time, though. That, and a whole bunch of Asian dramas. We managed to watch every version of *Boys Over Flowers* there was—as it stands, we remained divided over which was our favorite: 2008's Japanese drama *Hana Yori Dango* or the original Taiwanese live-action, *Meteor Garden*, from 2001. To my mother's deep exasperation, we indoctrinated Trinity, too, and she agrees with me—*Meteor Garden* is clearly the best.

A half hour into the Sailor Moon movie, I hear the garage door open again and I contemplate whether I should hide my indiscretion or not, but I'm still thinking about it when Trini bursts through my door with an accusatory finger. "YOU," she says.

I grin but don't move. "Me. Sorry I went through your stuff, kiddo."

She stares at me from the doorway in mock rage before shrugging. "I wanted to watch *Supergirl* tonight, but this works."

Then she drops her backpack next to my bed and shuffles in next to me. "I'm glad you won your race today."

She snuggles in to me, her mass of hair lodged beneath my chin. For the next hour, we sit like that, watching as the trusty sailor scouts fight to defend their planet from an evil alien. When the climax starts—Sailor Moon deciding to sacrifice herself for her friends—we're both wiping our eyes as if we haven't both seen this movie two hundred times. And then our favorite part starts—an energetic song with an '80s power beat about love. We barely need to exchange glances before we're on our feet, singing and dancing around the room and making a total racket.

"YOU'VE GOT TO BELI-EEVE. IN. THE. POW-ER OF LOOOVE." We repeat the words to each other even as we hear quick, heavy steps coming toward us. I'm certain it's going to be Mom, irritated at how loud we're being. And when the door swings open, there she is, her eyes ablaze—and full of mischief. Without skipping a beat, she dances into the room, her hips shaking and her arms pumping in the air as she screams off-key, "YOU'VE GOT TO BELI-EEVE. IN. THE. POW-ER OF LOOOVE."

Trini and I shriek with delight, but we don't stop. None of us do. We dance around one another, the Marshall women, loud and ridiculous. Free, for the moment. I want to believe that Mom is doing this for me—to celebrate me—and maybe a part of her is. But I'm sure she's doing this more for Trinity's sake, too. Because what has the littlest one done wrong other than just exist in this house where everyone else is angry about something all the time? And here she is, trying to have a dance party with her big sister. Mom can be a lot of things, but she isn't stupid. Today, Trinity is happy—and I'm happy. And maybe, if she dances with us, if she lets go, if she closes her eyes and pretends like she's somewhere else, she can be happy, too.

And Mom won't look at me, but I don't care for now, because she's holding Trinity's hands and spinning her in a circle, and when she lets go, Trinity falls into me, and we're laughing. The three of us, laughing, laughing, laughing, pretending happiness is a thing we can hold on to if we try hard enough.

Until the door swings open again.

Red eyes and the stench of liquor mute us all in an instant. Trini moves behind me, and Mom in front of me—the three of us in our places. I thought maybe he'd still be at the church, fixing the plumbing. It's not a big church, but it's old and he's been spending a lot of time there. But he must've gotten home early and heard us upstairs. Judging by the alcohol, he was not at church.

Quietly, I reach for the remote on my bed and turn the TV off.

What he says, he's said a thousand times before, this man who calls himself father, and husband, and man of the house.

We're being too loud, he says, and all three of us, down to the youngest, the baby, are all bitches. Unrefined. Undisciplined.

The things he says when we're having too much fun without him.

"You need to go," Mom says, and of course he doesn't. And she tries to push him out of the room, and of course she can't, because the minute she touches him, he jerks away and their usual dance begins, his hands against hers, limbs struggling against limbs as they both attempt to assert control. Mom wants him to leave, and he wants to stay, and so they just push and pull at each other, fingers grasping, teeth clenching, insults exchanged.

I don't watch them, because I know how this scene plays out. Instead I turn to Trini, but she doesn't play her part. This time, she runs around me and between them, screaming "STOPITSTOPITSTOPIT."

And because they are both surprised, their well-practiced choreography screeches to a halt. Dad stands to her left, breathing hard and clutching his left hand. Hazily, I realize that it's bleeding. Mom stands to Trini's right, her hand on her heart. Slowly, both of them uncertain, they reach for her, but I move quickly—always, of course. I grab Trini's shoulder and push her forward, out of the room—out of my room—and down the stairs, through the living room, and into our parents' room, where I lock the door, and turn the TV on as loud as it will go.

Thirty minutes later, Mom knocks on the door.

When I let her in, her eyes are red. "He's gone," she says, as if it means that he's not coming back. He will, we all know, but I move aside, and Trini runs past us, back up the stairs to her own room. Mom looks at me, then past me. I let her walk into her room. Then I leave, and shut the door behind me.

CHAPTER 10

The next day, I return to the field alone. There are no practices on Sundays, especially not right after a meet, so it's the perfect opportunity for me to be in my own head, away from people. That's why I don't text Naomi or Marissa for a ride. Instead, I walk the hour it takes to get to school without a car. I spent the morning convincing myself to leave the bed, so it's already midday.

When I get to the track, I stop at the water fountain right next to the gate, and then I see Tessa on the bleachers, rummaging through her bag. She's on the second row nearest to me. So much for being alone. She's probably here to practice after yesterday's failed run.

She waves when she sees me and then returns to whatever she was searching for. After a minute, she pulls out what I assume are headphones. Then she pops the speakers into her ears and jogs out onto the track. I guess I don't have to worry about being bothered, then. I hop onto the bleachers myself and drop my duffel bag a few feet away from hers, at a respectful distance. Then I join her on the track.

With each lap, the muscles in my body relax and I move through the air like it's part of me—like I'm returning to some essential self after years of being trapped in skin and bone. This is exactly what I need. A reminder that I exist outside of the nightmare of my house.

But as much as my brain wants to float into the ether, I still feel stuck in the here and now. I want to focus, but I can't stop my eyes from wandering to Tessa's sweat-drenched form each time she passes.

She's running too fast for the amount of times she's passed the track—a side effect of frustration, I'm sure. But she's also not stopping. I can tell from the taut muscles in her face and the frown she wears that taking a break is the furthest thing from her mind. She's in the ether, far away from the space we both share. I wonder what makes her run. I wonder what she's running from.

Or toward.

The sun drifts toward the center of the sky.

A couple of football players swagger to the track and drop their bags onto the field. They barely glance our way. One of them, a boy with shaggy brown hair and pale brown skin, pulls out a football and tosses it to his friend, a skinny guy with tightly coiled hair and shaved sides.

After about an hour, they leave.

We're still here.

Eventually, I admit to myself that I'm about as far outside my head as I ever have been when I'm running. I'm still here, because she's still here, and I don't want to leave. But finally, even my legs give out, and I retreat to the bleachers, sitting between her bag and mine. I try to appear casual as I lean back, my legs splayed out as I shove my hands in my pockets.

After another half hour, Tessa finally stops.

She looks up at me, and from my spot in the bleachers, I can tell that she's smiling. It's the first time she's acknowledged me since I appeared on the track two hours ago. She waits by the gate's entrance, and I walk to her slowly, trying not to smile myself.

"Hey there," I say, realizing too late that my voice has dropped. I clear my throat and try again. "I mean, hi."

"Hey, Aali."

"You feel better?"

Something in her eyes flickers, as if seeing me for the first time. She regards me with narrowed eyes, but her smile never waivers. "Yeah," she says, and it sounds like an invitation. A mutual understanding. Fear feels like acid in my throat, and I push it down, letting the burn fuel me. I've got this. I do know how to talk to girls. Especially girl teammates. I'm totally equipped for this completely normal human interaction.

I do some mental calculations. It's been a little more than a week since I got paid, but I could spare a few bucks. "You want to get some food?" I keep her gaze, even though I want to run far, far away.

She breaks out into a grin. "Yes."

I have never been embarrassed about not having a car until this moment, as Tessa digs for the keys in her gym bag and I stare at the road. It is the height of uncoolness to ask someone out to eat and then beg them for a ride. Not that I begged. But if Tessa is annoyed, she doesn't show it. Instead, she pops into the car like we've been doing this for years, leaning over to unlock my side of the door and then fidgeting with the radio station.

"You have a preference?"

"Ah, no," I say, buckling in.

"Hot 97.5 it is."

"Today's hottest music."

She giggles, and I'm suddenly elated that I'm privy to stupid radio slogans. Still, as a Shawn Mendes song starts to play, I become acutely aware that this is the first time in a long time that I've been in a car with someone other than Marissa or my parents. It feels nice, but weird—like I've achieved some teen rite of passage, declaring that I'm capable of having a social life. Still, it's a tight space with a pretty girl and this is the longest we've ever been alone together. I could do any manner of stupid things. Like pass gas, or make fun of a song she likes. Or what if I like a song and I sing too loudly? I absolutely *will* sing badly, and what if she hates that? Then we'd really be screwed. There's no coming back from someone who's offended by the literal sound of your voice.

"You okay there?" Tessa shoots me a look of concern as we pull out of the parking lot.

"Totally." I nod so hard my neck hurts. "You okay?"

"Why wouldn't I be?"

"I don't know. Do you often give rides to strange girls?"

"Absolutely. Especially the cute ones." She says it lightly, as if my stomach hasn't just plummeted to my knees.

"Great," I say, reaching toward the radio station. "That's. Good. This? Shawn Mendes, huh?"

She laughs and lets me turn the music up higher. This could be a sign that she's gay, but girls are weird. They flirt with each other all the time, and then say they're just *really* good friends. It's confusing, but straight girls seem to navigate it just fine— except at parties, when they make out with each other. Whatever. I decide to let it go for now, and when she asks where we want to go, I suggest the epicenter of hell, otherwise known as Town Square, because my brain is too fried to think of anything better. It's an outdoor shopping center just before the Strip, where pretty much everyone from our high school either works or hangs out. It's not bad, exactly, just boring and full of all the people you actively try avoiding at school, and who actively try avoiding you. It's like the cafeteria, or a crowded hallway, but with your parents tagging along for the ride.

Still, it's got decent food options.

As we drive, Tessa reaches toward her phone. "Do you listen to Shamir?" she asks. I shake my head no.

"Wait, are you serious?" She looks at me with big eyes. "Shamir! He's a Black, queer—agender—singer. And he's from Las Vegas." She's talking fast now, her eyes switching between the road and her phone. But the only thing I can think is how she said the word *queer* so casually, like maybe it's not a word she's heard other people use, but one she uses all the time. Perhaps to refer to herself. Plus, she just called me cute.

She switches to a song that is, admittedly, awesome. It's kind of a fast tempo, a dancy kind of rhythm. Not exactly my style, but I like the lyrics, and that Tessa is singing along to them. She's got a nice voice, but the song is more of a rap than a melody for the most part.

The song switches, and I use this opportunity to talk, but Tessa tells me to wait. She wants me to hear the next song. It's different, way different. Like something straight out of the seventies—or a cross between Jenny Lewis and Tracy Chapman, all guitar strums and slow drumbeats. I lean back against Tessa's seat and close my eyes.

"'Straight Boys,'" Tessa says.

I blink my eyes back open and turn to her. "Say what?"

"That's the name of the song. Good, right?"

"Fucking amazing. I'm in love."

She grins. "I'm glad you like it."

I take a deep breath and try to summon some bravery. "Do you listen to a lot of queer music?"

She doesn't look at me, her eyes still on the road, but her smile doesn't fade. "Gotta support fam, right?"

A million stars seem to explode right in front of my eyes. *She's gay, she's gay, she's gay, she's gay! Hip, hip, hooray!*

I nod. "Right," I say.

✳ ✳ ✳

Once we get to Town Square, we grab a hot dog for her and a burger with fake meat for me, and find a place to sit on the fake grass next to a tiny bridge that crosses a man-made pond just outside Express.

"So," she says as we take our first bites. "About the other night . . ."

I try not to cough up my vegan meat. "Oh God, I'm so sorry you had to witness that."

She laughs softly. "It's all good. I'm sorry *you* had to experience it. Radhika was being pretty tough on you."

"Yeah, well. I guess I deserve some of it."

"Can I ask what happened?"

My first instinct is to say no, but it occurs to me that out of everyone on the team, Tessa would be the most likely to understand. Which . . . feels sort of amazing. "Most of the team doesn't know this, but, uh . . . I got outed to my mom."

"Oh damn."

"Yeah. And . . . um. It didn't go over well, and then running kind of seemed like the last of my worries."

Tessa's eyes soften. "I'm sorry."

"Hey, you didn't tell my mom I was gay." Tessa laughs a little but is otherwise quiet. Her eyes don't leave mine, and I continue. "It's fine, though. I'm going to kick ass this year."

"Oh, I can tell." She waves her hot dog around a little. "You left us in the dust yesterday."

"Damn right." I give her a sidelong smile that she returns. Then she looks down, as if something just occurred to her.

"Hey, can I ask you something?"

"Shoot."

"Did you and Marissa used to date?"

This time, I almost choke. "No. Not at all. Tracey was just being a jackass."

Tessa gives me a thoughtful look. "Do you think it's because you guys are super affectionate?"

I frown. "Oh. That's just how some girls are, you know?" I mean, I think so. This is what I've been told. "Why? Do you think it's weird?" I ask.

"No," Tessa says lightly, playing with a strand of fake grass. "I was just wondering if you were ever together."

"Never," I say quickly. "At all. Just friends. Besides, she and Emmanuel are a thing now."

"Oh, I know," Tessa laughs, indicating that she, like the rest of the team, is very aware of Marissa and Emmanuel's postpractice exercise routine.

"Tell me about you," I say, because I want to change the subject. She smiles. My heart quickens, and I take a few more bites of my burger to give myself something to do other than stare at her mouth.

"But I want to hear about you," she says.

"Hmm." I pretend to think. "Did you know . . . that Emmanuel and I used to date?"

Tessa blinks. "Seriously?"

"Totally. We were very much the 'it' couple of sixth grade."

She laughs, and the sound is full, hearty. Beautiful. I take the moment to really look at her, at how the sun shines off her gorgeous Black skin, and the way the tips of her braids touch her waist. They almost make me jealous. She catches me staring, and her laughter fades into a shy side smile. She looks down.

I do, too.

Soon, the sun begins to set and we make our way back to her car. We talk a little about where she's from—Reno, hence the "biggest little city" shirt from day one of practice—and how I've lived in Vegas my whole life. I tell her about Trinity, and she reveals the strange experience of being an only child. We talk about little things—light things. It's not long before we reach my house, and as I open the door to leave, she calls out to me:

"Aaliyah?"

"Yeah?"

"Let's do this again sometime."

My smile is megawatt as she drives off, and just like that, the summer is over.

CHAPTER 11

"You did just fine your freshman and sophomore years." Miss Eccleston is going over my school reports, thick square black glasses perched on her nose as she clicks through various windows on her computer. Naomi is sitting in the chair beside me, a binder open in her lap that I assume is filled with tidbits about my various failings. "So let's talk about junior year," Miss Eccleston continues.

Yes, because that's exactly how I want to start senior year. I shrug and lean back. "I just got overwhelmed with classes. I'll do better this time."

She blinks at me, and then at Naomi, who's dutifully looking at neither one of us. "Okay. We can talk more about that later. In the interest of time, we'll move on. I assume you received Miss Pratt's email about preparing a list of colleges. Can you please share that with me now?"

Oh, damn. I actually forgot about that. I glance at Naomi, who smiles sweetly at Miss Eccleston. "That's actually one of the first things Aaliyah and I are going to work on. This week, in fact."

Miss Eccleston looks at me to confirm, and I nod as if that's something we had absolutely discussed. "Okay, then. Well, do you have any idea right now, Aaliyah? A place to start?"

"No," I say at the same time that Naomi says, "Didn't you used to talk about the University of San Diego all the time?"

The glare I send her could burn a hole through the wall, but Naomi doesn't look at me.

"Oh, that's lovely. A Catholic institution, right? Are you religious, Miss Marshall?"

"No," I say. It comes out so easily, I almost want to take it back. But I don't.

"Oh. Well, that's fine. All kinds of students attend all kinds of schools. What were you hoping to study?"

"I don't know." I know I'm making this harder than is necessary, but I suddenly want to be literally anywhere but here. After a few more minutes of fruitless prodding, Miss Eccleston dismisses us.

"What's wrong with wanting to attend USD?" Naomi asks once we're outside the administrative building.

"Nothing," I say. "It's just . . . stupid. I can't leave Vegas."

"Why not?"

Because I have a family to protect. "I gotta go," I say. "See you at practice."

I don't wait for her to respond, thankful that we don't have any classes together for the rest of the day. I do, however, have calculus with Tessa, which makes math my new favorite subject. She chooses to sit in the seat in front of mine, and I hope that's not by accident.

"Hey," I whisper to Tessa before Miss Adebayo walks in.

"Hey, yourself," she says with a quick wink, and it feels like I'll be floating on air for the rest of the day.

By the time class ends, it's clear that she and Miss A are going to be the best of pals—math nerds for life. I don't linger, though. We're not quite there yet, and I don't want to push it. Instead, I just think about her "hey, yourself," until the last bell of the day rings.

✳ ✳ ✳

Marissa's making a group of kids laugh when I walk into the theater classroom, which is behind the stage of the actual theater. It doubles as "back stage" during productions, and I feel like a VIP when Marissa stops whatever conversation she's having to pull me into a hug and plant a kiss on my cheek.

"Hey, bestie," she says as if introducing me to her new friends. They smile and wave even though they probably recognize me from my Yasmin days. I wonder what they must think of me now that I'm Marissa's new shadow, but I don't have time to think about it. With a wave to her adoring fans, Marissa ushers me out of the classroom and into the hallways, toward our lockers.

"Class was awesome today," she says, her arm wrapped around my shoulders. "Seriously, babe. I can't thank you enough."

"For what?" I say as we stop in front of my locker. Hers is next to mine, but evidently, she doesn't need anything from it. Instead, she leans against the door and watches as I switch out the books I'll need to study tonight.

"For not bailing on me when I decided to switch to the dark side." She says this with such matter-of-factness that I don't realize I should dispute her until her attention has already switched to something new, as demonstrated by the way her jaw dislocates itself from her mouth. "OHMIGODLOOKBEHIND-YOU," she whisper-shrieks to me. I do, and see Naomi and Curtis standing close to each other down the hall. Whatever they're talking about, it's probably not necessary for there to be less than two inches of space between them. Curtis has his hand above Naomi's head as the other clutches his backpack, and Naomi's normally pale cheeks are brushed with pink.

"Holy shit," I whisper-shout back. "Holy shit!"

We watch until Curtis turns away, walking in the opposite direction. With twin grins, we move with unspoken agreement toward Naomi, who has only just spotted us and whose pink cheeks have now lost all their color.

"Haaaay, girl," I say emphatically. "What's new?" Whatever remnants of irritation I had this morning have evaporated in favor of my absolute thirst for dating gossip.

Naomi glares at me in a way that's too adorable to be intimidating, and Marissa's Cheshire cat grin only grows. "Yeah. What's Curtis up to these days?"

"Nothing," Naomi says. She slams her locker door and hurries away without a glance back. As she leaves, Marissa and I stumble over each other in utter delight.

"I can't believe it—"

"We totally saw it coming—"

"Their babies will be adorable."

"I. FREAKING. KNOW."

"We have to confirm—"

"I'm already on it." I type out a hasty text to Naomi: Details and I'll forgive the USD thing.

My phone vibrates a moment later with textual confirmation, and the whisper-shrieking begins anew, ringing through the halls as we pass through the exit toward the parking lot. "He asked her out! They have a date this weekend! Tomorrow! I'm so excited!"

And it's surprising, actually, just how true it feels. How giddy I really am, because we get to witness an unusually wholesome event that naturally has a mass stamp of approval. Even if I didn't know Curtis, I would trust Naomi's taste in love interests, because she's got a better head on her shoulders than any of the rest of us.

Exhibit A: Yasmin, standing next to what I can only

assume is Daisy Skye Cloud's car, a beat-up black Durango, as Marissa and I make our way over to Marissa's barely breathing Bug.

I immediately feel numb, which is a feat as it is literally 97 degrees today. Marissa nudges my arm, and I realize that I, like an idiot, have stopped walking. Long enough, it turns out, for Yasmin to notice me, because she waves, and I wave back and then suck in a breath and walk the lonely, miserable, achingly distant ten feet to Marissa's side door.

"You okay?" Marissa asks as she tries to start the car.

"Sure," I say.

"Okay," she says, and then turns her attention back to the car for the next few minutes until it finally roars to life and we set off onto the road.

"How was class with her today?" I ask after a couple of minutes pass.

She shrugs. "We didn't talk."

Suddenly, her phone buzzes from the drink holder between us. "Oh," I say when I read it for her.

"What?"

"Um. Emmanuel wants to know if you want to make it a double date. The thing with Curtis and Naomi." I try to measure her reaction without giving away too much of my own. Not that I'm not thrilled. I'm, uh . . . fine. It's fine.

Marissa sits there, blinking. "Oh. Well, this is new."

I let her phone drop back into the cup holder. "Aren't you guys, like . . . dating already, or whatever?"

"No," she says, which is unnecessary, because I already knew that. She glances at me. "Do you think I should?"

I shrug. "I mean. Do you like him? I mean, other than the . . . you know. What you've been doing."

"Yeah," she says slowly. "I do. I mean. I just haven't really considered anything more than that."

"Seriously?"

"Yeah. We have fun, I just . . ." She glances at me, and then starts biting the side of her lip, which I take as a bad sign. "Aali, if I said something to you right now, would you promise not to freak?"

Oh God. It's her serious tone again. I hate her serious tone. It always makes me feel things I don't want to feel. "Absolutely not," I say, hoping a joke will defuse the situation.

"No, seriously." She taps on the steering wheel for long enough that I realize she's really weighing her words. She takes a few deep breaths and then turns toward me. "Do you remember the night of that house party back in April?"

My heart beats so fast that I think my head will explode, which is both emotionally and anatomically confusing. I don't know what she's about to say, but I know whatever it is, it's not something I want to handle right not. "Nope." I smile.

"Aaliyah," she groans, but I keep going.

"I mean, let's think about it," I say quickly, picking her phone up again. "You two obviously have great chemistry, and it's not like you don't have things in common. Cross-country, at least."

She stares at me for a while. A long while. Then she rolls her eyes and nods. "Totally. You're right."

"Right?"

"Yeah," she sighs. Then she starts the ignition.

"And Emmanuel's actually incredibly sweet," I continue.

"He is, he is." She begins to back her Bug out of the parking lot. "I don't know, maybe it'll be nice to get to know him better outside of. You know. The back of this car."

"Oh, ugh. Gross." I lean forward in my seat, as if it will put enough distance between me and everything that has ever touched the interior of this dying insect. I knew they had sex back here, but I didn't need the reminder. "So does that mean you're gonna say yes?"

She's quiet for a moment and then turns to me with a smile, her eyebrows waggling.

"Yeah. Why not?"

The grin is off, even as it lights up her eyes, and when I text back to let Emmanuel know Marissa's in, I can't bring myself to smile back.

✷ ✷ ✷

The next day, I'm official lady-in-waiting to Marissa's fashion show, helping suggest outfits that I know she will turn down because I don't understand her style in the slightest. Casually cool former-lead-singer-turned-theater-queen going on her first date with a guy she's been hooking up with for three months? Not my area of expertise. Very patient best friend? Present!

Naomi refused when I asked if she, too, needed three hours of unpaid consultation, but that didn't stop her from sending pictures of at least three different outfits, followed by "???" I told her Curtis would love them all, which is true, but we finally agreed to a long and pale blue dress that fits loosely at the top and bottom and cinches in the middle. That process took all of maybe twenty minutes this morning.

With Marissa, we are very close to hitting the two-hour mark. I'm sitting on the silk sheets of her bed while she stands in front of a full-length mirror—an antique her mother won in a bet once—and she is asking me, for the third time, if the red dress she has draped over her white tee and black jeans shorts is "too sexy" or "just sexy enough."

"He has seen you naked, no?" I dodge the dress when she aims it at my head and then add it to the growing pile of discarded clothes at the foot of the bed. She riffles through her drawers beside the mirror and then pulls out a short black leather-looking skirt.

"It's not real," she says, even though I haven't said anything. Then she makes quick work of removing her top and jeans and slipping the skirt on—a process she's now done more than a dozen times. She stands in front of the mirror with her hands on her hips, probably trying to figure out the right top to go with it. Eventually, enough time passes that I begin to actually notice that she's shirtless, revealing her bare stomach and a lacy pink bra. For a second, my brain goes on the fritz and I remember what it felt like to trail my fingers there, just over her navel, then higher, to just graze the skin beneath the wire.

Oh God. Stop, brain. Stop!

If I'd learned anything from Yasmin, it is to *not* make a big deal out of things like that. It was just something fun we'd shared. I avert my eyes and shift a little farther to the edge of the bed, becoming suddenly interested in the particular fabric of the red dress she just discarded.

"Such a gentle-lady," she says to me mockingly, probably noticing my obvious discomfort from her mirror. She turns and cups her chest with her hands, shimmying forward so I can get a better view.

Which I don't want. Honest to God.

"You are a shitty person, Marissa."

She winks at this and then returns to her drawers. "And you are ever so sweet. When's the last time you got laid, by the way?"

"Never," I say, which she already knows, but she looks up like what I've said is news.

"Oh, right." Then she shifts onto one leg and places a hand

on her hip, conjuring up an impossibly coy look. "Do you want to?"

It's her turn to duck now, as she just barely avoids getting smacked in the face with the white tank she was just wearing. When she pulls it from the floor, she jumps up and down. "That's it!" She turns back to the mirror, holding the white tank to her chest. "This is perfect! This is what I'm wearing tonight." She puts the shirt on quickly and then, with an evil glare in her eyes, shoves all the clothes on her bed onto the floor. "I have done it! I have conquered the fashion beast!"

"Wow. Good job, Mar." I'm holding a pillow to my chest like it's armor.

She turns to me, all the playfulness and theatrics she previously exhibited now faded in favor of a shy smile. "Do you think I look good?"

And she looks so oddly earnest in this moment that the sarcastic comment I was originally going for dies in my throat. "Yeah," I say, my throat suddenly dry. "You look incredible."

For a second, I feel the slightest shock of electricity from the way her gaze holds mine, like if I said something right this moment, she'd push me back on the bed and we'd get lost in the tangle of her sheets. But I don't say anything and the moment is broken with a bat of her eyelashes. "Of course I do, babe," she says. And then she's off to the bathroom, where I can only assume is where she'll take another six years putting on her makeup.

"Achievement unlocked," I text to Naomi as I move from Marissa's closet of a bedroom to her vaguely larger living room, where it will be easier for me to be on hand as she moves in and out of the bathroom.

Naomi texts back a smiley face, and then I wait as three dots indicate she's going to tell me more. Then: Tessa's coming.

And with those two words, my heart nearly stops.

Oh. My God.

"With who?" I text back, slowly, as if Naomi's words will disappear if I move too quickly.

"Could be you, if you get dressed fast enough," her text reads. Then I'm barraged with what amounts to roughly five hundred winking smiley faces.

When Marissa emerges from the bathroom, her neck now adorned with a black choker, I must be as pale as a ghost, because she takes one look at me and stops dead in her tracks. "What's going on? What happened? Is it your dad?"

"No, no," I say quickly, running more calculations in my head. "No, it's . . . uh . . . Tessa."

"Tessa?" She frowns. "What about her?"

I take a slow unsteady breath that transforms into the goofiest of all smiles. "I think I'm crashing your double date."

CHAPTER 12

Three hours later, Marissa and I appear together at the movie theater attached to the local hotel casino, where Naomi and Curtis are already waiting for us. Naomi is in her pale dress, her dark hair half up and half down, while her freshly curled bangs brush the tips of her eyelashes. Curtis is in a white button-down and dark-wash jeans. It's always startling to see them out like this—all appropriately showered and dry and breathing normally, instead of baking beneath the heat in running clothes. They look good together, even as they stand awkwardly apart from each other.

But as we walk up to them, just outside the movie theater, Curtis's hand swings toward Naomi's and then they move toward each other until their pinkies are just barely touching. I wonder if it's because Marissa and I are holding hands—something I hadn't thought twice about until just now. I disengage her fingers from mine, and she gives me an odd look before shrugging and then squealing, hopping toward Curtis and Naomi and throwing her arms around both pairs of shoulders.

"YOU. BOTH. LOOK. SO. GOOD," she says, and now the entire hotel casino complex knows we're here.

"So do you!" someone shouts from behind us. It's Emmanuel, hurrying down the hill from the parking lot we just came from. His short black hair is slick with gel that makes his curls bounce, and he's wearing an outfit not unlike Curtis's except that his shirt is navy and tucked into his jeans. "Como estas, mi bella?" he says breathlessly as he catches up to us. His accent is so terrible that I know his abuelita is rolling over in her grave. But at least he's trying. Coach feels weird about it, I think, but Marissa told me that his mom is ecstatic.

When he reaches Marissa, he grabs her around the waist and spins her. She giggles effusively while Curtis and Naomi look on with bemused expressions. Now it's just me, standing awkwardly in a dark green dress I stole from Marissa's closet. I'd stared at myself in the mirror for a long time, assessing my appearance: My hair. If jeans or a dress or heels or sneakers made the most sense. What would make me look good without making me stand out?

Or what would make me stand out without making me look *off*? What did girls wear on dates with each other? What if we both showed up in dresses? What if she showed up in a dress and expected *me* to show up in pants? I'd wanted to ask my mom for help, but it was another one of those things I just had to figure out without her.

I'd been almost catatonic until Marissa shoved her green dress at me and told me to chill out. "You will look fine," she said. "More than fine. The benefit of being on this team together is that we have all seen each other gross and sweaty, some of us more than others"—she winked at me—"so it can only go up from there."

Now here I am, with my short hair, and my simple dress, and my white Chucks. The dress doesn't have pockets, much to my despair, so I was forced to borrow one of Marissa's shoulder bags, too. The hopelessness of it all is mildly funny until I realize, watching Naomi and Curtis and Marissa and Emmanuel, that out of everyone, I truly have no idea what the hell I'm doing. There's no shortage of teen movies that indicate all the ways straight kids are supposed to behave, from attraction to flirtation, to kissing, to dating, to sex, all the way down to the white picket fence and 2.5 kids. But queer kids like me are in the lurch.

"Hey." I turn at the sound of Tessa's voice and see her walking from the entrance of the theater. She must have come through from the casino side of the complex. Her green and white box braids are wrapped into one large braid that falls over her right shoulder. She's wearing an off-the-shoulder black romper, and a simple gold chain falls from her neck, accentuating the darkness of her bare collarbones. I catch my breath at the sight. As she approaches, I'm forced to look up just a bit more than usual, because she's wearing heeled red sandals that give her an inch or so over me.

"Hi," I say, and it comes out so low that even Curtis snickers. He claps a hand on my shoulder and motions us all into the theater. We take our places as we walk—Curtis and Naomi at the front, of course; Marissa and Emmanuel behind us; and Tessa and I between, not touching, barely speaking, but something passes between us nonetheless—a quiet sort of joy and hopefulness that I haven't felt since Yasmin and I kissed that first night so long ago. It feels soft, and warm, and full of possibility—just like they say in the movies and television shows that I always thought were for other people.

But tonight, it's just for us.

Even though we're on time, the theater is already packed, so we seat ourselves in the first row nearest to the doors. Emmanuel and Marissa are at the farthest end from Tessa and me, and I can already tell that being so close to the screen doesn't bother them in the slightest: The chances of them actually watching are nil. Curtis and Naomi are between us, with Naomi's hands fidgeting in her lap while Curtis repeatedly tries and fails to casually put his arm on the back of her seat. Finally, he drops it on his armrest and sighs, which causes Naomi's face to turn the brightest red I've ever seen on human skin. Tessa, who's between Naomi and me, catches my eye and winks. In that moment, everyone else totally disappears. It's the first time I notice just how pale her brown eyes are—not quite hazel. More of a liquid brown, like specks of cinnamon dancing in the light of the screen's glow. She gives a coy smile, and that's when I realize I've been staring.

"Sorry," I whisper.

Her smile widens, and my heart starts to dance.

"Shhh," someone says, and I glance around to find Marissa's pale finger pressed against her lips. To my surprise, she and Emmanuel are not deep in the midst of coitus, but sitting relatively upright in their own respective chairs, though Emmanuel's arm is draped lazily around her shoulders, while her other hand is propped on his knee. Like a proper couple.

Huh.

Marissa gives me a pointed look and nods to the screen, which I realize has just begun the first few seconds of a trailer. I didn't even notice the theater going dark. Damn. I let out a loose breath and sink into my seat. *It's okay*, I tell myself. *I can watch the fun superhero movie and not creep out my super cute teammate sitting next to me. That's a totally possible thing that I can achieve.*

"Hey," Tessa whispers into my ear so softly that I almost jump three miles into the air.

I look back at Marissa, but she's no longer paying attention. "Hey," I whisper back as low as possible.

"Is this a date?"

The bluntness of the question throws me off. My eyes widen into saucers. "I. I mean, I thought. But really it's . . . did Naomi tell you it was . . . ?"

Tessa shrugs, and I watch her braid move with her. "No, but . . . I thought so."

"Oh. Good!" I say too loudly, this time earning me more *shhh*'s from the audience behind us. The trailers have gone off, and the beginning movie credits start to roll.

"I'd like to hold your hand, if that's okay," she says. And it would be okay, if I weren't suddenly aware that my hands are gross, clammy petri dishes of doom.

"I have to go to the bathroom," I respond. Quickly, I stand up and rush out of the theater, nearly knocking over an entering attendant. In the open air of the lobby, I take a deep breath of buttered popcorn and curse myself for being vegan. What I wouldn't do for the sweet, melty comfort of fermented milk right now. Instead, I focus on the all-gender bathroom across the way and dash toward it as if my life were on the line. After I burst through the doors, I scan the empty room quickly and decide that I'd better be as prepared as possible for the next hour or so, because God knows the last seventeen years have left me wildly unskilled in this new era of movie theater dates.

Once I've done my business, washed my hands while singing the birthday song, and triple-checked my teeth for excess greenery, I'm left with just my reflection in the mirror beneath the fluorescent lights. I turn my head side to side to check out the shorn curls I can't uncut. I wonder, still, if I like them yet. Tessa told me she did.

I stare at myself for just a second too long before the thought I've been avoiding for the past year speeds through my brain.

Nice, but not enough.

I blink, and steel myself against the oncoming storm of berating thoughts. I breathe in slow. Breathe out slow. I think of the sun, and the grass, and my feet against the earth.

And I try not to think about—try not to consider—running.

I try not to think about the girls like Yasmin's girlfriend who just *look* like they know who they are, what they're about. The girls who take risks; the girls who don't care what you think.

The kind of girl other girls leave you for.

I stare at my reflection again and square my shoulders.

It will have to be enough.

Finally, I dry my hands—although, by this point, they've dried on their own—and I step back into the lobby, where Tessa is waiting for me.

She leans against the wall across from me, her midnight-black arms crossed and those golden-brown eyes lit up again, this time by nothing but their own fire. I can't tell if she's mad or concerned. Maybe she can't tell, either.

How long was I in the bathroom?

"Are you okay?" she asks, and I can tell that's not the question she wants to ask.

"I'm sorry I left the theater," I say, walking toward her. Her eyes search mine as I approach, and when I stop a few feet in front of her, they drop.

"I can be a little blunt sometimes," she says. "I'm sorry if it freaked you out."

I go to stuff my very clean hands into my pockets, only to remember I don't have any. Awkwardly, I let my hands fall back to my sides. "It's fine. You're fine. I just . . . freaked out. But not because of you!" I say quickly, realizing I've just validated her fears. "Because of me. Er, well, because of . . . ah. I've never been on a date before."

Tessa cocks her head, her eyebrows furrowed. "What do you mean?"

I frown back. "What do you mean, what do I mean?"

"Naomi told me you were dating this girl last year?"

My frown deepens. I knew they talked, but damn. I look up at the ceiling, choosing my words slowly. "Oh. Yeah. Well, we weren't really dating. It was a whole situation. We were friends."

Tessa touches my arm, and I look at her. "Got it. I'm sorry; I shouldn't have assumed."

"Nah, it's cool," I say, but I don't move away from her touch.

I keep my head down until she ducks her head to try to catch my eyes.

"Really?" she says.

"Yeah," I say. I smile, and then she smiles, and we stay like that for a few seconds, dopey smiles both, not knowing what to say, but not minding the moment.

The buzz on Tessa's phone makes us both jump.

"Wow. The vibration on that thing could wake a cemetery. You might as well have it on sound."

"Yeah, yeah." She takes out her phone. "Naomi says that the group thinks we've died," she narrates slowly, "and will be sending state troopers soon. Wait—never mind. Curtis sent another text; says that was Marissa's idea. Then he sent an emoji of the Black power fist."

I cover my mouth to keep from laughing up a lung. Tessa gives a little laugh. "So," I say after I can breathe again. "Shall we go back in?"

"That depends," Tessa says, her mischievous smile returning. "Can I hold your hand?"

✷ ✷ ✷

By the time the movie ends, Curtis has finally managed the art of seduction, with his arm lightly placed on Naomi's shoulder, and Tessa is fully under my arm, her head tucked up under my neck. I'm pretty sure the movie was fine, but I've gotta say, I wasn't paying attention.

When we leave the theater, Naomi asks Curtis if he wants to go to the arcade around the corner. It is, pointedly, not a group invitation. The rest of us barely manage not to knock each other out and lose our sight with all our winking and nudging as the two walk away from us hand in hand. Naomi promises to text Tessa later.

"And me!" I shout at her retreating back.

"You two want to come with us back to the house? Mar and I were thinking of smoking a bit," Emmanuel says, his arm wrapped around Marissa's shoulders.

"Hookah, too, babes," Marissa chimes in for my benefit.

Tessa looks at me as she laces her fingers into mine. I look back at her, as if we're already at the level of reading each other's minds. But I'm caught by her eyes again, and the dimple in her left cheek, and the beauty mark on the right side of her mouth that I hadn't noticed until now.

Tessa must realize that my brain has lost its ability to process information, because she breaks her gaze with me. "Do you mind actually if we hang out later?" The question is directed toward Marissa and Emmanuel, like she already knows my answer.

And she does.

Marissa's eyes flicker toward me. "Totally." She presses on a smile that doesn't reach her eyes.

Emmanuel, on the other hand, breaks away from Marissa to give two huge thumbs-up. Maybe he ships us as hard as we all ship Naomi and Curtis.

"See you," I call to them as they walk out of the theater, leaving us as the last couple in the lobby. Hand in hand, we walk together into the night, which is blustery but still warm. Despite the streetlights of the manufactured shopping square across from us, the stars above are still bright. Once upon a time, I could name each constellation. I could tell Venus from Mars, and what point the moon was in its cycle. We all had to learn this stuff in elementary school, and then most of us forgot. I don't know when I did, but I wish I hadn't.

"Cassiopeia." Tessa's voice comes to me as if through water.

"Sorry, what?" I return my gaze to hers.

"That constellation right there," Tessa says. Her fingers draw a map of the stars. As if she knows exactly what she's looking at. What she's looking for. Her hand stays in the air as her eyes fall back to mine. "You zone out a lot, by the way."

Heat rises to my cheeks. "Yeah, I've heard. Sorry about that."

"I don't mind. Your absentminded-professorness is kinda cute."

"Professor?" I say as we begin walking toward the empty shopping center. It's too late for most of the shops to be open, but I'm sure we'll stumble upon a Coffee Bean or something. In any case, Tessa doesn't seem to mind wandering. "You're the one who seems to rock at math and, apparently, astrology."

"Astronomy," she says with exaggerated surprise until she sees my smirk. Her thumb runs across my knuckles as we continue walking. Then she shrugs and looks back at the stars, moving closer to me, trusting me to guide us. I'm not sure that's the best idea, but I'll try to live up to her expectations. My arm slips to her waist as my heart pounds. My throat dries. I feel a little small, but I push that aside and breathe in. I can do this. I can be brave. I draw her in a little closer, and she doesn't move away. She might even get closer.

"Is that what you want to study?" I ask, after my breathing returns to normal.

"What?" Her gaze is soft as she looks back to me.

"Astronomy."

"Ah." She smiles. "Maybe. Something like that. I want to go back to Reno—to the university there—and study something science-y. Probably the stars." I try not to let my disappointment show when she mentions Reno. If I do go to USD—or even if I stay here, which is more likely—Reno is still far away. We'd be in a long-distance relationship . . . assuming we even got that far. But I don't want to think about that right now. Thinking too far ahead has gotten me in trouble in the past, and all I want to do now is focus on the moment. I squeeze her waist and smile.

"Maybe you could be my tutor."

"Oh yeah?"

"Yeah," I say. "You help me improve my abysmal calculus grades, and I'll help you improve your running." That's when she stops walking with such abruptness that I almost stumble over her. *Well, goddamit.* "Sorry," I say. "Sorry, I shouldn't have brought that up. You're an amazing runner. Like, completely incredible."

"I just suck at competitions," she says. I'm too busy stammering in my own head to respond immediately, so she just sighs and walks toward one of the benches in front of a closed Paper Source. I don't know if I should sit next to her or not, so I just stand there.

"I wasn't trying to imply anything," I say quietly. "Sometimes, I say stupid shit. I'm sorry."

She shakes her head, and the movement makes the light of a streetlamp reflect off the beads in her hair. I hadn't noticed them before, but now I see that they're a burnished gold, nestled into a few individual braids. I keep my focus on them as she speaks. "No, you weren't wrong," she says. "It's just . . . you know. Shitty. To run so well at practice and then bomb when it matters most." She doesn't move away when I finally sit down next to her, which I take as a good sign.

"I get it," I say. "Last year, my running was a shit show. *I* was a shit show. I could run circles around most of the team during

147

practice runs, but when I was out on the field, it felt like someone else was in my body. I couldn't get out of my own head."

"Why?" She asks this with genuine curiosity, her eyes watching me with such alertness that I nearly choke on the lump in my throat.

Instead, I slump back against the metal of the bench and look at my knees. If my mother could see me, she would scold me for not sitting like a proper lady in a dress, but no one is here besides us. I glance at the scars on my knees from years of roughhousing on the playground and around the neighborhood. I can barely remember where I got most of them, while others, I could remember as if it were happening all over again.

"Um." I cross my legs, wishing I could cross my ankle on my knee like I've seen Curtis do a million times. "Bad breakup." Tessa waits for me to continue. "Sort of, anyway. This girl, Yasmin, and I were really good friends. And, uh, then we became something more. Sort of. It was never really very clear. And then she decided she wanted something else. Which is fine," I say quickly. "Totally fine. It just would've been nice if she had told me that before she found it."

"Ah," Tessa says.

"Yeah. I mean, it's whatever. It just . . . made things harder for me. A lot of stuff happened with me and my mom last year . . ." Tessa quirks her head, but I hurry on, not presently interested in rehashing the details. "And Yasmin was there for me—like one hundred percent. She was being a really good friend, and I didn't want anything more from her than that. But then suddenly, you know, she kind of kisses me out of the blue and it's like . . . oh, okay, are we doing this?"

I reach down and pick at the soles of my shoes, remembering. When Mom still thought Yasmin was my rich, straight friend, she let me hang out with her sometimes between my forced Bible study sessions. After one particularly grueling session, Yasmin showed up at my door, all smiles and innocence. She asked my mom if she could give me a driving lesson, even though she technically wasn't old enough to take me on her own.

This was hilarious for multiple reasons—one, because Mom doesn't trust me to drive. I scratched her car once when I was first trying to learn, and she banned me from her car for life. That left me with my friend's cars to attempt to learn in, or Dad's car. He was good at giving lessons when he was sober—infinitely less anxious and judgmental than my mom. It was all *turn here, baby. No, you gotta put your blinker on—right, like that.* Mom couldn't get through a streetlight without declaring I was going to kill us all.

So no lessons from her, and Dad was good but frequently drunk. So I spent a lot of time figuring things out from Yasmin anyway. Yaz quickly determined then that the best way to get me out of the house for longer stretches of time was to convince my mom that *she* would be my driving instructor. She even promised to put on a Bible podcast. My mom agreed—she thought herself generous, for that. And so for the next few weeks, Yaz and I drove aimlessly through the city, me behind the wheel.

Then it was time for me to parallel park. Now, since we lived in the suburbs, there weren't a ton of opportunities to practice, which is why Yasmin decided to drive us to downtown—the only part of the city that actually *feels* like a city. I sucked at it—like, truly, and fully, could not fucking understand how to get Yasmin's car from the middle of a busy street to an empty spot sandwiched between two cars. Not to mention that it was rush hour, and since it was autumn, the sun was going down earlier in the day. We spent twenty minutes with Yasmin standing on the sidewalk, attempting to coax me into this space designed for clown cars.

And then it happened.

The grace of God smiled upon me, and as Yasmin's Bible podcast shared verses from the Song of Solomon—she'd put it on because she thought it was funny—I finally got the car into the spot. One wheel was on the curb and I was still kind of peeking out into the street, but whatever. I'd done the damn thing. Yasmin cheered, and I turned the car off. With a stupid grin on my face, I ran circles around her like I'd seen a guy during a football game do once on TV, and I fake cheered. *And the crowd goes wild. Aaaaaaaah!!!*

It was the happiest and most accomplished I'd felt in a long time. I picked Yasmin up—she's a curvy girl, but I was stronger than her from all the cross-country—and spun her around. I was feeling silly, and having a good time, and when I put her down, she was looking at me with something weird in her eyes. Something like curiosity.

It made me feel funny, but I pushed it aside until we got back to her house. Yasmin had convinced my mom to let me stay the night—and turns out that was fine, because she and Dad were fighting again. We went to bed, same as always, and that's when Yasmin asked if I wanted another lesson.

We didn't go far—not that far. It was my first kiss, my first anything, and I wanted to savor it. *Kiss me and kiss me again, for your love is sweeter than wine*—that's exactly what it felt like. Song of Solomon, chapter one, verse two.

But then I didn't hear from her for two weeks. No responses to my texts, or to my DMs. To have someone ignore you after something like that probably feels pretty shitty. To have someone you love do it—who's supposed to love you—feels like . . . well, like someone scooped out your heart, put it in a blender, and then spat on it.

I flinch when I feel Tessa's hand press into mine, as if she's grazing raw, open skin, but I force myself to breathe and relax back into the present, into the softness of her skin, into the wholeness of my own. "Anyway," I whisper after I finish recounting the memories to her, "the point is—it was probably my fault. I missed some social cue or whatever telling me to back off." I pause, suddenly completely done with reliving one of the most humiliating experiences of my life. I turn toward Tessa, ready to bring us back to what I've learned is one of her favorite topics. "So I think that's why I suck at word problems."

"Oh?" Tessa says, her eyes lighting up with amusement.

"Yeah," I grin, excited to shift us back into a better mood. "Yeah. I need parameters; a clear set of instructions of how to get from A to B. If you sit me in front a puzzle and want me to make sense of it, I will be stuck there for years."

"Well," she says, scooting a little closer to me. "I can help you with that. Math, and word problems, and all of that. I can see a straight path in pretty much anything—and I'm very direct."

"Yes, I know," I say, and she laughs. "So what's your deal? With the running, I mean, now that I've revealed my deep, dark lesbian past."

Tessa sobers, which was the opposite of my intentions, but she doesn't let go of my hand. "To be honest, I feel pretty silly now. It's not that deep."

"I'm not comparing."

"I'm new." She lets out an exaggerated sigh. "That's it. I'm just . . . new here. And it's hard. I spent my whole life in Reno, in the same neighborhood, and I knew all the same people from when I was a kid. And then, you know, my parents decide that married life is kind of a drag, and then they split, and my whole life implodes. Or it feels like it does." She sits back against the bench the way I had moments ago, until we're in parallel positions, except that her feet are crossed at the ankle. "And now I'm here, trying to piece it all back together. And the running . . . when I'm running, I feel free. Like I'm in control and everything is exactly as it should be. But when competitions roll around . . ."

"The pressure is crazy like it is at home and everywhere else."

"Exactly. Exactly! And I feel like I have to perform, again. Like I have to be on point. And it makes me do totally the opposite. Like you said, I can't get the fuck out of my head."

"Totally," I say, and that's when we look at each other for the first time. Apparently, we've both moved closer, slowly, imperceptibly, so that we're sitting in the middle of the bench with a person-sized swath of space on either side of us. "I can help with that, I think. If you want."

"I'd love that," she says. And then I decide something then and there—because this is an actual, real live date, with a girl who might actually like me.

"Do you mind if I kiss you?" I whisper it quietly, as if I'm not totally sure I want her to hear.

"No," she murmurs. I take a breath, lean down, and press

my lips to the corner of her mouth. Suddenly, I feel her body shake and I fill with panic when she moves away from me.

"What?" I say, failing to mask my alarm.

"That's what you meant?" Her voice is filled with so much amusement that I think the mirth will kill me.

"I want to move slow." *And I don't want to fuck this up.* I clear my throat as if that will distract her from the blush warming my cheeks and neck. "At least, off the field."

"Okay," she says. "That's totally fine with me." Then she presses a soft kiss into my cheek. It sets my entire skin on fire.

"Hey," I say after a moment of comfortable silence. "Can I ask you a question?"

"Mm?"

"Why haven't you accepted my friend request on Instagram?"

Tessa chuckles softly. "Wow, Aali."

"My bad." I smile. "I know you don't want me to find out about your other girlfriend back in Reno."

"Well," Tessa says, and my heart speeds up rapidly, "I don't have that." I breathe a little easier. Of course. Right. Thank God. "But it's what I use to keep up with my friends back there. I added a few people on the team here in Vegas when practices first started, but then they started commenting on things and it felt like . . . I don't know, like I was erasing my old life. So I made it private."

"Oh." I squeeze her hand. "That makes sense."

"Honestly, I didn't actually know that you sent me a request. I don't look at it that often anymore. It's . . . hard."

I feel bad that I brought it up to begin with, but I understand. The past is a hard thing to examine—especially when it's something you sometimes desperately wish you could return to. I put my arm around her shoulders, and she snuggles closer to me.

Slowly, people begin to filter out of the movie theater again. Some folks pass us on the way to the car or perhaps to the mysterious Coffee Bean we didn't bother to look for. A few minutes pass until we're alone again, but we're both so quiet that I can't tell if Tessa has fallen asleep or if we're both too comfortable to speak. Then, I feel her adjust beneath my chin, and her hand finds my knee. She says nothing, and neither do I.

Instead, we sit there beneath the stars and streetlights, wrapped in the warmth of the night and letting ourselves remember what it's like to be still.

CHAPTER 13

Alas, even with the heavenly embrace of a blossoming romance, I must still contend with the eternal damnation that is academic probation. Thankfully for me, Naomi is a living saint. I mean, she is *truly* anointed, as the churchfolk would say, because I know that I am getting on her last damn nerve, and she still hasn't cussed me out.

This is our first one-on-one meeting with her as my "peer adviser," and we've been sitting here at Starbucks for the better part of an hour. So far, she's managed to get me to list, oh, two colleges. One of them is in Narnia.

She wrote it down anyway.

"Okay," she says finally. "Let's talk about USD."

Boooo. "Naomi. I told you. I'm going to the community college. If I go anywhere. Or maybe UNLV."

She nods enthusiastically. "Great. That's two local schools, and I think those are perfectly acceptable choices."

"Cool. So can we go?"

"No, because you need to list eight more that exist in this universe."

I groan. "Fine. Nevada State College."

"Great! Okay, that's three. Seven to go."

"I can't think of any more colleges in Las Vegas."

"What about the university in Reno?"

"That's too far."

"Aaliyah," she says, showing the barest hint of frustration. "Can I ask . . . why are you so obsessed with staying here?"

"Why are you so obsessed with me leaving?"

At this, she takes a deep breath and squares her shoulders, taking a moment to choose her words carefully. I don't know why I'm being an asshole—I could just put her out of her misery—but I'm getting the tiniest bit of glee seeing Naomi frazzled.

"It's not necessarily any of my business," she says. "But from what you told me last year, your house doesn't seem like . . . the safest place."

Oh. I shift in my seat. "It's fine."

She does her adorable nose twitch and then sighs again. "We don't have to talk about it. But, as your peer adviser, and your captain, it *is* my job to support you."

"You don't need to worry about me, Cap. I'm not going to fuck us over again this year, I promise."

"That's not—" Naomi cuts herself off as her phone buzzes

on the table. Not surprisingly, a text message from Tessa pops up. My heart does a little jump, even though I'm not the one she's texting. Plus, it's probably about school. One may not guess it from appearances—Naomi's got a much simpler style to Tessa's more eclectic choices—but the two are oddly similar. Both calm, down-to-earth, and nerdy as fuck. Since our group date, they've created their own little study pod for geniuses. The only reason Tessa's not here now is because peer advisory sessions are mandated one-on-one, unless a counselor is also present. "Reduces distractions," and all that crap. So instead, I'm reduced to getting all fluttery at the mere sight of her name.

Naomi sends a quick response to Tessa's text and then turns back to me. "Okay," she says, smoothing down her completely unwrinkled shirt. "I'm going to get another iced tea. You want something?"

I shake my head no. As she gets up to go to the counter, I check my own text messages, hoping that I'm on Tessa's mind like she's on mine and—yup. There it is. A flirty little message that is . . . also about school. "Study session after class on Monday?" Of course. And we absolutely *will* be studying, because Naomi and Tessa are friends now, and they're both deeply invested in my academic potential. I want it to be annoying, but . . . it's not. Plus, Tessa and I have barely done anything but hold hands, and that's perfectly okay. That makes my heart skip, too.

"Absolutely," I text. "Can't wait."

As soon as I hit send, a message from Marissa pops up: "Hey, stranger," it reads. "Hang tonight? I miss you." She ends it with a frowny face.

I don't know why, but I hesitate. It's only been a couple of weeks since the group date, but things have started to get weird with us. Well, not weird. Just . . . different. We still text every day, but it doesn't feel like "just us" anymore. Between planning a study schedule with Naomi, and the time I've been spending with Tessa, Marissa and I haven't had a whole lot of face time together. Especially now that she and Emmanuel are . . . a thing. I assume Curtis and Naomi are doing great, too, judging from the fact that they now walk into practice together almost every day holding hands.

Honestly? It's been weird having a whole social life again. It feels nice, but tenuous. Like the whole thing could blow up in a matter of mere seconds. Maybe that's why I've been giving Naomi a hard time today. Tension feels more familiar than progress.

I shoot off a text to Marissa suggesting we hang after my session with Naomi, and then pull up something I haven't looked at in a million years: a doc featuring my list of dream colleges. I made it with Yasmin at the beginning of junior year, and haven't touched it since . . . well. You know.

There's Colgate University, American University, Wellesley

College, Chapman University, Regis University, and a whole bunch more. Big universities, small colleges, and in cities across the country. Totally different in every way except that they all had . . . um. "Peace studies." Like, you could study things like violence and conflict resolution, and, I don't know, that seems cool. Necessary. Like something I could actually apply to my family's life. USD became my number one choice at some point, because it was by the ocean, not too far from home, and I thought my mom would like that I was studying at a religious school.

I thought she'd be proud of me, but hey. I thought a lot of things back then.

"What are you looking at?"

Naomi has returned with her iced tea and, of course, a tall chai latte for me. Now I really feel bad for being so difficult today. But that's me, right? Making everyone else's life harder than it needs to be.

"Nothing," I say, pocketing my phone and taking a sip of her peace offering. "And thank you. You didn't have to." As she takes her seat, I surprise myself with a question. "Hey. What do you think your parents would do if you were gay?"

Her eyes go wide. "Oh. I don't know."

"Would they still love you, do you think?"

"Oh," she says. "Um, yes. I . . . think so."

"But it's not very Mormon, right? To be a flaming queer?"

At this, she chuckles softly. "For some people. I don't think that way." Suddenly her eyebrows furrow in alarm. "You *know* I don't think that way, right?"

I wave her away, still lost in my own line of questioning. "Yeah, of course," I mutter. "But, like . . . you're religious, aren't you? You follow certain rules, like not cursing and stuff."

"Yeah." She's looking at me with too much concern right now. I should stop, I *want* to stop, but the words tumble out before I can control them:

"Do you think God hates me?" The question hangs like a sinking ship, but I don't feel anything. The question should be monumental, I guess, or super powerful, but it feels anticlimactic to me. Like I've just asked her what the weather is. Still, I'm curious about her answer.

"Oh, Aaliyah," she breathes. "No. Not at all. And I don't think that, I *know* that."

"Huh." That's all I can muster, for some reason. Just "huh." The weird thing is that I believe her. I don't think God hates me. I'm fairly certain he doesn't. But Mom?

Now that's the real question.

That's the answer I'm not ready to hear.

"Anyway." I exhale deeply, like that'll dissipate the tension that's consumed us like smog. "Yeah, colleges. Um. Anything I can commute to. That's nonnegotiable."

Naomi is still staring at me, and I know what's she thinking.

Poor Aaliyah. But I'm no charity case, and I'm not delusional, either. Unlike what most people may think, I know exactly what I'm doing.

Naomi takes another deep breath and then flips a page in her binder. "Okay. Let's talk about European History."

CHAPTER 14

Despite the weirdness of having a social life outside of the two of us, Marissa and I snap back to normal the second she shows up at my door. She immediately plops onto the couch, turns on the TV, and beckons me over like it's *her* house. Once we settle in, engrossed in an episode of *House Hunters*, she turns to me with a bright gleam in her eyes.

"Hey. Aaliyah."

Oh no. I know that voice. It's the *I bet you don't want to do this thing I'm about to suggest, but I'm gonna suggest it anyway because you looooove me* voice. "What?"

"So, Halloween is in a few weeks."

"Uh-huh."

"And there's this new haunted house near The Strip . . ."

Hell no. I guess I've forgotten to inform her in the friendship contract we signed last spring that I *hate* all things scary—clowns, zombies, creatures with scythes. Not my thing.

"But I promise to protect you," she says, throwing her arms around me as I pointedly try to ignore her.

"Nah," I say. "I'm all the way good." When she tries to cajole me further, I pick up my phone and start scrolling, in a very obvious attempt to get on her nerves.

"Stop texting," Marissa whines. "I'm serious! It'll be fun! The chain saws aren't real, and neither is the blood. It just *looks* real."

"That's a huge nope, my friend."

She sighs dramatically, and I lift my phone up even higher as she rattles off reasons why haunted houses are the only thing that makes Halloween worth celebrating. I'm just about to google "haunted house–induced heart attacks" when a message from Tessa pops up on my screen:

"Was just thinking about you today, and what it'd be like to kiss you."

"Oh dear God." I shift so that I can look at Marissa. I can't remember the last time I thought straight, but now is not one of those times. "Tessa wants to kiss me."

Marissa holds the pillow she'd clearly been planning to throw at my head. "Wait. You haven't *kissed* yet?"

My cheeks color, and I finally put the phone down. "No."

"Why NOT?" Marissa asks, and I remind her, frantically, that Trinity is home and Mom is sleeping off last night's shift. Dad, supposedly, is out on another job—after he fixed the church's pipes, another parishioner asked if he'd help with repainting their house.

"Because," I whisper harshly. "We just started . . . you know. Dating, or whatever."

"But it's been almost a month!"

"Which is an eternity to you, I know, but this is new to me! I've never dated anyone before, and"—I pause, my heart pounding—"this would only be my second *real* kiss."

At this, Marissa frowns but tries to keep her voice light. "Third, dude," she says.

"You don't count." Even though I'm joking, the look on Marissa's face tells me that I'm not being funny. "Anyway," I say quickly, "I just want to take my time. Tessa is, you know, special. I don't want things to catch on fire like last time."

Marissa rolls her eyes and sits back on the couch, her phone suddenly appearing in her hand, and I know she's texting Emmanuel now, apparently ready to finish our conversation. "Yasmin was a unique case, babe. She's an arsonist at heart." I take a breath, suddenly feeling frustrated. Now that Tessa and I are finally starting to pick up, things with Yasmin don't seem so bad anymore. It was shitty, sure, but I have to think she had a good reason. Maybe something was going on with her— something at home, or maybe she had a depression spell. Don't we all deserve second chances?

I don't know why I feel the need to defend her, but I do. "You don't know her," I say quietly. Marissa gives me an unreadable expression. Then she shrugs noncommittally. For a while, we sit there in silence as she texts and I stare at the TV, pretending to care about houses being flipped in Orange County. Finally, after several minutes of Marissa dislodging a series of difficult breaths, she puts her phone down and stands up.

"I'm making us sandwiches," she says, and before I can stop her, she's in the kitchen, gathering bread and tempeh and vegetables. I follow her and begin pulling out plates and napkins. Within minutes, we fall back into sync as usual, letting anger and frustration dissipate into friendly familiarity. Her fingers brush my back as she moves around me—it's a light touch, but it still sends a jolt through my skin. I jump away from her, but I can't tell if she notices because I'm too busy grabbing things from the cabinet, putting things back in the refrigerator, and otherwise trying to get my breathing back to normal.

Finally, I clear my throat. "So how's theater?"

"Great!" She lights up, and then she shrugs. "Well, boring. Well. It's fine."

"Uh-huh?" She laughs at my confused look.

"Okay, well, obviously Yasmin is, like, around or whatever. We don't really talk, of course. So that's awkward. But Mr. Chisholm gave us two options for the winter musical: *Dear Evan Hansen* or *Spring Awakening*—"

"Wow, both of those are deeply depressing."

"Guy's got a hard-on for misery. Anyway"—she pops a piece of red pepper into her mouth—"we picked *Spring Awak-*

ening. Which is fucking awesome. I am planning to sing the shit out of 'Don't Do Sadness.'"

"Isn't that the boy's part?"

She winks. "I'm sure I could convince him to let me try for it." Her voice turns comically husky as she drapes an arm around my shoulder. "I'm very persuasive."

I try to maintain the humor. "Yes, I know," I say, shifting a little farther away.

She kisses my cheek and starts stuffing our sandwiches with vegetables, apparently ignorant of how blanched my skin just became.

"So," I say, trying to stay focused. "When are auditions?"

"Tomorrow," she says.

"Right. Yes. That's in my calendar. And you're definitely going for Melchior?"

She rolls her eyes. "Nerd."

"Takes one to know one."

"Uh-huh," she says. "You're going to be there, right?"

"If you want me there, of course." I pop a slice of cucumber in my mouth. "Do you think Coach will be pissed we're missing practice?"

Marissa stops me from stealing another slice of cucumber—we need it for the sandwiches. "Yes." She wags her finger at me. "Just don't make a habit of it."

"Har har."

She winks. "I'll text him about it tonight." She takes her plate to my couch, and I follow. "So," she says. "Fine. Haunted houses are out. For now. But what about Emmanuel's party on Halloween. You're going, right?"

Ew, no. "And be smothered by a bunch of drunks?" I say. "No, thank you very much." I literally have zero interest in seeing Emmanuel and Marissa swap spit for the rest of the night. I mean, I guess I could bring Tessa, but I'm kind of scarred from the last party Marissa and I decided to go to. Not that we'd ditch our paramours to make out with each other, but it would feel weird for us to be at a party together now—out of place, maybe. But I can tell she's offended. "What?"

She shrugs. "I dunno. First of all, *I'm* not going to drink. At all. So you don't have to worry about that. But also . . . we're teammates, and Emmanuel's my . . . you know."

"So? It's a party, not a championship game. You don't need me there for moral support."

I ignore her frown by taking a deep bite of my sandwich. It's followed by a sharp jab to my leg. "Ow!" I say. "What?"

"Why are you so far?" Her frown has turned into an adorable pout. Marissa is rarely adorable. That's why it works so well. I muster up a long-suffering sigh and, just to make her suffer, snuggle farther against the armrest on my side of the couch. Then I drape my legs over her thighs and adjust for the optimal position to both eat and semi–lie down at the same time.

Marissa makes a sound of annoyance but when I look at her, she's smiling.

Once we've eaten and the dishes and food are put away—save for the sandwiches we made Mom and Trinity—we return to the couch, both our phones discarded somewhere in the folds of our seats. My legs return to her lap, and her hand finds my knee as we watch the adventures of people far richer than we'll ever be complain about the cost of tile.

At some point later in the night, I tap on Mom's door to ask if Marissa can stay over. It's a pretty bold move, but that's how I've been feeling lately. A little more brave, a little less constrained. There's silence behind the door that feels like it stretches into eternity before Mom calls back: "Keep your door open."

Oh my freaking—

I clench my teeth so hard I'm surprised my permanent retainer doesn't break. I could say so many things right now, but fuck it—I got what I wanted. Permission to have a friend spend the night. I will take my victories where I can find them.

"Of course, Mom," I say, church-daughter voice on full display.

Maybe if Mom knew that I was dating Tessa, she wouldn't assume I was sleeping with Marissa, but maybe she just thinks I want to screw anything that moves, as long as it's not a cisgender dude. Who knows?

But I don't care.

I mean, fine—she's not even wrong. I *have* kissed Marissa. I *have* been kissed by Yaz. Why shouldn't she think I have ulterior motives, even if she doesn't know the whole story? If Marissa were a boy, Mom would've said the same thing, right?

Always assume your kids are having sex; never assume they're feeling confusion, or heartbreak, or betrayal, or any other fucking emotion that comes with it. Never assume they might need guidance, or comfort, or support.

That would be asking entirely too much.

Marissa gives me a sympathetic smile, but I just roll my eyes and gesture toward the stairs. We stop at Trini's room, and I slip in to grab Marissa's discarded laptop. Trini's sleeping form is curled around it as the credits to an anime roll. She sleepily allows me to tuck her in before I switch off the lights and meet Marissa in my bedroom.

For the rest of the evening, we switch between texting our significant others, watching TV, and pretending to do homework. At some point, we throw on an old British mystery about a town trying to solve the murder of a twelve-year-old boy and it makes me sad, so we turn on *Captain America: Civil War* instead. Eventually, we fall asleep, both of us splayed on top of my sheets, a mess of teenage limbs.

It's dark when I wake up, with only the glow of Netflix asking if we're still watching to guide my eyes. But it's not the light that woke me; my phone is buzzing frantically, as one text after another comes through. I register four text messages before the burst of buzzes becomes consistent and I realize someone is calling.

I reach over the side of my bed, careful to neither fall over nor bump Marissa's sleeping body. I lift my phone and try to clear my vision as the words "Yasmin Reyes" come into focus.

CHAPTER 15

Marissa is going to kill me.

CHAPTER 16

If I had just blocked Yasmin's number, I wouldn't be here. I'm not allowed to drive Mom's car—I have very explicit instructions. But I've never been rational when it comes to Yasmin.

That's why I'm already in her driveway, having sped through the neighborhood like I was possessed by Marissa. But when I put the car in park, I hesitate. It's feels weird to be back at her house like this—as if there should be bells or a ceremony welcoming me back to what is essentially her father's mansion.

Mr. Reyes owns a real estate development company, which operates both here in Vegas and in the Philippines, where he's from. He had this house specially commissioned for himself, his wife, and Yasmin. You can tell it's custom from the way it stands out from the rest of the neighborhood—a massive boxy slab of concrete and glass. On another night, I'd remember that I used to find it gorgeous. The kind of sleek, *postmodern industrial design* they talk about on housing shows with people who have too much money to spend. Like Curtis's house, the landscaping matches the natural desert, but the design is more minimal, with concrete made to look like marble and a burst of green foliage next to the front door.

When Mrs. Reyes bailed seven years ago, Mr. Reyes started traveling and spending more time at his other properties. I mean, I guess he *technically* still lives here since it's not like Yaz is emancipated, but she also hasn't had a babysitter since we were eleven.

From fifth grade to tenth grade, I spent nearly every afternoon with her in her backyard, swimming in her ten-foot-deep pool, warming up in the firepit out back, and trying not to set the house on fire when we tried to use the outdoor kitchen. I never really picked up a decent level of cooking skills, but Yasmin became a chef of epic proportions.

I tap on the steering wheel, the last ten years of our lives flashing before my eyes. We really had been best friends. Now, we're barely acquaintances. So what am I doing here?

"Aali?" I can hear her voice from the crack in my window. I look up and there she is, leaning against the railing of her dad's massive balcony, the glow of the streetlamp nearby casting her brown skin gold. She disappears through the doors, and a moment later, her front door opens.

Even if I wanted to leave, it'd be too late now. Besides, I know why she called. This isn't the first time I've heard her frantic voice in the middle of the night, and even if I hate myself for being here right now, I'd hate myself more if I left.

I shut off the engine and then walk toward her open door. Her short black hair is plastered to her face as if she's been sweating, and her pale brown skin looks pallid, the golden glow from earlier diminished with the sheen on her skin. Her eyes are dull, red. I can't tell if she's been drinking, but I know she's tired. Without needing to ask, I reach for her wrist, careful to avoid the newly open wounds and the specks of blood that have bubbled up. Instead, I run my finger over her palm.

"I'm sorry," she starts to say, but tears and hiccups interrupt her. I pull her into me, her lips muffled against my shirt. When her sobs quiet, I hum past her, pulling her into her house and shutting the door. I lead her to her bathroom and sit her on the edge of her bathtub. It's all muscle memory; a scene we've played out ever since we were kids. It's been a while, but certainly not long enough.

A little water, a little alcohol, a little gauze.

She'll be all right.

She sniffs as her eyes follow my fingers. We barely exchange words.

When the wounds are clean and the supplies put away, I stand against the doorway, ready to leave because I don't know what else to do. This is the part that's new for us. I don't know how to speak to a stranger.

But then she says my name again.

"Aali." It comes out as a whisper. My eyes flicker down, and for the first time tonight, I'm the one who's vulnerable.

"Look at me," she says, her voice stronger this time, and I don't know how she does it. I don't know how she can assume control like this so quickly, so easily.

I lift my chin and force a smile. "It's not so bad this time around, huh?" I say.

She forces a chuckle, and her eyes are suddenly clearer, calmer. As if she's never shed a tear in her life.

"Are you hungry?" she asks suddenly. "I have some leftover lumpia in the fridge." She nudges me, an insider gleam in her eyes. "Or pancit. I know those are your favorite."

I fake a smile and shake my head. "No. I'm vegan, remember?"

"Ah. Right." She looks down. "It's been a while. Since when, again?"

"About two years ago," I remind her. That was before everything happened, but she must've forgotten.

"Right," she says again. "Skye is vegan, too." She pauses, probably remembering our run-in the other day. Then she lets her shoulders drop with a sigh. "I'm sorry I made you come here."

"You didn't make me do anything," I say too quickly. I bite

the inside of my cheek, take a breath. "Where is your girlfriend, by the way?"

"I should've called her, I'm sorry." If she apologizes one more time—"But," she continues, "I guess I just thought of you first." The smile she offers is so impossibly Yaz; so completely the girl I used to know since I was eight years old. A radiant sight of white teeth against smooth sand-colored skin.

"Yeah, well. Habit," I say, meaning nothing. Suddenly, it's too hot in here. Too closed in. My senses are on fire, and I know that if I don't escape, this room will swallow me whole. But she brushes her fingers over my arm, and I still. Slowly, her fingers trail up, up, up until they reach a patch of skin a shade darker than the rest of my arm. To most, it's a birthmark—a quiet reminder of a peaceful beginning. But Yaz was there when I pressed the flame of a lighter to my skin. She's the one who took it away in the morning.

The day I got outed to my mom, I was talking with Hayley Gomez at the queer center. Nothing happened; we were just sitting outside, our knees a little close together maybe, maybe our pinkies were touching. And then suddenly a woman appeared, angry blue eyes, white-blond hair. I recognized her immediately—Michelle Taylor, one of the women who helped run some of the church's volunteer activities. I didn't know her well; maybe we smiled at each other a few times in passing, or exchanged a few "how are you's" during coffee breaks after the sermon was over. But now here she was, a raging bull of a woman yanking Hayley away from me as if I was going to send her right to hell with a touch of my arm.

Turns out Hayley was Michelle's niece, and we were both the devil incarnate. It was scary—the first time someone who wasn't my dad screamed at me like that. A volunteer ended up driving me home, and for the first time in my life, it wasn't the usual stench of whiskey on Dad's breath that greeted me, but scriptures my mother wielded like knives. Miss Taylor had apparently found the time to call my mom and inform her of my heathenry in between promising Hayley eternal damnation. I bolted, like I'd always done when Dad was drunk, and then called Yaz to pick me up in the parking lot of one of the shopping centers nearby. She did—she always did, I could never forget that—and when she fell asleep later that night, I rummaged around for her razor, and her lighter.

I started with the fire, just to see how it would feel. Then Yaz knocked on the door of the bathroom I hid in. I didn't let her in—not for hours—but I put the lighter down. Left the razor untouched. And Yaz waited outside the door until the sun came up.

"Hey," Yaz says, bringing me back to her. "You cut your hair." She reaches toward my face, and I stand so quickly that we're both nearly knocked off balance. But she keeps me right side up, her left hand on my shoulder, the fingers of her right suddenly laced into mine.

"I should go," I say, but her hands keep me in place.

"I like it," she says. "You look different." My lips pull into a thin line, and I can only offer a brusque thanks before moving around her toward the door. Again, she blocks my path. "Please, Aali. Stay the night?" she asks.

I want to say no, but we both know I won't. How could I?

She lets go of my hand, and I follow her to her bedroom, although of course I know the way. There are still pictures of us in the hallway; sixth grade Halloween together; both our elementary and junior high graduations. I don't look at them, but I know they're there.

In her bed, we lie beside each other, careful not to touch. Another new phenomenon. When we were younger, we used to make forts, pile things onto each other, a tangle of tiny limbs and snores. And then, we got older. We settled down, just two friends falling asleep.

And then one night she kissed me.

Our last night together in this bed.

I try not to remember, but I awake three hours later to find her arms wrapped around my stomach, just like lovers. For that brief moment, I'm lost.

For that moment, I think that the last nine months never happened. That our story was everyone's favorite meet-cute:

Two friends kiss, and fall in love, and the breakup doesn't happen until they get into different colleges and move away.

But Yasmin made a different choice.

And that choice wouldn't be too happy with her girlfriend spooning me. So I shift, stand. I need to get back to the house before Mom knows I'm gone and kicks my sappy ass. Quietly, I grab my things and head for the door, but as I'm slipping my shoes on in the next room, I hear Yaz behind me. It's her turn to stand against the door frame, and watch me without words.

"Sorry," I say, turning to face her. "I didn't mean to wake you. I just gotta go before my mom finds out I'm gone. Plus, class and whatnot."

Yasmin tilts her head, taking me in. Her arms are crossed, and her hair is shooting up in multiple directions, making her look a lot like a porcupine. I laugh, and her lips pull into a smile. "What?" she says. I think it's coy, until I realize it's insecure, and I curb my lips into my own small smile.

"Nothing." I shake my head. "You just look cute like that, is all."

She blinks a couple of times, and before I can register her movements, she's in front of me, her palm against my cheek, then just below my ear, behind my neck. She presses her smile into mine.

The kiss lasts longer than it should have, and she pulls away first. "I'll see you at school." She says it like a question, even as she's turning away, not waiting for the answer. From my spot in the living room, I can tell she's starting to get dressed and so I leave, nearly run for the car waiting for me outside. My heart is pounding, and my mouth feels like it's on fire. I wish I felt angry, but with Yasmin, I never know what to feel.

In the car, I stare at the dash blankly. It's 4:30 A.M. Three hours before we're supposed to be at school. In one hour, my mom will be waking up to get ready for her shift. I could be reckless—take the car and just drive somewhere. Clear my head. But I've made enough mistakes tonight.

Instead, I drive home, park the car in the carport in front of the house, and sneak quietly up the stairs. When I get back to my room, the light is on and Marissa is sitting up in bed, silently scrolling through her phone.

I try to speak naturally, but it comes out as a croak. "Hi," I say.

She looks up at me lazily, as if I'm interrupting something dreadfully important. Her eyes outline my frame, up and down, as she chews on her bottom lip. I know this look well. It's what she does when she's biting back a series of insults or curses. I've seen her do that the few times I've been in the same room as her and her mom. I continue to stand there, hands fiddling with the hem of my shirt, until finally she clears her throat, looks at her phone for a few more seconds, and then lets it drop back onto the bed. "So," she sighs, "what did she do this time?"

The question is both completely natural and totally enraging. Marissa knows about the Adventures of Yasmin and Aaliyah. Our history, and every detail of it. And I want to defend Yasmin, badly, but I also want to scream, and punch things, and dig my fingernails into my wrists. Not because of Yaz, not really. But because I don't know what I'm doing. What the hell I'm supposed to be doing. I settle for digging my nails into my palms instead and look at the ceiling, so that the tears that have suddenly sprung to my eyes don't fall. I take a deep breath and sit down next to Marissa's knees. I present the burn mark to her, and she flashes a glance toward my eyes before inspecting it thoughtfully. Gently.

Just like Yaz. Too much like her.

Marissa takes another deep breath and then releases the air over the puckered skin. The air is replaced with her lips, a light kiss. Then, to my forehead. She drops her knees, and I fall into her arms. She plants another kiss into my shorn hair and whispers, so quietly that it takes me a second to understand her: "Do I need to hide the sharp things?"

I choke out a laugh that becomes a sob I can't control.

I don't know how long we stay like that, or when we fell asleep, but the first thing I wake to is her dark red hair, the morning light streaming through my window, and the realization that we are two hours late for school.

CHAPTER 17

Normally, Marissa is the speed demon and I'm the one leaning back, casually letting my hands drift through the air that rushes by her open window. The thing is, Marissa drag races with phantom opponents because *she likes it*, not necessarily because she feels like we need to go somewhere important.

And it's not like I'm about to be valedictorian or whatever-torian ranks twentieth in their class, but I am also *not* interested in getting detention, having teachers call my mom to ask where I am, or letting it seem to anyone that the upward swing I've been on is crashing down yet again.

I am not fucking up again.

So even at a clip of sixty-five miles per hour in a zone of forty-five, Marissa is not driving nearly fast enough for my anxiety to be outpaced.

"Dude," I say. *"Please go faster."*

She barely quirks an eye at me as the speedometer keeps steady. "Why?" she asks. "The difference between ten minutes and fifteen is negligible when you're two hours late, babe. I don't even see why we're going."

"BECAUSE." I restrain myself from taking the wheel from her, but she tightens her grip as if she senses my wavering control.

"We'll be fine. Just walk in like you own the place, and no one will be the wiser. Except the teachers who marked us down as absent, but we can't do anything about that now, can we?"

Dear God, sometimes I could smack her.

But she's not wrong. In fact, it's not until we're turning the corner into the school zone that I really begin to think about what we're rushing toward:

1. Keeping my already sullied name less sullied than it was last year.
2. Yasmin, the girl who broke my heart and then kissed me last night.
3. Tessa, the girl I'm dating and who I've not yet kissed, because I "want to take my time."

"Wait, slow down," I say to Marissa as she pulls into a parking spot.

"Uh, done. We're parked."

"Does what happened last night with Yasmin count as cheating?"

"In my book?" Marissa shrugs. "No."

"Do you think Tessa will consider it cheating?"

"Dunno. You should ask her."

I give Marissa a glare I can't justify unleashing and then drop my head onto the dash. "God, I'm fucked."

I feel her hand on my back and try to relax as she begins to rub circles below my shoulders. "It'll be okay," she says, "I promise." Then she opens the door and lets it click shut beside her. A few seconds pass, and then I hear the door on my side open. "Now, let's go."

When I wander in twenty minutes late to calculus, Tess gives me an odd look that I avoid as I sink into my seat behind her. Miss Adebayo gives a "nice of you to join us"–esque comment to which the rest of the class snickers, but right now, my mind is on more pressing things than solving for x. Miss A resumes her lecture, and I proceed to doodle onto the blank page of my notebook, wondering how I will explain myself to Tessa.

Of course, I could *not* tell her about anything. But that would make me a terrible person, and I try to avoid that course of action when possible.

Then again, I didn't kiss Yasmin—she kissed me.

Then again then again, I was the one who drove to her house when she called. And slept in her bed.

Goddamit.

It takes everything in me not to just let my head bang against the desk a few times. Instead, I keep doodling, ignoring Tessa's attempts to get my attention, including the texts occasionally buzzing against my thigh.

When class ends, I swing past her, my backpack already latched onto my shoulders as I quickly make my way down the hallway. I can feel her eyes boring into me from the door, and I know I'm only digging myself into a deeper hole. I wallow there for the next few hours, dark thoughts and memories clouding my mind until a note in the middle of English class sends me to Miss Eccleston's office.

Great.

"Miss Marshall. Have a seat." I collapse into the chair across from her desk as she leans back in her own seat. "I prefer to not have to meet outside of scheduled sessions, but I heard from a couple of your teachers this morning that you didn't show up."

"I overslept."

She sighs like it's the oldest excuse in the book and then pushes aside whatever's on her desk to "really" look at me. "Aaliyah. What's really going on? You get As and Bs your first two years of high school, even the first semester of junior year, and then you nearly flunk out? That's unusual."

"Okay."

She tries not to clench her teeth, but she's doing a bad job of hiding it.

"Tell me about college."

"What about it?"

"Where do you want to go?"

"Nowhere. I don't know. CSN, I guess."

"Okay. What about USD? The college Naomi mentioned last month?"

I shrug.

"You're not interested anymore?"

"I don't want to go out of state."

"Why not?"

"Because." I'm snapping now, but I need to rein it in. I take a deep breath and don't say anything else.

Finally, Miss Eccleston bites the inside of her cheek and shuffles the stray pages on her desk. "Okay. Listen. You're doing okay this semester, so far. I hear you're doing well on your cross-country team—extremely well, in fact. So I'm not worried. Yet. But I don't want today to mark a pattern, or I'll be increasing your sessions with myself and Miss Pratt, including after-school sessions. Do you understand?"

I give some semblance of a response, and then she lets me go. I slink out of her office just in time for practice to begin. I distract myself from the inevitable shit show by finally checking my messages, scrolling through Tessa's pleas for an explanation.

As I walk toward the field, my feet move even slower. So slow, in fact, that I wonder if I'm moving backward, or at all. My armpits begin to sweat, my breathing quickens, and suddenly the field begins to waiver like a mirage before my eyes.

Is this what a panic attack feels like?

Okay, count to ten. Breathe. It's just like a competition, except with a higher possibility of face-planting. My fist opens. Closes. If I can keep my circulation flowing, then I can keep walking: one foot, now the other. I've got this.

When I finally reach the field, the world rushes at me as if my brain suddenly pressed *play*. "You're here!" Coach says. His voice sounds puzzled, and I give him a weird look as Naomi waves. She's sitting next to Tessa, who is sporting the deepest scowl I've ever seen. "Hi," I say to her.

"She speaks," Tessa says, and the sweat rushes back to my palms. Time to think of a reasonable explanation. Anything other than *I'm a cheating bitch*. But before I can explain myself, Coach's head bobbles into view.

"Tessa," he says with an ever-friendly grin, "want to run the stretches today?"

She agrees, bolting away from me and Naomi quick as lightning. Then we're off to a run, and Tessa stays as far from me as she can. She goes off on her own instead, and I try like hell to do the same, but I'm completely aware of where she is at all times, her eyes hardened, her lips a thin line, her body stiff. We're both running too fast and hard for a proper practice run, and Coach's whistle goes off madly, reminding us to slow down, to pay attention to our bodies and our breaths, to get back on track before we wear ourselves out.

At the moment, we both suck at listening.

By the time practice ends, we're both out of breath and sitting on opposite ends of our teammates. Coach shakes his head with a disappointed frown.

I guess today's his rainy day.

"I need you all to get your heads on straight," he says. "Our next meet is in a few days. I can't have my best runners out of gas before we're even halfway through the run. Got it?" He looks us both square in the eyes, and I push down the bile rising in my throat as Radhika and Tracey snicker behind me. Then Coach blows the whistle again, signaling that we're done.

As the team filters off the field, I imagine following alongside them. But I jog up to Tessa, who's at her backpack by the gate, digging out her water bottle. "Hey, can we talk?"

She turns to me with such immediacy that I think she's going to push me over. "Yes," she says instead. "What the hell is going on?"

Her response is too fast. I didn't really prepare an explanation, so much as prepare to give one. This becomes obvious, because it takes me a few seconds too long to respond. Her light brown eyes turn stormy, and she returns to shoving her water bottle back into her bag. With the bag on her shoulder, she looks like she's ready to leave, but she stands there, instead. Waiting.

"I kissed someone else." That's the best I can do.

She blinks several times, as if this is the last thing she expected me to say. "Oh."

"It was an accident, and it didn't mean anything. But I didn't know how to tell you, so I . . ."

"Made me feel like I did something wrong, instead," she answers.

"I'm sorry, Tess. I know I fucked up."

"Yes. So what are you going to do about it?" She's still standing there, scowling at me, but with no indication that she's planning to leave.

I nod quickly to fill the empty space left by her question, feeling an odd mix of relief and delayed panic. "Can we walk? Around the field, or something." She eyes me for a moment and then drops her bag.

"Fine."

As we walk, I tell her about what happened with Yasmin. I tell her about Skye and about why I started this year with a mane of curls before cutting it all off. I try to explain, and to apologize, and to rationalize all the ways in which I'm a complete and total idiot. She listens as we walk, and I'm grateful for her patience, even as I'm terrified that as soon as I'm done, she's going to leave and I'm going to be left with all my idiot mistakes again.

Instead, she's quiet. A lifetime passes before either one of us speaks again, and finally we find ourselves back at the bleachers, where this all began.

We sit together, my body angled toward hers and hers angled away from me. Finally, she speaks. "So. You still have feelings for her, then?"

I wish I could lie, but that wouldn't serve anyone. I release a loose breath and lean back on the bleachers. "I wish I didn't. And it's not that I'm actually interested in having something real with her. That's not an option. But, yes, she was the first girl I ever thought I . . . was in love with. That's not easy to shake."

"I understand." She stretches, leans back so that our bodies mirror each other. "Back in Reno, there was this girl I was wild about. We didn't go way back, like you and Yasmin, but we had that thing. That spark. It crashed and burned, mostly because her family is Baptist and when her mom found us necking in their garage, it was not a pretty scene. There's nothing holy about what came out of that woman's mouth." She snickers at the memory, even as it brings me back to darker times. "It was like two years ago maybe, and I haven't seen her since, but I still think about her. And if she were to suddenly pop up again after all that, I don't know what I'd do. Or how I'd feel." She lifts a hand toward me and runs her fingers around my baby hairs, which are dry and frizzy now that practice is over. She tries to smooth them out, even though we both know it's useless. Then her palm cups my face, and for the first time, she looks into my eyes.

"Thank you for telling me the truth," she says, and my heart thuds so hard that I think it's going to fall into my stomach. Then she runs a finger beneath my chin and pulls me to her so that her lips brush my ear. "And thank you for feeling bad about it." Then she presses her lips there, a sweet kiss. Forgiveness.

I don't realize I'm leaning toward her until she pulls away and I nearly fall to my knees at her feet. Quickly, I sit back up and nod with what is probably too much enthusiasm. "I. Yes. Of course." I try to rein in my breathing, and my heart. "I am sorry, Tess. Really."

A wide smile finds its way back beneath her beauty mark. She reaches up and touches my hair again, gently pulling out the curly strands and letting them spring back into place. Her gaze is far away, and I watch her eyes, trying to understand what she's thinking.

"So you don't like your hair now?" she asks.

I let out a breathy laugh and lean back into her touch as she continues messing with my curls. "I mean, it's fine. Kind of shaggy now, actually. I've seen this cut on other girls and stuff, and I like it *on them*. But it feels . . . off to me. Like I'm trying to be something I'm not."

"We could dye it," Tessa suggests. Her eyes sparkle. "Bleach blond on top, get some cool designs shaved into the side."

"Like Aquaman?" I ask, while Tessa cocks an eyebrow. "He's a DC character. Like, in the comics—"

"I know who Aquaman is." She smiles. "You nerd."

"Your mom's a nerd."

"Wow. Nice one." Then she moves closer to me. "So. Blond?"

"It looks good on him. I don't know about me." The fact that I'm able to form coherent sentences while she's so close to me is a mystery.

She kisses that spot again between my ear and my baby hairs and then stands, pulling me up with her. "Okay, we'll think of something." And with that, I'm tugged off the bleachers, barely reacting enough to grab my bag—and hers—before we appear before her car.

"Where are we going?" I ask, although I'm slipping into the passenger seat as she gets behind the wheel.

"We're exorcising your demons," she says. Then the car starts.

CHAPTER 18

Hair is an absolute minefield.

I'm trying not to show my absolute ignorance by keeping Google alive and well on my phone as Tessa speaks, but I can't type as fast as she throws out terms and hair care techniques: the difference between individual braids and crochet braids, and Senegalese twists versus Havana twists, and jumbo versus medium, and *I think my head is going to explode.*

Other than my family, I've spent the past seventeen years surrounded by non-Black people with straight-to-wavy hair. Even my church is mostly white. This is new territory for me, and while I'm happy to tag along with any adventure Tessa wants to go on, I'm feeling just a little overwhelmed.

Like, maybe I'm a little bit of a fraud, sitting there with my cropped curls and blank stare as Tessa begins to relay the subtle differences between a sew-in weave and just going with a wig customized to one's hairline. Finally, we pull into the strip mall parking outside Greg's, but I assume we're not going there, because right next door is a Sally's. She sits back and turns to me expectantly. "So," she begins. "What'll it be?"

"Um." I stall for time, trying to wrap my head around what felt like an intensive astronomy class. My brain struggles to connect the dots between her hair theory course and what actually applies to me. "Wellll," I draw out. "My concern is this: If I get braids, will people think we're twins, instead of girlfriends?"

She lets out an adorable snort that sobers into a thoughtful frown. "Are we girlfriends?"

My attempt at evasion has backfired spectacularly. "I. I mean. If you . . . would like to be? Not that I'm trying to rush you. Not that I don't want you to be! I mean. Um." I sink into my seat and sigh so deeply that it almost comes out like a neigh. The panic forming in the pit of my stomach subsides as her lips meet the warmth spreading throughout my cheeks.

"We look absolutely nothing alike," she says. "But I get it. People are wild, so maybe we won't go with a style that looks exactly like mine." She shakes her head to demonstrate the pile of green and white braids piled atop her head. "But you can get different colors, and different kinds of twists or braids . . ."

"Right," I say quickly, afraid that she'll go back down the hair rabbit hole. It's not that I'm uninterested—totally the opposite in fact. But it's bad enough that this all has to be explained to me to begin with. I open my door, and she follows suit. Then

I face the store, and my feet root into the ground as a world of too many possibilities stands imposingly before me. Tessa comes around to my side and wraps her arm around my waist. Without thinking, I rest my head on her shoulder, and we both spend a few seconds contemplating our next move.

With her body so close to mine, I'm feeling a little less bad. A lot less.

It's like magic.

"Hey." I turn her toward me. "I'm both completely terrified of what will emerge from this store and extremely curious. Excited. You make me feel both, all the time. And I'm sorry that I made you feel more terror than excitement today. I'm sorry I made you feel like shit. And, I'm sorry I cheated."

Tessa's eyes follow mine as I speak. She lets my apology hang suspended between us, and then lifts my knuckles to her lips. They brush my skin for the briefest moment before they suddenly disappear. She spares me a glance and then walks into the store alone.

I could take any of that as a good sign, or a bad sign, but I decide I'll just have to wait and see. Just as I'm about to follow her in, though, I see Lonnie coming out of Greg's. They're pushing a row of carts and giving me the thumbs-up.

★ ★ ★

I've been in Sally's about three hundred times, but I've always ignored the aisles of real and synthetic hair, ashamed of my own weird mix of curiosity and ignorance. Now, equipped with the world's fastest crash course, I'm wandering through as if I know what I'm looking for, as if these things of which I've just learned will finally show me who I am. I'm in front of a packet of simple dark brown crochet twists when a package of curls catches my eye. The hair looks a lot like mine, except that it's longer, of course, and the tips are dyed royal purple. I look at the model on the cover. Laid out, the hair is a little bigger than I recall mine being. A little bolder.

In my hands, the package is lighter than I expect, although I realize I'll have to grab a bunch for the desired result. But I feel silly for considering it. Didn't I cut off all my hair so that I didn't look like this? Didn't I want something different? And besides . . . why would I put *fake* curly hair on top of my *real* curls? I picture my mother's disdain, and Yasmin's indifference. Just as I'm about to return the package to its rightful location, I feel Tessa's cool breath on my neck and her arms wrap around my waist again.

"You like that one?" she asks into my ear.

I relax into her arms, even as I start to frown. "Yeah," I say, and I hate that it sounds like a whine. "I do. But I think I should get something different. Something wild."

"Do you like something else?"

I pull out of her arms briefly to take a cursory, meaningless glance around. "Everything here looks pretty amazing actually.

But I don't know. I guess I want something that feels familiar." I gesture toward the package. "And that looks just like my hair if I grew it out again."

Tessa reaches around me to inspect the package. She turns it over in her hand, looking at the back cover and then the model on the front. Then she shrugs. "There's nothing wrong with looking like yourself, babe."

My eyes widen. "Babe?"

She ignores me. "You'll need about six, I think." Then she pulls out the required number and brushes past me, but the motion is anything but cold.

It's electric.

I float behind her as she walks to the cash register. She's already pulling out her wallet, which is ridiculous, so I nudge her aside and hand the cashier my debit card, trying not to wince visibly at the price. Sixty dollars. Jesus Christ. "Wait," I say, turning back to Tessa just as the cashier rings up the first package of hair. "What's next? Don't I need to set up an appointment somewhere? I think it might be too late to call my usual stylist." *Plus, I can't afford to.*

A wicked grin grows on her lips as she reaches up to smooth my baby hairs again. "What are your plans tonight?"

"Oh, um." I pretend to think. "Nothing."

"Good." Tessa's voice turns singsong. "'Cause I'm doing your hair."

She grabs the bagged packages of hair and prances out of the store before I can stop her. The cashier, a Black woman with a straight blond bob, tries to hide a smirk and gives me my receipt. "Have fun," she says.

"Thanks," I mutter, following Tessa out to her car, where she's tossed the bag into the back seat. Once we get on the road, she starts tapping out a song I can't decipher on the wheel. My own terror and excitement yield to a weird sense of joy. "You're amazing," I breathe out, and I don't know if she heard me, but a few seconds later, her hand drops to the console between us. I drop my hand into hers without hesitation.

CHAPTER 19

About fifteen seconds after Tessa announces we're near her neighborhood, I receive what is probably my third phone call from Mom in the past ten minutes. I figure she's catching up on all the voice mails my teachers left her, so I'm not exactly keen to answer. But Tessa gives me a long look after my phone buzzes for the fifth time.

"Sorry," I say, turning my phone to silent.

"Maybe you should answer?" Tessa asks as we pull up in front of what I assume is her house. I want to take it all in—the brown Spanish-style roof and the grayish blue walls, with the bright orange door. Clearly, her mom has eclectic taste. Which, taking in Tessa's assorted braid colors, shouldn't be a surprise. But I glance at my phone just as I'm about to shove it in my pocket for good, and a barrage of texts from my mother stops me cold. The newest one reads: PLEASE PICK UP TRINI FROM HOME. NOW. She probably thinks I'm with Marissa. It wouldn't be the first time we made an emergency trip home.

"What's wrong?" Tessa walks around to my side of the car,

her arms wrapped around herself as if she's sensing that something is totally off. I lift my chin to indicate I'm not ignoring her, and then dial my mom back. She picks up on the second ring, and the familiar scratchiness of her throat does not set me at ease.

"What's wrong?" I echo Tessa.

"Your father is home. He's drunk. Trini called, and I can't get out of my shift—"

"Got it, I'll get her." I take a breath and try to sound nicer, even as my blood pressure spikes. "Don't worry, Mom. It's all right."

"You'll get her?" Mom suddenly sounds hysterical, as if she's been holding herself together just long enough to hear salvation. "Oh, thank God."

"Uh-huh. Get back to work, Mom. I'm on my way now."

She tries to tell me she loves me, but I just uh-huh her off the phone. I think about throwing it clear across the driveway, but I've already terrified Tessa enough today. I take a few breaths and turn to her. One of her arms is still wrapped around her own waist, while another holds on to the back of her neck.

"Hey, I hate to do this but . . . can we pick up my sister? She's . . . ah, she shouldn't be home alone right now. You can just drop us off at, like, a Starbucks or something until my mom gets home and we can do this"—I gesture vaguely to the hair strewn across her back seat—"later."

"Of course," she says, returning once again to the car. "And we can come back here." I blink at her quick acquiescence, but now's not really the time to play coy. Instead, I follow her into the car and hold my breath as we take off back toward my house.

Ten minutes later, we pull into my neighborhood and as we turn the corner toward my block, I see Trinity. She's sitting on the brick ledge of our front yard that hangs over the sidewalk. Her head is bobbing up and down as she looks at her feet, her Spider-Man headphones blocking out the rest of the world. As soon as I step out of Tessa's car, I can hear music blasting out of the house; not because it's loud—though it is—but because every window and door is wide open.

Trini looks up at me as I walk toward her, and her eyes are both tear stained and defiant. I bend down to her level, my hand on her knee, and she wraps her arms around my neck without saying anything. "It's okay, honey," I say, although I know she can't hear me. Paramore is blasting out of her headphones. Then Dad stumbles out of the garage. In his hand is a sixteen-ounce can of Corona.

"My girls!" he says, a wide toothy grin on his face as he approaches. He sticks one hand into his pocket and takes a sip of his beer. "The little girl call you?" he asks, lifting his beer toward Trini.

"Mom did," I say as Trini's grip tightens.

"She called your mom?" He puckers his lips in thought. Nods. Takes another sip of beer. "Snitch."

"What'd you do?"

His calm veneer drops for a second, and I see the rage in his red eyes appear. "Not a goddamn thing."

"Dad." The warning is in my voice, but it's not like I know what my threat would be. Whatever it is, though, I swear I'd do it.

"I ain't touch that little girl. Did I ever touch you? Have I ever fucking touched you? No." He spits, takes another swig of beer. "I came upstairs, wanted to talk. Ask her how her day was."

"He was already drunk," Trini whispers in my ear. "He fell down when he came in."

"What'd she say?" His voice rises just as I hear Tessa's door click open. Fuck. I forgot she was here. Fuck fuck fuck.

I turn just enough to see her standing in the open door of her car, one hand on the hood. "Trini, honey. Get in the car, please," I say. She nods, and I drop her gently to her feet. She continues looking down as she walks away, and I keep my eyes on our father.

"Who's that?" he asks, gesturing toward Tessa. I don't look back. He looks me up and down. "Where's your other friend? The redhead?" He takes another sip, and then sighs as if it's the most refreshing thing in the world. He waits for me to respond. "Where's Yasmin?" Then he laughs. He squeezes the can and drops it on the grass. "Play on, playa." He winks as he turns around and heads back into the garage.

If this were the first time, or the tenth, I would be concerned about the neighbors watching. But we're going on year thirteen that I can remember, so I just take a deep breath and turn around. At least no one called the police this time.

When I get back into Tessa's car, no one says anything for the whole drive back to her home. It's not until we pull into her driveway that I grab her hand, to keep her from putting the car in park. "Look," I say. "I'm sorry I dragged you into this. If there's a Starbucks or whatever nearby, you can just—" But I don't get to finish my sentence. Tessa's lips are on mine—a firm but gentle kiss.

Our first one.

"Get inside," she says with a smile. Then she turns off the ignition and turns to Trini. "So you're a Spider-Man fan."

Trini looks up from her hands, her headphones apparently turned down. "Yeah."

Tessa quickly lists each Spider-Man movie in her collection. Which is every one that's ever been made. "All on Blu-ray," she says, "so we don't have to worry about any shi—crappy— Wi-Fi connections. What's your poison, little lady?"

Trini's eyes sparkle. "All of them." Then she looks at me and gives a shy smile. "Please."

CHAPTER 20

Halfway through *Spider-Man: Homecoming*, Trinity's fast asleep on her side of the couch. We're all curled up in Tessa's living room, the afternoon light streaming in from the sliding glass doors that lead to her backyard. Her mom won't be home for a few hours, but Tessa's been insisting that she call to see if we can all have a big "sleepover." But I can't stop thinking about what she saw, what she heard, and what she must think of me. I can't stop thinking about our first kiss, and the fact that it happened after she saw what I come home to every day, what my life is usually like.

I'm dying to be her girlfriend—not her charity case. I need her to know that. Just as I start to open my mouth and explain, once again, that Trinity and I would be fine taking refuge in a coffee shop somewhere nearby, Tessa leans over. "You ready?"

I glance back toward Trinity, who is well and truly gone from this world, and then at the TV screen, where Peter is starting his preparation montage for the school dance with his crush, Liz. I take a deep breath and rake a hand through what's left of my own natural hair. "How long's it gonna take?"

Tessa pulls on my hair briefly and starts a practice cornrow for a moment. Then she shrugs. "Three, four hours tops."

Okay. It's late afternoon, and Mom should be home in a few hours. Maybe she'll be able to book a hotel room for the night so that we don't have to mess with Dad's foolishness . . . How much money do I have left? I can't believe I blew sixty bucks on fake hair. Sixty dollars could get us a motel on the Strip for a night—

"Aali?"

I look up to find Tessa's concerned face. "Sorry," I say. "That's okay with me. Although I really, really don't want to impose—"

"You. Are. Not. Imposing." Tessa fixes me with a glare that could rival Marissa's. "Come on." She pauses the TV. Then she pulls me up, the bag of fake hair suddenly appearing in her other hand, and walks me upstairs to her bedroom.

Which I realize, as we enter, I've never seen before.

Tessa pushes me onto her bed and disappears into the bathroom we passed down the hall. I take this moment to look around. Steady myself. Her room is surprisingly femme. The walls are painted a pale pink, and her duvet has a floral pattern crocheted onto it. In one corner of her room is a horde of variously sized stuffed animals of myriad colors and species. I spot a stuffed Groot nestled in with a smallish Porg, beside an impossibly large elephant of no discernible fandom. It's not a big room, although definitely larger than mine, and I'm curious for the first time about what her mom does to be able to afford a three-bedroom house like this on her own.

Her walls, unsurprisingly, are also covered in a mix of Marvel movie posters, a Janelle Monáe poster, and some singers I don't recognize. Then I glance behind me, and notice for the first time a huge poster of Whitney Houston above her bed, with the word QUEEN scrawled beneath the singer's face in bold red marker. I smile at the word.

I don't know what the protocol is for riffling through your maybe-not-quite-girlfriend's things yet, so I'm angling over Tessa's bed, trying to get a good look at the pile of LP jackets stashed under the record player on her bedside table when she walks in with a handful of hair products in her arms. She peers at me above the collection of items in her hand. "Whatcha doin'?"

I pull myself right side up with a sheepish smile. Then I nod toward Whitney. "What's your favorite song?"

"Um." She takes a moment to adjust her stance, and I realize that I should probably stand and help her. I begin taking moisturizers, combs, and whatever else she's got stacked in her arms and place them, according to her direction, in a coherent pile at the foot of the bed. She puts a hand on her hip as she stares at Whitney. Then she grins impishly. "'It's Not Right But It's Okay.'" The one about a dude cheating on her and Whitney deciding that she'll be perfectly all right without him.

"Wow." I nod in approval. "Yeah, okay. I deserve that one."

She sticks her tongue out playfully and directs me to sit on the floor. Then she deposits herself at the foot of the bed among her pile of products. "Hmm. I'm too high now." She leaves and comes back with a chair from God knows where. I take my seat there, and she returns to her spot on the bed.

"What's your favorite song?" she asks as she begins to play with my curls, running her hands over my scalp in a light massage. It feels incredible.

"That's a tough one." I lean into her hands. "Mom and I like to sing that Deborah Cox duet with each other sometimes. 'Same Script, Different Cast.'"

"Can your mom sing?"

"Absolutely not."

Tessa chuckles, then she sighs so hard that I can feel her eyes roll. "What's up?" I try to angle my head up so that I can see her, but she's already moving off the bed.

"I almost forgot the most important step," she calls to me as she walks out of the bedroom, leaving me bewildered. When she returns again, she has a towel in her hands.

"So you need to wash and condition your hair. Then I'm gonna blow-dry it, okay?"

"Oh." My eyes widen at the sight of the towel. "Wow, this is all very complicated."

"Don't worry, Aali," she says. "I'm not going to walk in while you're showering."

Suddenly, my mouth feels like sandpaper. "Yup, okay." I take the towel from her hands and hurry into the bathroom in the hallway as she shouts directions at my retreating back. "Yup, the stuff's in the place. Got it." The door slams behind me, and I lean my head back against it. "Well, fuck."

Then I glance around for the products she indicated I should use. They're in the corner of the bathtub, as instructed. Heaving a deep sigh, I take the plunge and strip off my clothes.

Beneath the lukewarm droplets of water hitting my skin and hair, my body relaxes. For the first time today, I realize how tight the knot in my stomach has been. How long has it been since I saw Yasmin—was it only last night? It feels like an eternity now, since walking in late to school, since having to explain myself to Tessa, since having to deal with Dad—again, always. Since Tessa "met" my dad, and since we kissed.

God, we kissed.

And I haven't even said anything about it yet! Ugh. My head dips so that the water drips down my face, and I fasten my eyes onto my feet. What is even happening right now? I thought I was past all of this last year, but here I am again, totally drowning.

It must be women. Women, like my dad says, are always the problem.

Then again, my dad is always wrong. So.

Whatever.

What I do know, though, is that Trinity is asleep on the couch downstairs; Tessa is here, and waiting for me outside. And it felt really good when she kissed me. Like, insanely good. Like, everything in the world is maybe okay if I let it be. And if I just stand here under the shower, and let the water sink in, I'll be able to get through this day, and this week, and this life, just fine. Just fine.

I don't know how long I stand there, but it feels good not worrying about it, or anything else, for once.

✷ ✷ ✷

When I finally emerge from the shower, dried and dressed in the clothes I came in, Tessa's sitting on her bed with her cell phone pressed to her ear. She gives a weak smile and lifts her finger to indicate that I wait.

I lean against the door, trying to calm my growing anxiety toward whatever this new development might be. Instead of letting my panic spawn thousands of possibilities about impending forms of doom, I close my eyes and let my mind wander. A moment later, Tessa concludes her call with an "Okay, hon. We'll see you soon."

"What's up?" I ask.

She shakes her head. "Naomi and Curtis broke up."

"Oh shit." I stand up straighter. "Why?"

She shrugs. "He's not Mormon, and her parents found out."

"Oh wow. So . . ."

"So she's on her way over. She's kind of a wreck."

"Tessa's Home for Lost Souls."

She smiles and pats the spot next to her. I take her invitation, and then decide to go a step further. As smoothly as possible, I slip my arm over her shoulders. She leans into me without hesitation. "It's not so bad, actually," she says into my shoulder. "I moved here without any friends. And now here I am, with a full house."

"Sure, that's one way to look at it."

She gives me a gentle shove that barely moves me. Then she reaches up and pulls on a strand of curly, wet hair. "We might have to do this later. Naomi should be here really soon."

"I'm game for whatever."

"Oh yeah?" A light dances in her eyes.

"Yes," I say, a little more breathlessly than I intended.

"Then I'm going to kiss you now," she says quietly. "If that's okay."

"Okay. Yes. Very okay." I barely have the words out before we fall onto her bed, and the only thing I can see is pink walls, black skin, and the word QUEEN fading in and out of my vision.

CHAPTER 21

Naomi shows up a full hour later than we thought she would, and when she appears at Tessa's door, her arms are filled with half a dozen grocery bags from Greg's and Whole Foods. "Dinner?" she asks as she walks into Tessa's living room. Then she beelines for the kitchen. "I'm great at lasagna, Aali," she calls from the kitchen, "and Tessa, I hope you don't mind, but since Aali is vegan, I stopped at Whole Foods for vegan cheese and ricotta. But if you do mind, I bought regular cheese, too, so we can have either or both. Or neither, if you prefer I make something else. I don't mind going out again."

Tessa and I look at each other and the still-open door that Naomi walked through. "I don't think I've ever heard Naomi say so much in such a short period of time," I whisper.

Tessa shuts the door. "Looks like she's a stress-cooker, too."

"Yup."

"I'm gonna call my mom," she says. "Can you . . ."

"Yup," I say again, and she places a quick kiss on my lips before heading in the direction of her room, where we left our phones. It leaves me a little breathless—not just the memory of her lips on mine but the knowledge that there's more to come. That its brevity was only an indicator of our relationship's next step, and not its end.

When we were lying on her bed a couple of hours before, breathing hard and arms wrapped around each other, I was full-on shaking, feeling like my entire body was buzzing with kinetic energy. Our shirts were off, and Tessa was running her fingers over my collarbone, occasionally placing a kiss that followed the trail her fingers left. It was a slow gesture, like we had all the time in the world to learn each other's bodies, each little mark and hair on our skin. Her hand had hovered over the burn mark on my arm like a question, but I'd used the opportunity to gently push her on her back and start our kissing anew. I didn't know what I was doing—not really. But this wasn't new for her and she'd given me instructions—*Kiss me there, on my neck— yes. And you can go lower, I don't mind.* I'd stopped just at the top of her bra, at the swell of her breasts, wondering if I was ready for that. But as I hesitated, Tessa pulled me back up to eye level and kissed me again. *We don't have to rush*, she'd said. *Lying here with you is just fine.*

Part of me would have liked to stay unrushed upstairs in her bed, but we'd thrown on our shirts and made our way downstairs soon after, knowing Naomi was on her way and my little sister was going to wake up at any time.

I still haven't moved from my spot at the door, so I force myself back toward Tessa's kitchen to aid in Naomi's stress ritual. By the time I make it there, the oven is already on and she's begun to lay pasta sheets into a pan. "Wow, yes, hi." I try in vain to grab Naomi's attention long enough for us to stop and talk, but she's clearly uninterested. I decide to be her sous chef instead. "What do you need?"

"Do youuu"—she drags out the word as she sprinkles mozzarella cheese onto the baking pan—"want to get a second pan out," she continues, moving toward the refrigerator, "and start the vegan version of the lasagna?"

"Of course," I say, and we move in tandem, me following her directions as we slice vegetables and prep for our impromptu Italian meal. A moment later, Tessa returns and watches us with an amused expression.

"Mom is going to go out with some friends tonight," she says. "She'll be home later. You two, and Trinity, are welcome to stay the night. We have another bedroom, and the couch is a pullout."

"I can't stay the night," Naomi says, scrubbing an errant dish in Tessa's sink, "without my parents' approval. Because I can't do anything without their approval. Or the temple's approval. I don't even know if I've submitted the proper forms to make lasagna tonight."

Whoa, Tessa mouths to me.

"Right, well," Tessa continues, "the offer still stands. You, too," she says, giving me a pointed look that I dodge as I begin drying dishes that Naomi's cleaned. "Also, I have a dishwasher, guys."

We ignore her, and she rolls her eyes, taking a seat at the dining table. "I would help, but it looks like you've got things under control."

"I control nothing," Naomi mutters morosely, just as I mutter, "I'm always in control."

God, are we a team.

"Aaliyah?" a small voice calls from the other room. Tessa stands and takes my place in the kitchen as I let her dishes drop gently onto a drying rack. I walk quickly back into the living room, where my sister is sitting up and drying her eyes.

"Hey, kiddo," I say, scooping her into my arms.

"Where's Mom?" she asks through a yawn. Then she takes a look around. "Oh," she says, apparently realizing that we're not home. Then she frowns. "Where's Dad?"

"Not here," I say. "We're at Tessa's, remember?"

She nods, a pout forming on her mouth.

"We're making dinner. You want to help?"

She pulls her pout to the side and looks toward the kitchen, where we can see Naomi and Tessa behind the counter. "Hi, Naomi," she calls.

"Hey!" Naomi shouts. Then she shuffles to the living room

door, a dishrag in her hand. "I'm making lasagna. Is that okay with you?"

"Yeah," Trinity says.

"Good girl." Naomi smiles and returns to the kitchen.

I pull Trinity into a hug that she only half accepts before reaching for the remote on the coffee table. "Can I watch more *Spider-Man*?"

I laugh and ruffle her hair, which has flattened from her nap. "Of course."

As Trini snuggles into her blanket, starting the film over from the beginning, I dash back up the steps to find my phone. I have a few notifications from Marissa, but I don't read them—I'll text her later. Instead, I text Mom to tell her we're staying over at Tessa's house. A few seconds later, I get several heart emojis back and a request to call in the morning. Then I return to the kitchen, where Naomi and Tessa have made themselves comfortable at the table. With nothing left to distract herself, Naomi sits with hunched shoulders, a frown pulling at her lips. Tessa has an arm wrapped around her.

"Food's in the oven?" I ask, sitting on the other side of Naomi.

They both nod, and I place my own hand on Naomi's other shoulder. "You okay?"

"I'm okay," she whispers. She lets out a little laugh and

wipes her eyes. "It's not as if we would've gone to the same college anyway."

Tessa and I exchange looks. "Probably not," Tessa says, nodding sympathetically.

"But who knows?" I offer, then shrug at Tessa's glare. I don't know! Should we dash her dreams, or give her hope? This isn't really my forte. But Naomi shakes her head and sighs.

"Definitely not. He had his heart set on Rice University. He's got family in Texas." She sits a little straighter, and I'm happy we at least have her talking. "I don't know what I thought when I told my dad Curtis and I were dating. I guess I thought he'd be okay with it—Mom was Catholic when they met and she converted before they got married. Not that I was thinking about marrying Curtis. Which is stupid. Of course I should be thinking about marriage soon."

Tessa blinks in surprise. "Like, as in right after we graduate?"

Naomi laughs. "No. I have my mission, and I need to prepare for it. Decide where I want to go and finalize the details. I'll be gone for three years, and . . . and dating someone right now is stupid. I know that." She sighs. "And Curtis is so sweet, and so funny, and so *kind,* and just . . . he'd make a great husband." A blush creeps across her face. "Not that I was thinking that."

"Sure you weren't." Tessa waggles her eyebrows, and Naomi

covers her suddenly beet-red face. "Speaking of college. Do you know where you're gonna go yet?" Merciful Tessa. How kind of her to change the subject.

"No, not yet . . ." Naomi trails off, letting her hands fall back to her lap. "To be honest, I'm not even sure about BYU. I've heard Southern Virginia University isn't as strict, so . . . it might be a nice change. Farther away from home." She lets the statement hang before suddenly releasing a long groan. She turns to me, her eyes bright with fresh tears. "Oh God, I'm so sorry. I've totally ruined your date."

I run a hand over my curls. "Trust me, it was ruined before you got here."

"What do you mean?"

I give a sidelong glance to Tessa, who shrugs before I sigh, placing my hands on the table in front of me. "My dad. You know."

"Oh. Aaliyah." Naomi wraps both her arms around me—a startling movement. Naomi's always been sweet, but never affectionate. I stiffen beneath her and then relax. We're all vulnerable tonight. "You okay?"

"I'm okay," I say. Then I look at Tessa. "Are you okay?"

She laughs. "As long as my friends are okay."

"Great!" Naomi gives a little clap. "So now that we are all okay"—she turns to me, her teary eyes turned mirthful—"I was told that you had a hair appointment?"

"Oh. No." I put my hands up to ward off the mischievous gleam that has made its way to both their eyes. "I am all good here, guys. Seriously."

Tessa shrugs as she stands and walks to the oven. "We've got at least another half hour before the food is ready. I'm sure we could get a few cornrows in."

They both look at me expectantly.

I sigh. "Will it make you happy?"

Tessa grins. "Immensely."

I stand and offer a bow. "Then I am at your service, milady." Tessa squeals and races into the living room. I don't hear what she says, but a moment later, I hear a loud "YEAH" booming from Trinity's voice and then two pairs of feet patter up the stairs. I glance at Naomi, whose wide smile has dampened just a bit, her eyes off to the distance.

I bump her shoulder with mine, and then offer her my arm. "My other lady, if you would."

She smiles and loops her arm through mine. "I would, indeed." She leans her head on my shoulder as we make our way up the stairs together.

CHAPTER 22

Something feels different. That's the first thought I have the next morning. It's not just the crocheted hair, which does look so curiously like my own but with sprightlier curls and that pop of purple. Or my skin, which is the same shade of light brown it's always been, darkened by the weeks I've spent running in the sun. It's my face, too.

I'm not trying to smile, but my lips haven't gotten the memo. With every move I make, as I shake out my curls, or brush my teeth, or put lotion on my arms, my mouth quirks, as if it's permanently pleased by some private joke between it and the universe.

Downstairs, in the kitchen with her mother, Tessa is singing.

I get dressed in her clothes, which smell like lavender and jojoba oil, and take my time walking down the stairs. Trinity and Naomi are in the living room, deep in discussion on the couch. "And then," Trinity whispers, "it turns out that the bad guy is the girl Peter's crushing on's *dad*."

"Oh my goodness," Naomi whispers back, her eyes wide as

if genuinely surprised. She looks up when she hears me pass and winks before returning her full attention to my little sister.

"Good morning," a woman says when I walk into the kitchen. She's like an older version of Tessa, but with long locs instead of braids. She's also much taller, with thick round glasses and a big smile. Abruptly, Tessa stops singing, a bloom of color reddening her brown cheeks. She turns away quickly, and her mom breaks out into a loud guffaw. "Aww, my baby girl is embarrassed!"

"Mom!" Tessa shrieks, and it only makes her mom laugh more. I continue to stand there awkwardly. I've yet to complete the queer girl mating ritual and ask Tessa how her mom feels about the whole super gay thing, so I don't know if I should feel welcome or apologize for interrupting.

"Okay, okay, I'm sorry," Tessa's mom says to her. Then she returns her attention to me. Her hand is wrapped around a spatula that she gestures my way as she stands in front of the stove. "Come help me flip these pancakes, would you?"

"Of course, ma'am," I say immediately.

"She's so polite," Tessa's mom stage-whispers to her. Tessa groans behind me, and I hear the clink of dishes being set up. "Miss Marjorie is fine, honey. Now, was it you or the young lady in there who helped make such delicious leftovers?"

"Both of us," I say as I flip the pancakes. "But mostly Naomi. I don't really cook a lot on my own."

"Neither does that one over there." Miss Marjorie nods to

her daughter as she supervises me, her arms now crossed as she looks across the kitchen, as if mapping out our breakfast for the morning. "Syrup and orange juice," she says to herself as she opens the fridge. "And I don't really cook, either, if I'm honest." She places the items on the table. "That was something Tessy's dad usually did," she sighs. "You know how it goes."

Tessy? I mouth to Tessa. She just shakes her head as Miss Marjorie shuffles over and whispers something in her ear. Tessa shoos her away, but spares a smile toward me. I have no idea what they're talking about, but they seem happy. Comfortable. Like Mom and I used to be.

And Miss Marjorie seems completely unbothered by my presence, which is nice. Honestly, it's wonderful. I continue supervising the pancakes, popping stray pieces of fried batter into my mouth.

"So." Miss Marjorie reappears behind me so suddenly that I jump. "What are your intentions with my daughter?"

I nearly choke. I look toward Tessa, expecting her to interject, but she just raises her eyebrows and keeps laying out the dishware.

"Oh, I. You know. She's great." I clear my throat. "Which you know, of course. So my intentions are. To. Can I?" My throat is so dry it hurts to think. "I'd like to date her." I turn toward Tessa again. "If that's . . . You want to."

Tessa holds back a laugh, but Miss Marjorie doesn't. "Oh-ho, I like this one, Tessy!" she exclaims. "Come on, baby." She grabs the spatula back and gently pushes me aside. "Go on and tell Naomi and your sister to come back in here and eat." But before I can go, she grabs the sleeve of my shirt and pulls me in close, her voice low. "You and I will talk more later. But for now, I just want you to know that I expect you to treat my baby well. You understand me?"

"Yes. Ma'am. Of—totally." I'm pretty sure there's a sentence in there somewhere.

Miss Marjorie pats my cheek and relinquishes my shirt.

After breakfast is served and we're stuffed with pancakes (and eggs and bacon for everyone else), Miss Marjorie offers to take Trinity to school. I protest, but I learn quickly where Tessa learned how to stare someone down. Trinity pops into the car with Miss Marjorie, leaving me standing between Naomi and Tessa on the driveway.

Naomi heads to her car. "I have to call my parents," she says by way of explanation, and I realize that staying over at Tessa's house is possibly the most rebellious thing she's ever done—besides dating Curtis.

"Good luck," I call to her. She waves and shuts the door, and it occurs to me that I haven't looked at my phone in hours. I glance at it quickly, long enough to see a friend request from none other than Lonnie Martinez, along with a DM. "Got a gig coming up. Bring your girl?"

It shouldn't make me smile, but it does.

"Ready?" Tessa asks as I put the phone away. I grab her hand and stand up a little straighter.

"Absolutely."

★ ★ ★

The rest of the school day goes by without incident, which is a welcome reprieve from the events of yesterday. In fact, given the whirlwind of the past twenty-four hours, I'm feeling pretty good. Practically walking on air in fact, which is why I don't notice when Marissa pops up beside me at lunchtime. "Where were you yesterday?"

"What?"

"My audition," she says. "You weren't there?"

Oh. Shit. So much has happened that I can't even begin to think of an answer. I think back to the texts I ignored from her—she was probably trying to figure out why I ditched her. I could tell her it was my dad again, but that happened later. Missing her audition was really and truly my bad. Before I can even think to apologize, though, let alone explain, she tugs on one of my curls. "And what happened to your hair?"

"Oh," I say. I have to stall for time. There is way too much to explain here, and I can't think clearly. Confessing to Tessa, confronting my dad, comforting Naomi . . . and what did any of that have to do with my hair? "Tessa did it," I say finally, landing on the fastest thing. Something to start with.

"Oh." Marissa shrugs. "Okay."

"And, um. I'm so sorry, but I totally blanked on the audition. Stuff happened with Tessa, and then my dad . . ."

"Oh, right. Totally." She nods, but I can tell that's not enough. God, I'm an asshole.

"Marissa." I try to reach toward her, but she steps away.

"So," she says lightly. "You decided you wanted to look normal instead of like some super dyke?"

Whoa. I face her full on now. "What did you say?"

Something I can't decipher clouds her eyes. "I said—" She stops herself and rolls her eyes, settling for a frustrated sigh instead. "You look good, Aaliyah. I was just joking with you. About Yasmin and cutting your hair, you know?"

I don't say anything, and an uncomfortable silence settles over us. I don't understand how she thinks she can use *that* word; something so crude and . . . and violent. Yeah, sure, it's been reclaimed or whatever, but reclaimed by *us*—fellow queer girls of the world. Like Skye and her tattoo of the upside-down pink triangle. Words and symbols have power, and it freaking matters who wields it.

I decide to tell her that. "You're not allowed to use that word."

She blinks, clearly taken aback. "Oh? And why not?"

"Um, because you're not gay? Just because *we* kissed one time doesn't mean you get to suddenly don the rainbow flag and throw yourself a parade."

A few people throw us strange looks as they pass by, and it occurs to me that I should keep my voice a little lower. Mar cocks her head at me, her eyes narrowed. "O-kay. So just so that I understand this right, you're saying that, um, *you* get to decide if I'm queer or not. Is that right?"

The fact that we're even having this conversation is ridiculous. She knows what I meant. "Come on, Marissa."

"Whatever." She takes a deep breath and moves as if she's getting ready to walk away. Before she does, she raises her shoulders and drops them. Her mouth opens as if she's trying to find the words to fit them. She settles on, "So, speaking of 'actual' queer girls,then . . . I assume you told Tessa about Yasmin?"

"Yeah." My response is short. I'm still coming down from my anger-fueled adrenaline rush. She pulls her bottom lip between her teeth.

"I'm glad you made up, then," she says. It doesn't really sound like that's true, but I nod anyway.

And then, because I'm still feeling salty, I say, "Lonnie has a gig coming up. I might take Tessa." Marissa gives me a long stare, and I immediately regret being an asshole. Just because I'm hurt doesn't mean I can be hurtful right back. "I mean . . . sorry, it's not like we've been hanging out or anything. I ran into them when Tessa and I went to the hair store. Together. To . . . um. And then Lonnie DM-ed me later."

"You missed my audition so that you could hang out with Lonnie and do your hair with Tessa?"

"No! No. Yesterday was just such a weird day." Neither of

us speaks for a moment, and suddenly the silence feels more painful than anything we've said to each other in the past few minutes. "Marissa," I start to say, reaching for her out of instinct, but she flinches away. It's so quick that we both jump like an electric shock has run through us, but it's different from the one I'm used to. This one hurts.

"It's cool, Aaliyah. I'll see you later?" And she walks away without waiting to hear my response. Emmanuel waits at his locker down the hallway, though he's pretending to be deeply engrossed in his phone.

I lean my head against the locker hard enough to feel the metal push back against my skull, with whatever lightness I was feeling this morning completely sucked away and vacuum sealed. Then I feel arms wrap around my waist.

I turn to look into Tessa's lovely light brown eyes. "Hey there," I say.

"Hey, yourself," she says, and leans in for a kiss. Just as I'm about to shut my eyes, Naomi comes into view. She slows as she takes in our embrace.

Our kiss turns quick, and Tessa's eyes open with surprise. Then she notices Naomi, too. We lace our fingers together but move a few inches apart, aware that of the three of us, one just had her heart broken the night before.

"Hey, guys," Naomi says. She glances at our fingers. "You don't have to do that."

"Do what?" Tessa asks coolly. She reaches forward with her free hand and pulls Naomi closer. "Be gal pals?"

"Be what?"

"Gal pals! Just a couple of ladies holding hands and being friends."

"Totally not romantic at all," I play along, and wrap an arm around Naomi's shoulders.

"Nope," Tessa agrees.

"You guys are so sweet and completely ridiculous." Naomi laughs, but leans her head on my shoulder. "Thank you both for last night."

"I didn't do anything." I nod at Tessa. "You're the one who sheltered us from the cold harsh world, Tess."

Tessa rolls her eyes, dropping both our hands to cross her arms. "Whatever. You're both dorks."

"And you loooove us," I singsong, but she's not looking at me anymore. I turn and see Curtis's long lean legs striding toward us, and when I look up, he's only a few feet away. His usually cheerful smile is at half-mast.

"Hey, guys." He gives us both a small wave. "Hey, Naomi."

She doesn't look up from my shoulder. "Hey, Curtis," she whispers.

Curtis frowns, but it's so brief, it's as if the wind blew it away. He puts a hand on her shoulder, glances at Tess and me, and then walks away. It's only when he passes us that his shoulders droop so low that his hands nearly touch the ground. When he reaches Emmanuel and Marissa, they both touch his back. Marissa doesn't look our way.

"I'm grounded," Naomi says after they've turned their backs on us. "First Curtis, then staying over your house last night . . ." She sighs. "It's a crap show."

Tessa nods and squeezes Naomi's shoulder. "Look at it this way, Naomi," Tessa says. She pauses until Naomi looks up at her again, then she puts on a sage look. "At least you're not a lesbian."

Naomi's horrified shriek bounces off the walls. I try to muffle my laughter as our classmates turn to stare at us, but Tessa's grin is so massive that I can't help myself. She's holding a newly petrified Naomi in her arms, and Naomi is chastising her for being so "politically incorrect." Eventually, I get my laughter in check and the hallway returns to normal.

Except that I catch Marissa's glance just as she turns away. Just as Emmanuel places his hand in hers, his other hand clasping Curtis on the shoulder. I can't read Marissa's expression as they begin to leave, and I hate it. It's the weirdest thing. It's the worst thing. Somehow, in less than a day, I've managed to turn yet another person I love into a stranger.

CHAPTER 23

Eight days, twelve hours, and sixteen minutes.

That's how long it's been since Marissa and I have talked. And other than passing her in the hallway, we've not seen each other, either. She's been spending almost every day after school in theater, so I've barely seen her at practice, and when she has shown up, we avoid each other. I keep telling myself that I'm going to text her, or do literally anything more than nothing, but every time I try to think of the right thing, my brain goes blank.

And each day the gulf between us grows wider.

Some days, I tell myself that if she cared, she would text me, too. But even I know that I'm the one who made things weird for no reason. I just don't know how to stop it.

Now, we're at this stupid meet in the middle of North Las Vegas in 110 degree weather, even though it's late October. Marissa is exactly two foot away from me, but it's like we're on two different planets. She's with Curtis, Emmanuel, Cody, Jason, and a few other teammates, talking about God knows what, and Naomi, Tessa, and I are in a circle with Tracey and Radhika, getting our final stretches in before the big run. At this point, I should be completely locked on, going over each step I'm planning to take to finish first. Instead, I'm running circles in my own mind, digging myself deeper into a ditch.

For the second time in less than one year, I miss my best friend, and for the second time in less than one year I'm going to completely fuck up another race because I can't get my shit together.

The fact that I'm digging my nails into my ankles as I stretch is the only thing keeping me together. That, and Tessa's casual hand on my back as she whispers something conspiratorially into Naomi's ear. I take a deep breath in and try to return to the conversation, although it's clear that I've totally missed everything that's going on.

"Right, Aali?" Naomi says to me, and I nod as if I was listening. Then, a whistle blows in the distance, indicating that it's the girls' time to get into position. We stand together, but Marissa makes sure to put Radhika and Tracey between us. I shouldn't notice right now, but I do.

Just run, I try to tell myself. *Please.*

Naomi mutters a prayer beside me, and for some reason it calms me. I square my shoulders, bend my knees. Get into position.

The whistle sounds again, and we take off.

I let several girls from the other team take the lead. I even fall behind most of my team, and at first, this is just strategy. It's just me letting the others tire themselves out before I burst forward and take my rightful place at the head of the pack. But as I weave through the crowd of girls, I make the mistake of glancing to the side instead of straight ahead, and I see Marissa staring straight at me.

I falter, and then I trip. A few girls from the other team stumble behind me. "Sorry," I mutter, and they barely spare me a glare as they help one another up and speed past me. Marissa looks surprised, and suddenly I want to scream.

No, I want to apologize.

I want—

"What are you doing?" Marissa hisses as she grabs my arm, lifting me up and onto my feet. I always forget how strong she is. She doesn't hesitate as I regain my footing, already racing ahead of me. But when she realizes I'm still behind her, she slows down again.

"Whatever you're thinking right now, don't," she huffs beside me. "Be better than last year. Remember?"

I open my mouth to speak, but she just shakes her head. She speeds up again, but just before she's too far ahead, she turns her head toward me and shouts, "I thought track was for pussies, though? Shouldn't you be kicking my ass right now?"

That breaks the spell. Suddenly, my legs move for me and

in moments I'm beside her, then in front of her, then in front of the girls I knocked down, and then I'm not paying attention anymore, because nothing else matters.

Nothing matters but the earth beneath my feet and air pumping through my lungs.

And I'm not going to let anyone get in my way.

Not even me.

When the meet ends, I come in at a solid fifth, which isn't the best, but it's better than last. Naomi's second, Tessa's seventh, and Marissa comes in at eighth. I'm waiting for her at the finish line, but she barely spares me a glance when Emmanuel wraps her in a massive bear hug. They share a kiss that is, to them, brief, and then Coach ushers Marissa away so that the boys can prepare for their run. Instead of coming back, Marissa wanders toward a free patch of grass and starts stretching alone. I want to talk to her, but I'm getting the distinct impression that she doesn't want to talk to me.

So I do the easy thing.

I walk away.

CHAPTER 24

Fourteen days, six hours, and eleven minutes.

CHAPTER 25

For most of my classmates, Halloween should be the night of shit-facery and getting laid, or going trick-or-treating with your siblings and then pretending you did the first two things. For me, the ritual for most of high school had been Yasmin and I indoctrinating Trinity with the *Buffy* sing-along episode, and then gorging ourselves on candy.

But a lot can change in a year. So much so that, tonight, I have no idea where my old best friend is, and my new best friend is off playing hostess to most of our teammates at my old boyfriend's "to-die-for" party while I take my little sister house to house in her Spider-Gwen costume.

I'm always down for sisterly bonding, but I seem to be colossally failing in the friend department. But at least I have a girlfriend? And said girlfriend is texting me now, to tell me she's on her way to pick me up for Lonnie's gig.

"Is your sugar craving successfully satisfied?" I ask Trinity, although we've only got two more houses to ransack anyway.

She looks up from counting her loot, her teeth already smeared with peanut butter cup.

"Mm-hmm." She grins wider, and I cover her mouth.

"Great. Last two, then home," I say.

Mom greets us at the door when we return, the doorbell barely rung before she dashes outside with a massive pail of assorted candies. She frowns when she sees us.

"Oh." Her shoulders slump. "It's just you."

"Don't worry, Mom." I smile as Trinity and I walk around her. "There will be more neighborhood kids to spoil, I swear." Somehow, this seems to cheer her right up because she returns to the couch, perched on the edge, with the pail still in her lap, waiting. One would think that all the churchiness would mean Mom hates Halloween and its affiliation with ghouls and demons, but she gets a kick out of holidays. We skipped last year, but the year before, she even sat outside with a hockey mask. Trinity sits beside her while I pop in our *Buffy* sing-along DVD.

Some traditions are sacred.

"Where's Dad?" I ask, and Mom just shrugs. I don't push, because I don't care. As long as he's outside terrorizing other people tonight, I'll be just fine. I join them on the couch as Mom skirts glances at the door, as if a desperate child begging for chocolate might appear at any moment.

Ten minutes later, someone knocks and Mom springs up. Before I can stop her, the door swings open to reveal Tessa. The girlfriend I thought would text me when she arrived but instead has appeared just outside like a harbinger of doom.

The girlfriend my mother has never met before.

"Hi," I nearly scream when I stand up. "This, Mom, is—uh. My friend."

Tessa allows me the slight fib and gives my mom her most dazzling smile. Mom shifts the pail so that she's holding it with one arm and looks Tessa up and down.

"Hi," she says. It's a formal but polite tone. An entry point.

"Hi, Mrs. Marshall. I'm Tessa Jones, Marjorie's daughter. It's nice to finally meet you. I'm here to take Aaliyah to her friend Lonnie's gig." Tessa assumes the voice of a highfalutin telephone operator, for which I'm eternally grateful.

Mom continues to take Tessa in. It's slow and agonizing, her one eyebrow arched, the plastic pumpkin head grinning ghoulishly from beneath her arm. She glances at me, then past me. Her eyes cloud over again, before she leaves the doorway like a ghost being summoned to the afterlife. "Have fun," she says over her shoulder as she returns to the couch.

I breathe out an unsteady sigh—from relief or nausea, I have no idea. "Thanks, Mom!" I step outside, careful not to grab Tessa's hand like I want to as I shut the door behind us.

★ ★ ★

"So Marissa's not coming?" Tessa asks once we're on the road.

Oh, Tess. Literally nothing escapes her attention. But I don't have the answer she wants, so I take the opportunity to look at her outfit and stall. She's wearing a fuzzy pink jacket over a black skirt and knee-high boots. Her braids are pulled up into two buns atop her head, and her lips are gold and glittery, to match her glitter eye shadow. She's supposed to be a rave kid, and I have no idea if she's pulling off the costume or not, but I know she looks very, very attractive. But she's clearly waiting for my response. Honestly, I have no idea if Marissa is going to come to Lonnie's gig tonight. She's probably too busy shoving her tongue down Emmanuel's throat.

The thought pulls at my stomach. I'm not sure if it's the image that upsets me or my own pettiness.

"No," I say finally.

"Do you think she'd be mad that you're going to her ex-drummer's show?"

"Nah," I say, but I don't entirely believe myself.

Tessa gives me a look that says she doesn't entirely believe me, either, but she lets it go. Instead, she finally takes in my costume: a black pleather dress that I got from Hot Topic, a pleather choker and wrist cuffs, and an ugly short brown bob I bought from Sally's, complete with dark blue eye shadow and plum lipstick. "Oh my God," she says. "Are you *Whitney?*"

I grin, feeling extremely proud of myself. "From the 'It's Not Right But It's Okay' video? Um, absolutely."

"I hate you so much," she says.

"I doubt that's true."

"I swear I could kiss you right now."

"Now you're just playing with my feelings."

By now, Tessa's laughing so hard that she struggles to keep her eyes on the road. "I like your makeup," she says. "You don't wear it a lot."

"YouTube is a godsend," I say. Then I sober. I wanted to ask Mom, but then she might've asked more questions—like why I chose my costume, or why I was going with Tessa and not Marissa. Or she wouldn't have asked any questions at all, and that would've hurt more.

Better to do it on my own and save us both the disappointment.

We don't say much after that, but my mood lightens each time I catch Tessa steal glances at my low-cut dress. She keeps gripping the wheel like her life depends on it, and that's a first for me. I could get used to it.

In a few minutes, we arrive at Container Park, an outdoor shopping center and music venue off Fremont Street in Downtown Las Vegas that's known for being made out of mostly shipping containers. It's been around for just a few years, and already it's one of the most fun things to do here that isn't inside a casino. It's at the very end of Fremont Street, where the older, lesser known hotels like the Golden Nugget and the oddly named California Hotel & Casino are. When I was younger, this was the area kids and tourists were told to avoid—where the glitz and glamour of the Strip ended. But in the past few years since that billionaire decided to tip his hat toward Vegas, things like Container Park have appeared and made the area more exciting and kid-friendly. A lot of new restaurants and stores have pop-up shops here before launching into the real thing, and the same goes for bands.

Tessa and I make our way through the park, heading to the large open performance space past all the stores. Lonnie's already onstage, with their two other bandmates—Mychal on bass and Teresa on keyboard. *Oh wow.* So it's literally just Light Pollution sans Marissa. Damn. They're getting their instruments together or whatever musicians do before a set, while I try not to feel like Judas incarnate. I focus on their Halloween costumes instead. Mychal kept it cool: aside from ripped jeans and a black tee shirt, she's just wearing a set of what I assume are alien antennae, whereas Teresa is dressed in a giant banana suit. This is just a Halloween show; no big deal. No massive betrayal. It's all good.

Since the band's not playing yet, the Killers is blasting over the stereo and a handful of people are clustered in groups on the turf. Tessa motions toward one of the restaurants as the music gets louder. "Shirley Temple?" she yells.

"Seltzer!" I yell back. I try to dig for my wallet, but she's already making her way to the bar. I start to follow, but a hand on my shoulder stops me.

"You made it!" Lonnie says into my ear, and then they pull me into a massive bear hug. Tonight, their locs are split into pigtails, and they're wearing overall shorts with one strap off the shoulder, and a white shirt and striped red-and-white knee-highs. I assume they're some version of Pippi Longstocking, with dark purple lipstick like mine and a perfectly executed cat eye to boot. Lonnie starts to take in my costume, but they look away almost immediately. "You! Wow. Great!"

I blush. I'm really starting to like this feeling.

"What are you supposed to be?" they ask, studying my face extensively, only taking quick glances below my neck to get the full picture. Suddenly, they gasp and cover their mouth. "GIRL," they shout. "You are not Miss Whitney Houston." Then they pull me into another bone-crushing hug. "I knew I liked you."

When I'm back on my feet and able to breathe again, Lonnie starts to scan the room.

"Are you looking for Marissa?"

They blink back at me in surprise. "What? Nah. I mean . . . I invited her, but . . ."

"You invited her?" That's surprising. "To perform with you?"

"Nah. I mean, not that that's not on the table. But I thought it'd be cool to just, like, touch base and whatnot. See how she's doing, if things are a little better than last year."

"What happened last year?"

Lonnie gives me a surprised look and then puts their hand out for me to take. I do, and they give me another quick hug. "Don't worry about it, bruh. S'all good. I'm glad you came." They start to walk back toward the stage, and then turn back to me suddenly. "You look good. I'm glad you came!" Then they disappear in the crowd of bodies.

✶ ✶ ✶

The space is filled now. Tessa's still waiting her turn at the bar, and she's texting me a series of OMFG WTFs to keep me updated with her progress in line. I'm too busy responding and trying not to think of the mystery that is the breakup of my favorite band to notice Yasmin step in front of me.

"Hey, stranger," she says, a can of cider held to her lips. Her dark hair looks windswept and falls across her face in very loose waves—she didn't straighten it tonight. She's got dark green eye shadow smudged around black liner on one side of her face, and the other is painted black and white—like a skeleton. It nearly distracts me from the fact that she's wearing the tightest black dress I have ever seen her wear. I try not to stare so hard, but my heart still tries to hammer out of my chest.

"Wow," she says, getting a good look at my costume. She's

the total opposite of Lonnie, taking the time to really look at the whole outfit. "You look so different."

"Thanks?" I clear my throat. "Um, thanks. How'd you get that?"

She looks at the bottle in her hand and then winks at me. "Fake ID."

"Ah."

"Want to say hi?"

She nods to the front of the crowd, and I follow her gesture toward the back of Skye's white-blond head. She's standing with a group of kids in front of the stage, and I recognize a handful of them as people from theater. One kid points toward Yasmin, and Skye turns around with a smile, waving enthusiastically.

"Oh," I say. How do I explain that I'm not alone? That my girlfriend—who I have definitely kissed more than once—is grabbing us nonalcoholic beverages? Does that make me sound silly? Stupid? Childish? By the time I settle on the right insult, she's already shepherded me to the group of theater kids. Fuck. "Hi," I say, feeling like many insults all at once.

"Aaliyah!" some kid says to me, and I recognize her vaguely as Kyle—Kylie? Keisha. Keisha, who I think I shared freshman English with. She's dressed now in a Pikachu costume. "Where's Marissa?" Kyle/Kylie/Keisha asks. I decide immediately that I hate her.

"Yeah," Yasmin says, turning me slightly toward her with the back of her hand. "I thought she'd definitely be here tonight."

"She's busy," I say, trying not to dig my nails into my palms. "Out with her boyfriend, I think."

"Oh, at that party," some other random theater kid whose name is maybe Josh says. "Emmanuel's."

"Yeah." I nod.

"That sucks," Yasmin says, and I glance at her in surprise. She shrugs and takes another sip of her cider. "She might be a megabitch, but she was a kick-ass singer."

"Good to see you again," Skye says, probably because I haven't acknowledged her yet. I mean, it's really loud.

"Remember when we used to come here all the time?" Yasmin says, looping her arm through mine. Her mouth is incredibly close to my ear, and I can smell the alcohol on her breath. Oh. She's already drunk. *That explains it.*

"Yeah," I say.

"That's how you met Marissa, right?" Skye tries again.

I lean in closer to Yasmin. "What?"

Skye lifts her drink. "Yaz told me you met Marissa here last year."

"What'd she say?" I ask Yasmin.

Jesus, it's loud.

"She said," Yasmin almost shouts, pressing her lips against my ear again, "that you and Marissa met here last year."

"Oh," I say, turning back to Skye finally. "No, I didn't. I mean, Yasmin and I used to watch Light Pollution all the time, that's all. They played every Thursday night, and we were basically obsessed, so. I obviously knew who Marissa was, but she didn't know me."

Yasmin cuddles in closer. "No way, dude. You used to stand right fucking here in front of the stage, talking about how hot the lead singer was, and Marissa would totally make googly eyes at you, too. Like, every fucking night."

I roll my eyes. "That's not true. First of all, Marissa is straight. And yeah, I thought she was hot because I have eyes, but it wasn't anything serious. Then we officially met in class last semester, and we became friends. That's it."

"Ooh, you became friends *after* her public meltdown," Keisha says.

I frown at her. "Her public what?"

"You were on lockdown," Yasmin whispers to me just as someone says, "Yeah, she shoved her whole foot in Lonnie's drum and then barfed all over the stage."

What the hell? "What are you talking about?"

"Bruh," another person says from beside me. "Aren't you two best friends? How do you not know about this?"

The next thing I know, someone is shoving a phone into my face with a video of Marissa onstage. She's clearly sloshed. "Sorry I don't have a guitar tonight, folks. Mommy dearest sold

245

it for a pack of cigs. But we can still rock!" She falls over on the last word, but I see Lonnie trying to catch her. She pushes them back so hard they tumble, but Marissa doesn't seem to notice. She's rocking out, lost in her own world to some music that's clearly in her own head, and she's so frantic that she doesn't notice Lonnie's drum set next to her. She kicks at it, and her foot goes through it, causing her to hit the ground and the entire drum set to come with her.

"That's it tonight, everyone," the keyboardist, Teresa, says, right before she goes to pick a drum off of Marissa. Mychal is still helping Lonnie off the ground when the video ends.

"Holy shit," I say. I guess I'm shaking, or maybe I look surprised—I guess I could be triggered? But suddenly, I feel Yasmin's arms around me. Maybe I shouldn't—maybe I should move—but seeing my best friend plastered onstage is jarring. It's . . . it's scary, and I shouldn't feel scared, and maybe Yasmin knows that. Maybe she understands, even when she's drunk— but, God, *she's* drunk, too. Why the fuck can't anyone be sober?

Just as I start to pull away from Yasmin, and maybe every teenager on the planet . . . Tessa appears. She's holding two nonalcoholic drinks in her hands and looking at Yasmin's arm wrapped around my waist.

"Hi," she says.

"Hey!" I shout. I nearly rip myself from Yasmin, stumbling

as I reach for Tessa. "Babe"—I lay the word on thick—"this is, uh. Theater people." I gesture to the group.

They save me with their own names. I was right about Keisha. Maybe-Josh is actually named Robert. Then Yasmin introduces herself, and I realize too late that I am in the deepest shit.

"Nice to meet you, Yasmin," Tessa says, looking at me. "What did I miss?"

"We were talking about how Aaliyah's friend Marissa used to eye-fuck her from the stage before she barfed on everyone and got kicked out of the band," Keisha sums up with a laugh.

"What?" Tessa faces me. Wow, seriously. Fuck Keisha.

"HELLO, LAS VEGAS," a warm voice blares over the speakers as the lights dim. The crowd goes quiet, but I feel Tessa's glare boring into my neck. "Thank you so much for spending your Halloween with us tonight. As you all know, Lonnie, Teresa, and I used to perform under the name Light Pollution." Mychal pauses to let the crowd scream. Yasmin screams beside me, and I try to join, but I can't seem to find my voice.

"Unfortunately, we had to put Light Pollution to rest," Mychal continues as the crowd boos, "but tonight we're trying out some new songs for you, some new sounds that we hope you'll enjoy. Thank you, Las Vegas!" And with that, Mychal lets Lonnie intro a song with a rapid succession of beats on the drums. They sound incredible, like I knew they would. I've never seen them look so good—fierce, determined, but relaxed, like they were born to perform.

I wish that this were it; just me sinking into the pulsating rhythm and Mychal's sweet, scratchy voice. It sounds nothing like Marissa's deeper, smoother tone, but it's passable. Enjoyable. But the thought of Marissa's voice makes me remember the days before we met—when I really was just a face in the crowd. Keisha was exaggerating, of course. I really think Marissa only ever saw me as a groupie at the front of the stage. If she didn't, I don't think she would've kissed me at Susannah's party. Still, I did stand there all the time, totally captivated. She *is* beautiful—anyone would admit that. And when she got really into a song, she would just let go, thrashing around the stage, hair, blond at the time, flying everywhere. And then there were the slow songs, when all that impossible energy seemed to still, and she'd just stand there with the mic in her hands, eyes never closed, gaze drifting over the crowd. And sometimes, yeah. I could feel—in my daydreams, I might even swear—that she was looking right at me. Maybe only at me.

I want to text her. Tell her I'm sorry. But then I remember the video of her drunk and out of control. And then I remember Tessa, who's barely moving to Lonnie's crazy drums. She's just standing there, and though her eyes are on the stage, I can tell her mind is elsewhere. I let go of my phone and try to grab her hand, but her fingers are limp. I glance back at the stage, not wanting to lose the moment—the memories. But I have to do something. "Come on," I whisper-shout into her ear. She looks at me and then lets me pull her toward the exit.

Away from the crowd, the air is still warm with a chill that falls on the wind. Tessa and I find a table near the park's entrance. The sky is black and dotted with stars, and in the distance we can see the lights of the Strip.

"What's up?" I ask, even though I know exactly what's bothering her.

She sighs and fixes me with a look. "Is that Yasmin the Yasmin you told me about before?"

"Yes," I say, because there's no point in lying. "But I swear, it wasn't what it looked like. Her girlfriend is Skye, that Asian girl with the multicolored blond hair, who looked like a werewolf."

"Sure, but that doesn't explain why you looked so comfortable with Yasmin draped all over you."

I roll my eyes and stare at the cars. "It wasn't like that, Tess."

"You haven't given me a great reason to trust you."

I look down. She isn't wrong. "Sure. Yeah."

"And what were they saying about you and Marissa?" The tone of her voice is full of incredulity and frustration, and I swear that Keisha is my least favorite person on earth right now.

"They were being stupid," I say, reaching for her hand. "Marissa used to be the lead singer for the band—"

"I know."

"—And we, Yasmin and I, used to watch her—I mean, you know, *Light Pollution*, play all the time. I thought Marissa was hot. That's all. I didn't know her then."

"So you don't think she's hot now?"

I pull Tessa closer. "Come on, that's not fair. I think Marissa's beautiful. She's also my best friend."

Tessa plays with the neckline of my shirt, thinking for a moment. "So there's never been anything between you two."

I frown. *Technically*, no. The night we kissed was a fun and lazy experiment—the kind where you let hormones overtake rationale. If things had escalated before Yasmin, I might've let myself believe there was something there, but I knew better by then. It didn't mean anything. If she were here, Marissa would say so, too. And if Tessa weren't looking at me the way she is now—lips pulled into a frown, eyes filled with questions, I might not say anything at all. But I realize I need to. All secrets—intentional or otherwise—out on the floor.

"We kissed once," I say finally. Tessa's head snaps up, but she doesn't say anything. "Just once," I barrel on, my hand tightening around her waist. "It was late last semester, and we were, I don't know, hanging out, at this party. Yasmin was there, and I was being sulky, so Marissa thought we should make her jealous. She said it'd give me a better memory. So she kissed me."

Tessa's breath tickles my nose as she stares into my eyes,

and I want to stop there because I can feel my words digging a hole beneath me. But I know I have to tell her everything. "We made out later that night—against my front door."

Then Tessa turns away from me completely. She takes a few steps and then stops. Her shoulders rise and fall, and I'm overtaken by the realization that she might decide to keep walking. Away from me.

I want to say something else. Anything else. But I don't.

Finally, she turns back around. "It didn't mean anything?" she asks. I have to lean toward her to actually catch the words.

"No," I say, because it didn't. It's never meant anything. Not with Yasmin, and not with Marissa.

Tessa studies me, then lets a small smile fall across her lips. "Aaliyah," she whispers, grabbing my hand. "Why don't I believe you?"

Her question stuns me into silence.

"I have to go," she says.

"Tessa—"

"I'll see you Monday."

She brushes past me toward her car just as the crowd inside begins to cheer.

I stay seated at the little table in front of the candy shop. I doubt there's anything vegan in there, but I still feel a craving for something sweet—something that will take my mind off the past five minutes. I could use a burst of dopamine right now. Alas, the shop is closed.

I stare at the sky instead. At the stars, which continue their nightly battle against the city's neon lights to be seen. To take center stage.

But light pollution always wins.

"What are you doing out here?" a voice says from behind me. I look at Yasmin, and the concern on her face is so laughable that I want to cry.

"Just staring at the sky," I say. She hesitates and then leans against a metal beam near my table.

"Where's your friend?" she asks.

I ignore her question. "What are you doing out here?"

"I missed you."

"What?" I'm so ready to scream that it's a miracle I'm even able to function. "What does that even mean? Your girlfriend and your friends are waiting for you. Go hang out with them."

"No, I mean. I've missed you." She raises her hands and then drops them. "For, like, ever."

I keep my eyes on the stars. This can't be happening right now. "You're the one who stopped responding to my texts."

She makes a sound, like she's going to protest, but then she says, "I know. I was—I just needed time."

I frown. "Were you depressed?"

She laughs, but it's a hollow sound. "At that particular point in time, no. I mean, I'm always depressed, Aaliyah, that's just how my brain works. But no, that's not why I disappeared."

"So, what then? What did you need time for?"

A sigh, and then—"To figure things out, I guess."

I shake my head. I don't have time for cryptic tonight. It's too much for me right now. If Yasmin wants to play games, she can do it with someone else. Preferably the chick she left me for.

"You keep doing that," I say. I stand and slip past her in time for the next song to start. Yasmin calls to me, but I ignore her. Someone deserves a good friend tonight, and it might as well be Lonnie.

CHAPTER 26

Nearly a full day passes without me hearing from Tessa. I'm so wired about it that I even skip my check-in with Miss Eccleston, opting to pace on the track until practice starts. By the next night, I'm sitting at the desk in my room, my phone in my hands as I try to craft the appropriate text to her, but I don't know what to say. I'm basically trying to will her to text me first when I hear the doorbell ring. I drop my phone and rush downstairs, ignoring whatever my parents are talking about in the kitchen.

It's Yasmin. She's just wearing white jeans and a hoodie today, with a butterfly pin in her hair. She looks like the twelve-year-old version of the girl I saw sloshing a cider around last night. I hold my breath, remembering how we left things. It wasn't one of my finer moments, but I'm having trouble caring.

"Uh." I lean against my open door. "Hi."

"Hey," she says. We stay there for a minute, so awkward that I think the ants in my dad's flower bed are cringing.

"What's up?" I ask.

Yasmin frowns at my head. "Did your hair get longer?"

I straighten up and try not to pat my newly wigless head. "Yeah, they're called extensions. Tessa—uh, my—she did them. I like it better that way."

"The girl from last night?"

"Yeah."

Her eyes brighten. "Your girlfriend, right?"

Her enthusiasm irritates me. "Yeah," I say. "She's cool. We're cool. Um." I take a deep breath in and close the door behind me, stepping forward so that she has to take a step back. I lean against the door again, this time crossing my arms. "What's up, Yasmin?"

She shifts her feet a little. "I, um . . . wanted to check in on you. After last night."

"Okay."

"You left suddenly."

"Yup."

"So." She sighs a little helplessly. Then she tries a different tack. "Marissa wasn't there last night. Is everything okay?"

"We're fine."

She raises an eyebrow again in a way that demonstrates she believes me not at all. "Are you sure?" I nod yes, but she keeps her brow raised. "I guess I just thought I would've seen you at rehearsals or something," she says.

"Oh." I shrug. "I've got other things going on. So."

"Right," Yasmin says.

"What part did she get?" I ask.

"Melchior," Yasmin says.

"Really?" I shriek. I remember myself quickly enough to keep from jumping toward her in elation, instead pulling further into my body. "I mean, that's awesome."

"Yeah, it is." She frowns. "You didn't know? She didn't tell you?"

"No."

"Okay. Sorry. Well, yeah, so. Rehearsals have been in full swing, and um . . . and it's not like I really like her all that much, and she *definitely* doesn't like me, but." She shrugs. "I noticed you haven't been around, like you were at the beginning of the year. We even had a little house party last week, the crew and cast, and you weren't there. So I thought maybe something happened."

"Why do you care?" I say, feeling every bit like the petulant child I sound like.

"Because I care about you," she says, with a kind of forcefulness that makes it seem like it's the most obvious statement in the world. "And I know Marissa does, too. I just want to make sure you're okay."

Her comments are about eleven months too late. I want to turn around and slam the door in her face, but I'm too tired to muster the energy. Instead I just stare at her, willing her to go away. Finally, her shoulders drop and she turns to leave, but I find my voice before I can stop it. "You're good? I mean"—I gesture toward the general direction of her forearms, whose latest scar has turned into a raised line of faded skin—"you've been okay?"

She turns back to me, but only just. "Yeah, I'm good. Doing my best." Her eyes hold mine, searching for a moment before she ventures for a smile. "You should come by again, sometime. Like you used to."

"Why?"

She casts her eyes down and then up again. "Because I'd like to be friends again." Then she leaves and I'm stuck standing there, alone again and not knowing why.

Upstairs in my room, I text Emmanuel.

He texts back fifteen minutes later, confirming that Marissa has indeed gotten the part of Melchior. "She's been so badass, dude," he texts.

"I bet," I text back.

"You guys cool?"

I hesitate, unsure of how to respond. Unsure how much Marissa's even told him, although I'm sure he's noticed how weird things have been. Clearly, she's not painted me as enough of a villain, though, because Emmanuel keeps blowing up my phone, first with excited recollections of Marissa's audition and then with details of Marissa's last few rehearsals and last week's house party and his preliminary plans to celebrate opening night.

Ugh, he's so sweet I could stab him.

I thank him for the details and then drop the phone on my desk. I lie back onto my bed and stare at the ceiling, letting the moment pass into nothingness. Then I hear the distinct sound of ceramic breaking against tile.

I'm down the stairs in seconds.

Dad's in the kitchen, throwing yet another bowl against the wall. Mom is sitting at the kitchen table, staring blankly at nothing in front of her. Dad is shouting obscenities, and I don't know what he's going on about this time, but I don't need to, to stand in front of him, to grab the next bowl out of his hand and slam it on the counter so hard that it, too, breaks. I take my position in front of Mom, and it's only then that I realize I should've checked on Trinity first. I can picture her in her room now. Hiding under the blankets, her Spider-Man headphones covering her ears, her face shoved in a book. I tell myself she's safe, but I can practically feel the therapy bills piling up in her future—and mine. I focus on Dad, who's standing in front of us heaving like a bull, his eyes red, and his hands clenching and unclenching.

Mentally, I dare him to hit me. I *want* him to.

Please.

Instead, he turns around and knocks everything on the

counter onto the ground. Then he grabs his beer and barricades himself in the garage, muttering about snitches. He's still angry about Trinity calling Mom when I was hanging out with Tessa.

Mom is shaking, but still she says nothing, her eyes glassy and unfocused.

"Let's go, Mom," I say.

"Where?" she whispers.

"World's our oyster." I shake her shoulder gently. "C'mon. Let's go before he comes back." I reach behind her and put her purse in her lap. I rummage for a moment and then pull her keys out, dangling them in front of her eyes. "Want me to drive?"

Her eyes snap to me. "Absolutely not." She stands then, ignoring my grin as she pulls the strap of the bag onto her shoulder. "Trinity!" she calls, and my sister appears at the bottom of the steps, her backpack already latched onto her shoulders. I sigh. She wasn't in her room after all.

"Ready?" I ask.

She nods, her frown older than her age. "Always."

CHAPTER 27

The lobby of the hotel is bright as day, and filled with so much noise that you'd think we were at a convention for family members of dysfunctional alcoholics. But it's just a bunch of locals and lost tourists blowing their rent on the promise of a million-dollar payout. Mom walks straight to the receptionist, and I follow her with our rolling suitcases in one hand and Trini's hand in another. We always keep runaway clothes in Mom's trunk. Just in case.

As she figures out our room situation for the night, I bend down and gently tap Trini's headphones. She turns to me, her look frighteningly vacant.

"Hey, kid." I give her the biggest smile I can fake and brush stray curls from her forehead. "How ya feelin'?"

She looks down and then pulls her headphones back around her neck. "I'm hungry," she says. I glance up at Mom, who's still talking to the receptionist.

"Well, lucky for you, we're at Sam's Town tonight. You know what that means?"

Trini's lips are pulled down, but they begin to quirk at the sides. "Burgerland?"

"Exactly! Burgerland!" I creep closer to her and grasp her shoulders. "Your *favorite*, right?"

"Right," she mumbles. I drop my hands to her sides, and she shrieks as I start to tickle her. "Yes," she giggles out, "I love Burgerland!"

"I know." I kiss her forehead. "So let's get the best freaking burgers this side of town, huh?"

Trini nods, sobering, but she's more alert now. Less distant. Mom reaches between us with a twenty. "Have fun," she says.

I grab the bill and shove it into my pocket. "Meet you up there?"

She gives me a tired nod. "You know what I like."

"Want to play a game?" I ask Trinity. She smiles, and we start to count the number of people we think are playing for retirement money versus a trip to Disney World.

✳ ✳ ✳

Upstairs in the bedroom, I find Mom sitting on the edge of one of the double beds, still dressed in her scrubs, her purse fallen over on the side of the bed. She's watching a newscast about some political disaster or another, but her shoulders are hunched and she's clearly thinking of other things. "Trini," I whisper, turning toward her before she can see Mom. "Why don't you take a shower before you eat?" Trinity peers around me and takes Mom in. Then she nods and walks into the bath-room.

The bed sags as I sit beside Mom, gripping the greasy Bur-gerland bag in one hand and wrapping another arm around her shoulder. "How are you holding up, Mom?"

She shakes her head. "I'm fine."

Wow. And the award for most in denial goes to . . . "Mom," I say. "Come on."

She doesn't respond at first. So we sit for a while instead, pretending to watch the news as we listen to the sound of Trin-ity's shower. In the quiet, I take the moment to build up my courage. "Mom," I say again. She sits up straighter. "Why don't you leave?"

Her laugh is coarse and bitter. "We can't all be running all the time, Aaliyah, doing whatever we want to do. Some of us have responsibilities."

For a moment, I'm taken aback by her bitterness. Not for the first time, I try to recall some distant memory of us smiling—laughing. Even in situations like this. A few weeks ago, I almost believed we still had it in us, even though I knew that we were mostly pretending. We still danced to an old car-toon like a family that still loved one another. Where did that family go?

"It's not my fault," I whisper.

She jerks her head up at me. "What?"

The words come out slowly at first, and then sharp. "I said—it's not my fault. I'm not the reason you're so damn miserable."

She laughs again, and this time any hint of mirth has been wrung out. The sound is hollow, incredulous. Angry. "You have some nerve, little girl." She stands and walks away from me, her head shaking again, one hand gripping the remote while the other is pressed to her forehead, like she's checking to see if she has a fever. Like maybe all of this is a hallucination—a terrible dream. She begins to pace, and in that moment I'm certain that neither of us know what she'll do next. For all I know, the remote could go flying, and I'll end up with another bruise on my cheek.

"'It's not your fault,'" she says, repeating my words. "So—so what." She turns to me, eyes flashing, and I know that right now, I'm not the one she's looking at. There's something past me—some wraith that only she can see, taunting her. Haunting her. "Is it me, then? Is all this my fault?"

"Mama, no," I whisper. "No, I didn't say that."

She shakes her head again. Again, again, again. Like she's trying to will away some voice in her head. I reach toward her, and she flinches so hard that I back away. She's scaring me—God, she's terrifying me. And I don't know what to do. I don't know how to handle this situation, or be the person she needs me to be right now. "Mom," I try again, and this time there are tears clawing at my throat. It sounds like a plea, and it is.

She turns away, head still shaking. Still shaking. Then she takes in a deep breath, lets it out. Turns back to me. Her eyes are clear now, and her voice is steady. "Your dad has problems, Aaliyah. He's not a bad man." She sucks in another breath and drops the remote to the bed. I feel safe for the first time in what feels like an eternity, but I still want her to say *Neither are you.* I want her to say *You're not a problem.*

I want her to say it's not my fault.

But she doesn't.

I grit my teeth as Mom sits back on the bed, reclaiming the remote in her hand. Silence greets us once again until Trinity comes out of the shower, fully dressed in her Supergirl pajamas.

"Trini, baby," Mom says, her voice suddenly saccharine. She's trying to pretend this moment away and act like things are normal. That the merry-go-round from hell is a cherished family pastime. "Come here and have your food. You, too," Mom says to me. I nod without saying anything, but my movements are mechanical. The burger tastes like cardboard, and my heart feels like all its blood vessels have been scraped off. But Trinity, for now, is happy. Dad is gone, and we're safe, at least as far as she can see. She must not have heard Mom before, and that's a good thing. She shouldn't have to deal with my problem.

"Can we order a movie?" Trinity asks. Mom hesitates, but I nod, subtly tapping the pocket that has my wallet. I'll be broke after tonight, but it'll be worth it to see Trinity smile.

"Sure, baby," Mom says after a beat. Trinity screams in delight and then snuggles against Mom's opposite side.

"MOM SANDWICH," she screams, smushing herself against our mom's body. Mom is stiff, resistant to the affection, but I want somebody in this room to feel free—to feel safe, and loved, and wanted. So I take a breath, and I smile.

"Mom Sandwich!" I yell with hardly half of Trinity's bluster. I wrap my arms around Mom, completing Trinity's circle despite how straight Mom's spine is. Then Trinity starts to wriggle this way; that way; back again. She moves so much that all three of us fall back onto the bed. Mom shrieks in surprise, but Trinity is persistent, and soon Mom is laughing as Trinity pretends to gnaw at her head and shoulders, muttering "om nom nom nom nom." I follow along, playing the role of big sister and loving daughter.

Mom giggles and starts to tickle Trinity until her fake feast ceases. "Okay!" Mom smiles and smooths Trinity's hair back. "Y'all want to watch this movie tonight or not?" This is the first time Mom looks at me since Trinity walked into the room.

"Yeah!" Trinity yells. Mom gives me a pointed look.

"Absolutely," I say.

Trinity flits through the channels until she finds a film she likes, and when it starts to play, she turns it up so loud that the room is filled with the sound of fiction, a made-up story of friendship, and love, and happily-ever-after.

CHAPTER 28

At first, I think it's the sun that wakes me, but when my vision clears, I see it's only the bright lights of the parking lot peeking in through the window. I brush sleep from my eyes and let the memory of where we are and how we got there set in.

When I was Trinity's age, this used to feel like a nightmare. An unfamiliar place in the middle of the night, my baby sister screaming from the complimentary plastic crib shoved between the bed and the window, and strangers drunkenly stumbling through the hallways, giggling as they bring new lovers to their beds.

The horror has waned since then. Visit a hotel enough in one year and it becomes like a second home. Visit it enough in ten and it becomes a sanctuary. Except my brain is quickly filling in the blanks of the night before, until the idea of staying in this room one minute longer makes my skin crawl. So I sit up, push to the side of the bed, and get ready to leave, grabbing my suitcase and changing into a new set of clothes. I'm not worried about waking up Mom and Trinity—they both sleep like the dead, and snore so loudly that I could conduct a parade and they still wouldn't hear me.

Then I grab one of the card keys to the room and head downstairs to the lobby. I'll have to go quickly—Mom hates when I disappear without telling her, no matter how many times I've done this temporary-escape routine. My guess without looking at my phone is that it's three or four A.M., but in here, it's bright as the afternoon, and the gamblers are still going strong. Naturally, there are no clocks anywhere to suggest anything different. I used to sit on the random benches scattered through the casino floor, and when a concerned patron would ask where my mommy or daddy was, I'd lie and say my daddy was out there, winning big. Raking it in. He'd only be a minute. I only had to wait just a little longer.

I ignore the casino floor now. Instead, I head straight to the business center, which is tucked away in a small musty room next to the all-you-can-eat buffet. A man in pajama bottoms and a bomber jacket is there with his headphones on, watching two talking heads argue about doomsday. He flinches when he sees me enter and then hunches farther over the keyboard, covering the screen.

I walk around him to the far end of the room and switch on the computer using our guest log-in credentials. As it boots up, I lean into my seat. I try to focus, but the longer I sit, the blurrier my vision becomes. There's a tightness in my chest that starts to burn, and for a minute, I'm positive—100 percent certain—that I'm about to have a heart attack. I gasp for breath, but my breathing is shallow. I try one deep breath—then two. I keep trying to focus. One deep breath. Then two.

"Are you okay?" I look up and Talking Head Guy is turned around in his seat, eyebrows furrowed. "Do you need—I can get you a tissue or . . . something?" And that's when I realize I'm crying.

"No, I—" I try another breath, but it comes out shallower than before. "Thanks, but I'm good." I stand up quickly, nearly knocking my chair over, and run before I know where I'm going. The man shouts something behind me, but he's already too far, his voice echoing in the halls. I keep running until I reach the sliding glass doors of the entrance.

Outside, the touch of the cool desert air calms me. It's not cold—not at all—but still I shiver, the darkness a harsh reality against the daylight-brightness of the casino floor. A tall man with shaggy gray hair is leaning against the building's exterior, smoking a cigarette. He looks at me, smiles, and offers me a drag, but I keeping walking, my arms wrapped around myself. I'm shaking, just like Mom last night. Shaking, and pacing, and I don't know what I'm going to do next.

I could text Marissa. Or Tessa. But that's—I can't do that. I can't call only when I need something; to beg for charity when I'm the one who's been fucking up.

So I keep pacing.

My body is shaking so hard that it feels like my brain is knocking against my skull, and my chest isn't tight anymore—instead it's loose, like if I move too fast, something will fall out. A lung might get displaced. I pull out my phone and scroll through my contacts, scrolling, scrolling, scrolling, scrolling.

Until one name makes me stop.

It's stupid, but I need to talk to someone. Anyone.

✳ ✳ ✳

Yasmin pulls into the parking lot thirty minutes later. She's dressed in bright pink pajama bottoms and a white tank top, her shoelaces untied but tucked into the sides of her Chucks.

"You didn't have to come," I croak out as she approaches. I don't know what I was expecting in response to my SOS—no response at all, probably.

She takes a seat next to me on the curb, careful not to touch me, as if I might implode at the slightest provocation. Then she fiddles around on her phone for a minute until a low song starts to hum from the speakers—an old Light Pollution song.

"Seriously?"

She leans back on her hands, stretching her legs out in front of her. "I thought it was necessary for the occasion. Bring back some good, old memories."

"If new memory serves, I think the lead singer now hates me."

"I thought you said you two were fine?"

"I lied."

She nods, but doesn't push, and we don't say anything more for a while, just letting the song play while the wind brushes by us. Slowly, I loosen my arms, feeling less like I might fall apart. I clear my throat and turn to her.

"Yaz?"

"Mm?"

"What happened?"

Then she looks at me, those dark brown eyes sweeping over mine, as if she's trying to figure out a puzzle. Funny—I think she needs a mirror for that. Then she drops her eyes to her knees, the wind rustling her wisps of short hair. Even though it isn't cold outside, I'm surprised that she's not even a little chilly in her flimsy pajamas. My hand brushes her bare shoulder—I don't know why. Maybe to check for goose bumps. "Honestly?" She takes a deep breath that comes out as a sigh. "I thought we could have fun."

I resist the urge to laugh. Whatever the hell occurred between us and after, it has been the opposite of fun. I tell her as much, and she chuckles a little. "I don't know," she says. "I did—really. We were friends, and we're queer, and, I guess I thought, wouldn't it be fun to explore things together? And I figured you liked me. I mean, I could tell—but I didn't, um." She pauses, and it goes on long enough that I speak for her.

"You didn't think it was that serious."

But she shakes her head. "No, I did. And I loved you, too. I mean, I love you . . . just not . . . that way."

This time, I do laugh, because the situation is so hilariously awful that I don't really know a better reaction. "You want to know what's funny?" I hear myself saying. "I didn't know. Not until you kissed me the first time—I had no idea. And I didn't even want—I didn't even *want* that. Not then. I didn't need it, back then. With everything else happening? I just needed my best friend, Yaz."

She nods as I speak, her eyes closed. "I know, Aaliyah."

"But no, you can't have known. Because you did it again last month!"

"I know." Now she's looking above us, at the few stars not washed out by the streetlamps in the parking lot. "I just—I wanted things to be normal. To be—to be *fun*, still, with us. Because we're seventeen—we're supposed to have fun, and fuck up, and not have the world end because of it. But I didn't . . . Aali, I didn't mean to mess things up so bad."

"Is that why you stopped responding to me? After the first kiss?"

She bites her lip and looks at me with her head only slightly turned. "I didn't know how to handle it. When I realized that it meant so much more for you than it did for me." She runs a hand through her hair. "I didn't know how much I hurt you."

"I think you still don't."

"No." She laughs a little, but it's not mean. "No, I think I don't."

We don't speak for another few minutes, just listening to the slot machines inside and the crickets in the dark. There's laughter behind us as a woman stumbles against her beau, wobbling in her high heels and slinky gold dress. The person she's with has a gold hoop earring that catches my eye, and they're wearing a pageboy hat and gray vest over a loose button-down. They'd be taller than the woman if not for the heels she's wearing. They have both arms around her as she continues to laugh and stumble, like there's a joke playing on repeat that only she can hear.

"Okay, Dana, let's get you to the car," says the person in the pageboy hat.

"Wait, wait—Jamie, I haven't even gotten to the best part!" the woman—Dana, apparently—chokes out, slapping her hand against Jamie's chest.

The two of them veer away from us, to the west side of the parking lot. Yaz has a bemused expression as we watch the pair. "They're cute together," she says.

I shrug. "Maybe they're just friends."

She looks back at me, her eyes sad—like maybe she means what she says. Maybe she really didn't mean to turn all of this to shit. After all, she did drive all the way here in the middle of the night. Granted, I did the same thing a few months ago—but that's what you do when you love someone, right? That's what you do when you care about your friends, even when they fuck up.

You show up for each other.

"I'm sorry, Aali," Yaz says finally, her eyes settling on mine, daring me to look away. To let it go. I don't know if I forgive her yet, but I know that I'm done feeling angry. It takes too much energy.

Look what it's doing to my mom. What it's done to my dad.

"I know," I say. "Thank you."

We sit together for a few minutes more. We don't talk about her girlfriend, or about my family, but she tells me her dad will be back in town for a few weeks. She says it might be nice for me to visit again when he's there, because he still asks about me sometimes. She says we could have dinner again, "like a proper family," and that makes me laugh. She laughs, too, and for the first time that night, she inches just a little closer. Our shoulders brush as the sun begins to rise.

CHAPTER 29

Yaz offers to take me to school, but I decline. It's one thing to sneak out in the middle of the night; it's another to disappear altogether. I'd rather not tip my mom into full-scale attack mode. When Yaz leaves, she promises to text me later and I decide to believe that she will. Then I make my way back to the hotel room. I spent too much time downstairs, so I know Mom and Trinity will be up by the time I get to the room. I decide, however, that I don't care. For once, I don't want to worry about how Mom is going to feel about me having emotions and experiences that she doesn't understand and therefore doesn't condone.

But when I walk in, Mom is sitting on the bed and reading the hotel's Bible. She glances at me, but says nothing. Just looks back down and keeps reading. I can tell by the yellow light that Trinity is in the bathroom, so I slip in to find her already brushing her teeth. She smiles wide when she sees me, her teeth covered in white foam, and tackles me in the doorway with a massive hug.

"Hey, what's that for?" I hug her back and push us backward into the bathroom.

Trinity skips to the mirror and spits out the toothpaste. Then she wipes her mouth. "I missed you!" she chirps loudly, as if we're in a concert hall.

I try to smile. This is Trinity when Dad's not looming over us like a cloud—carefree and full of life. Just like she should be. Like we all should be. I tussle her hair and then reach out for my toothbrush, waiting for me in a plastic baggie on the sink. As I brush my teeth, Trinity hums a song I don't recognize and tells me about Maisie, her new best friend, and how much she dislikes her English teacher, Mrs. Banks, because she keeps confusing her with the other brown girl in her class, Lillianna, and how much she wishes we could afford to buy a new bike that's small enough for her because my old bike is too big, and if she had a *new* bike that fit her, she could ride to Maisie's house after school and do their English homework *together*, just like real best friends.

She goes on like that for a while. Chirping and humming and skipping and talking and I smile, and listen, and nod, because I don't know when I'll get this moment again. This moment to just be the big sister to my baby sister, without any other strings attached.

Mom takes us to school an hour later. The ride is silent, except for Trinity's excited chirping. Then Trinity is dropped off and Mom and I are left alone. I watch the dry landscape pass us by as Mom stares straight ahead, the silence stretching on between us. I don't want to talk about last night, and I'm sure she doesn't, either, but I want to say something. Anything.

Mom surprises me by talking first. "Miss Eccleston called last night."

"Oh," I say. Anything but that.

"She says you missed class a couple of weeks ago."

"I overslept."

"And you had a session to address your academic probation yesterday. You didn't show up?"

"I was tired."

"You were tired. You overslept. But you seem to have enough energy to run around town with that girl."

Son of a—"It won't happen again, Mom."

"Like last year won't happen again?"

"Are you serious?" I turn all the way to my side to get a good, hard look at the woman who raised me. "Mom, what exactly do you think happened last year?"

"I know you suddenly stopped talking about college and quit cross-country after whatever happened between you and that little girl."

"No, I stopped talking about college and giving a shit about cross-country because of what happened between *me and you*, Mom." I know I need to stop talking, but I can't. Mom's opened the floodgates, and now I'm ready to burst. "I didn't *quit* cross-country, Mom, I *failed* at it. I was late to practices, and I sucked at my meets. Why? Because I was fucking *exhausted*, because my home life *sucks*. Because my dad is an abusive drunk, but my mom cares more about the fact that I kiss girls. Because I spent all the time I wasn't eating or sleeping trying to convince you I wasn't a fucking degenerate, and making sure that Trinity wasn't traumatized by the Marshall Family Blowouts.

"You want to know why I stopped caring about my classes? Why I stopped *gushing* to you about all the colleges I wanted to apply for? Because I knew it didn't *fucking matter*. I *have* to stay home, I have to *keep watch*, because I don't trust *you* not to fuck Trinity up the way you've fucked *me* up. I stopped trusting Dad a long time ago, but turns out you're not so great yourself, Mom."

I exhale, but my body is tense. I'm ready for a fight. Ready for her to scream, to slap me, to curse me out the way Dad has cursed us both out. I don't want to fight, but I will if I have to.

But Mom is quiet. She's glaring at me. Her jaw is tense. But she doesn't say anything. It takes me a moment to realize that she's pulled to the side of the road. Slowly, the rest of the world returns in a haze. We're a few blocks from the school. She unlocks the doors and turns away from me.

"Get out," she says.

And I want to be the biggest asshole. I want to shove my face in hers and grin and say something snarky like, "But, Mom,

I've *been* out," but my survival mode kicks back in like a stab through the heart. I grab my bag and run.

I barely have time to reach my first period class before I'm called away to Miss Eccleston's office.

Of course.

"Hey," I say, plopping into my usual seat.

"Miss Marshall. I spoke to your mother last evening."

"So I've heard."

Miss Eccleston raises an eyebrow. I'm not in the mood today, and it shows. "I take it you two have been talking about your academics, then. That's good."

"If you say so."

"Listen. It's not that I want you to get in trouble, but it's my job to make sure you graduate high school—"

"I will. My grades are fine. I might've missed a couple of sessions, but I haven't failed anything yet, and I'm not going to."

"Sure. And that's fantastic. But truth be told, I'm not just concerned about your grades. I'm concerned about your future. What do you want, Aaliyah?"

I huff and stare at the ceiling. "To survive."

"And then what?"

Her response is so quick that it jars me. "What do you mean?"

"I mean 'and then what?' What happens beyond survival. Roof over your head, food on the table, a safe place to rest—"

"I haven't gotten that far."

"How far?"

"The last part," I mumble. "The 'safe' part."

Miss Eccleston closes her mouth for a moment. "Okay. So let's start there."

Half an hour later, I'm holding a loose leaf of lined paper with the words *Safety Plan* scrawled at the top. According to Miss Eccleston, she's what they call a "mandated reporter," someone who has to let the authorities know if a house is unsafe. That could result in a lot of things, and I don't know if I want any of them. Child services, court appointments, foster care . . .

But that's down the rabbit hole, and only *if* I'm ready to talk about everything.

I'm not. I barely want to acknowledge there's an "everything" to talk about.

But she says I can start somewhere. Start small. So she gave me a list of numbers to call if I needed them and told me to write a list. "What would make you feel safe?" she asked.

I don't know. So my homework is to figure it out.

When I leave her office, I'm tempted to skip the rest of the school day—which is ironic, all things considered. But I'm consumed by the question: "What would make you feel safe?" It echoes in my head as I wander the halls, tune out my teachers, and stare blankly at my notebooks. It's only when calculus swings around and I see Tessa for the first time in days that

I come back to reality. But she ignores me. She takes her seat and keeps her eyes straight ahead, focused on Miss A.

It's in that moment that I realize I don't know what safety even means.

Before Tessa, I felt safe with Marissa. And before Marissa, I felt safe with Yasmin. But I don't know what it means to feel safe by myself. I don't know what it means to feel safe inside my own home. Or inside my own head.

Huh.

I take out my folded pieces of paper and stare at the empty lines until I feel a buzz from my phone. I glance at Miss A, and when she's not watching, I sneak a peek. It's a text from Yasmin:

"How are you feeling? Do you want to swing by rehearsal today?"

I shouldn't be surprised—she did promise she'd text me. Still, it's a new feeling—getting casual friend-texts from her again. I don't know if we can go from straight-up not talking to hanging out with hers *and* Marissa's friends in theater . . . but then again, I could finally see Marissa rehearse. Maybe I could talk to her . . . or maybe not. I don't really know how I feel about things with her all of a sudden.

But I guess I could figure it out.

"Yes. See you soon," I respond, and wait for the rest of classes to end.

When I get to the theater room, Marissa and Yasmin's

classmates greet me like an old friend. I see Keisha and Robert and decide to sit with them awkwardly until Yasmin walks out, heaving a massive bundle of metal rods. When I take a closer look, I realize she's also got a tool belt on.

And she's wearing wedges, because of course she is.

"Gay," I pretend to cough out, which prompts her to look around the stack of paraphernalia in her arms.

"Hey, you came!" she says, smiling.

"Yeah, well. You texted me." I nod at her hands. "Stage managing?"

"Stagehand, yeah." She grins. "I decided to take it a little easier this semester."

"Good plan. You need help?"

"Um." She shifts, and a rod threatens to tumble. "Yes. Absolutely."

I take two rods from her and follow her to a corner of the green room that doubles as a workshop. Just as I'm stretching out my back because those things were heavy as shit, a murmur erupts behind me. I turn. Marissa's standing there with more anger and hurt than I've ever seen in her.

"What are you doing here?" she asks.

"I, uh—Yasmin invited me," I say, which I realize too late is incredibly, unbelievably stupid.

"You came to see her?" Marissa laughs, and it's the most terrible sound in the world, but the worst thing is her expression. The wide eyes and the uncertain stare, waffling between shock and anger and . . . and heartbreak. But her classmates are watching. I'm used to scenes at home—the yelling, and the accusations, and the gawking from the neighbors outside when a police van pulls up.

I don't want to make a scene now.

"Marissa," I stage-whisper, as if that will somehow calm everything down.

"Are you serious? I get the lead in the winter musical and you don't show up, you don't call, you don't even fucking *text*, but your ex-girlfriend asks you to watch her *hammer* shit and you come running?"

"That's not what—" I try to say, but Yasmin steps in. Worse, she steps in front of me.

"Look, why don't you and Aaliyah talk later—"

"Oh, fuck off," Marissa says. "Are you kidding me? Was I even talking to you? How is it that you are just *every-fucking-where* all the time?" Marissa advances on Yasmin with every word, and I freeze. I don't want to see her like this—full of rage, venom dripping from her mouth. This feels too familiar, like a nightmare I can't escape, and suddenly my lungs feel like someone stabbed a hole in them. I can't seem to get enough air, and it's not until they're inches apart that I realize I should probably make another attempt at a full sentence.

Mr. Chisholm beats me to it.

"Marissa," he says, and his deep voice vibrates through the walls. He's standing in the middle of the room, looking not only pissed but *offended*, as if he can't believe our gall. "My office. Now." He points to Yasmin, too, and the two exchange glares before following him to the back room.

I'm tempted to keep standing there, because I genuinely have no better plan than that, but at least my lungs are working now. Slowly, the rest of the class turns to me, like they're ready for an encore. That's when Emmanuel walks in, a bouquet of flowers in his hand.

"What's going on?" he asks. The room is still quiet, and I must look miserable, because he places a hand on my shoulder like he's trying to keep me steady. "You okay?"

"Yeah," I say. I take a shaky breath and look at the flowers in his hand. "Those for Mar?"

His smile is dreamy. "Yeah. To celebrate, you know? Before her rehearsal schedule gets really crazy. A bunch of us are going out to Red Robin tonight." His smile dissolves into a confused frown. "Didn't you get my text?"

I blink at him. Either the text didn't go through or I didn't see it last night. Either way, Marissa probably doesn't want to celebrate with me now.

"Seriously, dude, you good?" He waves a hand in front of my face, and he's so genuinely concerned that it makes my stomach hurt.

"Yeah, Manuel. Yeah." I pat his cheek absently as I start to walk away.

"Where are you going?" he calls after me, but I don't bother to respond, or to turn around. I just keep walking, out the door, and off campus. I can't go home—not yet—so for now, I just keep one foot in front of the other, and hope that that's enough.

CHAPTER 30

When I hear from Emmanuel again, the sun has set and I'm nursing an iced tea in the Starbucks halfway between my house and our school. I've been tempted to buy another just so the baristas will stop glaring at me, but they weren't very happy with the quarters, nickels, and dimes I counted out for them the first time, so instead I've spent the past several hours scrolling through college lists and ignoring texts from Naomi.

Then I feel another frenetic buzz. When I see Emmanuel's name, I hold back a groan.

"Hey," I answer.

"Hi," he says. His voice is distinctly less cheerful than it was when I left him.

"How's the celebration?"

"Didn't happen. Marissa got suspended."

"Oh," I say.

I hear him take a deep breath. "Yup. So. Listen. I've been trying to coax her out of her house for hours now, and it's not working. I'm literally here, at her door, and she won't let me back in."

"So . . ."

"So get over here, dammit." The force of his frustration nearly knocks the wind out of me. "You're her best friend, right?"

"I don't think she wants to talk to me, Emmanuel."

"See, I think that's your problem. I think you both need to talk, like now. Please. She's gotta talk to someone, and she's not talking to me."

He doesn't wait to hear my answer—at least, that becomes clear after my protests yield no response. When I look at my phone, I see that he's hung up. I'm still tempted to stay where I'm at. To do nothing at all.

But I have to explain myself to Marissa. So I slide off the stool and start walking.

Emmanuel says nothing when I arrive. He just gives me a glare I know I deserve and pushes off from Marissa's door. Then he stalks to his car. A small part of me is happy that I'm the one he's angry at, and not Marissa.

I knock a couple of times on her door. "It's me," I call after a few tries. My heart is pumping, and for a moment, I'm convinced she's just going to ignore me. But after another few knocks, the door swings open and Marissa stands before me. Her eyes, normally perfectly lined, are red from tears.

"What?" she says, and it comes out as a croak.

"Hi."

"Aali, seriously?" She sounds tired. That's probably my fault.

"Can I come in?"

She glares but steps aside, so that I can walk into her small living room. The last time I was here was two months ago, when we went on our triple date. How has so much time passed already? I sit on her mom's lavish love seat—the one she got from when the Venetian did an overhaul of its hotel rooms. I pat the spot next to me, hoping for an easy resolution, but Marissa doesn't offer it to me. Instead she keeps standing, her arms crossed, waiting for me to speak.

"I, uh . . . ," I start. "I heard you got suspended. Are you out as Melchior?"

"No," she breathes. "Chisholm is cool. Pissed, but cool. If I had decked Yasmin like I wanted to, I'd be out as Melchior, but since I just cursed her out, I'm on probation."

"Don't say things like that," I mutter, and she looks away. I can see her fingers digging into her arms.

"Sorry," she says, and I know she means it. Neither of us wants to sound like our parents. Then she backs up so that she's leaning against the door, her eyes on the ceiling. "What's going on, Aaliyah?"

I don't even know where I would begin. But I figure I'll start with the easiest thing. "I'm sorry I went to see Yasmin, instead of trying to see you." Marissa takes another deep breath, but she doesn't look at me.

"She came over yesterday, and I shut her down, but then Dad had another one of his freak-outs, so we were at the hotel last night and—"

"What?" Marissa frowns. "Are you okay?"

I wave my hand as if it's not a big deal. "Yeah, I'm fine. It's whatever. I just—I tried to talk to Mom about it and *she* freaked, and it was just so much that I . . . well, I called Yasmin. You and I weren't talking, and Tessa isn't talking to me, either, so I didn't know who else to turn to."

"I would've answered the phone, Aali. You know that."

"Yeah, I know. I just didn't really feel like I deserved it, considering how . . . shitty I've been. Anyway. The point is, Yasmin invited me to come to the rehearsal today, and I thought I could use that as an excuse to finally come and talk to you. I promise—I really did want to see you."

Marissa nods. "Okay." She looks away, and I can tell she's battling with herself. Despite the weeks spent apart, this is the furthest I've ever felt from her.

"Marissa."

"Yeah," she whispers.

"How come you never told me about what happened with the band?"

She takes a sharp inhale of breath. "Oh, wow."

"Sorry," I mutter. "We don't have to talk about it. I just . . . someone showed me the video."

"Of course they did." She shakes her head. "I hate that. I hate that you saw me like that." She runs a hand through her hair, and in that moment, I want to touch her. I want to hold her hand, and pull her close to me.

"You don't owe me anything, Mar. We don't have to talk about it."

"It's stupid," she says. "I was just having a shit day. Mom sold my fucking guitar because she was strapped for cash, and I decided to pay her back by binging on her tequila. Turns out that was a bad idea." I don't say anything, just inch a little closer to her. "Anyway," she whispers. "It was a bad look for the band, obviously. So they kicked me out. I don't blame them. It's just . . . fucking embarrassing." She gives me a weak smile. "You notice I don't drink anymore."

I did notice that. I just thought it was for my benefit.

"I'm sorry, dude."

"Yeah, well. Like mother, like daughter, I guess. Everything I touch just goes to shit."

Oh, I know that feeling way too well. This time, I do take her hand. "You're *nothing* like your mom, Marissa. You're amazing, and one of the best people I know. We all fuck up. God knows I have. You're incredible, and I . . ." She looks at me with something indiscernible in her eyes, and I suddenly feel like I'm talking too much. "I missed you."

Marissa lets out a breathy laugh, but her eyes are brimming with tears. "Is that all?"

I lean in closer. "What?"

She wipes her eyes, trying to keep her voice even. "Is that all? You miss me?"

"I—yes?"

She sniffles a little and shakes her head. "Aaliyah. You're impossible, do you know that?" She takes a moment to take in a shaky breath, but she doesn't look at me. "Do you remember when we made out last year—at Susannah May's party? You keep avoiding the question, but I need to know what you felt. What you were thinking."

I swallow the lump rising in my throat. This isn't where I thought the conversation was going, but I guess I should've known. "I, uh. I thought you were playing with me. Like Yasmin was."

Marissa sniffles again. "Okay. Do you know that I wasn't?"

I think about the night of the party, and for the first time, I can see us clearly: Marissa's eager eyes, her hesitant kiss, the way she held me when we leaned against my front door, her lips pressed to my hair. I was too scared to believe that it was real, but if I think about the past few hours—the way she looked when she saw me with Yasmin, like her heart had broken into a million pieces, and the way she's looking at me now with tears in her eyes—the answer is obvious. It was real. But I didn't want to believe it then—didn't want to risk doing to our new friendship what it felt like I had done to my old one: wish for something more than what we had.

Slowly, I nod my head. *Yes. I know you weren't playing with me.* I think there's a part of me that has known all along. "Mar," I start to say, but she keeps her head down. "You have to understand that I was scared. Of turning it into something it wasn't. Or doing what I did with Yasmin and making a big deal out of something that turned out not to mean anything."

"So you did what Yasmin did and pretended like nothing happened instead."

"I—" Oh. The realization hits me like a gut punch. All this time, I'd been thinking Marissa was like Yasmin, but it turns out *I'm* the one who's been acting like Yasmin. The feeling knocks the wind out of me, and for a moment I just sit there gaping like a fish until I'm able to find my words again. "Mar . . . I am so, so sorry."

She shakes her head and lifts her hands to the top of her head as if that'll keep her from floating off toward the ceiling. She takes a few breaths and walks toward her kitchen a few steps away. She pauses at the dining table and, after a moment, turns back around. "I know I had shitty timing. But I kissed you because I wanted to kiss you. And then you pulled away, and that sucked, but then we fucking *made out* against *your door*, and you have pretended like nothing happened for the past eight *fucking* months."

"I know," I say, and I sound so much like Yasmin that it hurts. "I know. Seriously. I didn't—" Fuck. *I didn't know how much I hurt you.* I'm repeating words now. How did it get this way? How did we all fuck up this much? And that's when I realize—none of us know what we're doing. We're all just doing the best we can with what we have.

I stand and move toward Marissa, approaching slowly, like a sudden movement might scare her away. "I didn't mean to hurt you. I was trying to protect myself, and I . . . I feel like an idiot, because that night . . . it meant something to me, too." She looks back up at me then, her eyes searching. "I didn't want to admit it because I thought it was going to be like Yasmin again. I thought that you just wanted to fool around. But I thought about it every day. I still do." Then it's my turn to look away, because what I'm about to say next I don't want to say. Not really. But I had to have learned something this year. "I fucking adore you," I say, and her eyes follow my mouth, "but I'm glad nothing changed."

Then she laughs with so much disbelief that I almost feel hurt—as if she's the only one putting something at risk right now. I take her hands, and she doesn't resist, though I can tell by the tension in her wrists that she wants to. "I needed my best friend this year, Marissa. Not a girlfriend."

Mar's eyes keep searching mine. "But you're dating Tessa."

I shrug a little helplessly. "She's not my best friend." *And I don't know if we're still dating.*

"I wasn't your best friend when we met," she says quietly.

"Yeah, and I was a goddamned disaster, wasn't I?" She laughs at that, and it sets us both at ease. "It wouldn't have been good," I continue, "if we had started then. I think I would've broken your heart, and lost your friendship in the process."

Marissa raises an eyebrow. "I thought you were afraid that I would break yours."

"I still am," I say.

She sighs at that, and nods, more to herself than to me. Then I offer her a smile, weak as it is, and my arm, and we walk back toward the love seat together. When we sit down, she intertwines her fingers with mine almost on instinct, and lays her head on my shoulder. We stay like that for a moment, just listening to each other's breathing. I don't want to regret the past few months—I'm tired of that feeling. But sitting with Marissa now, our bodies so close together, our hearts beating in sync, I understand what I've been missing—like the other half of my soul was out there playing hide-and-seek.

I don't know how to say this to Marissa without messing up the moment, so I just lift her hand to my lips. I only meant for it to be that—innocent, and brief—but the way she looks at me stirs something in my chest and I keep my mouth to her skin, kissing each knuckle—*One. Two. Three. Four.* When I reach the knuckle of her thumb, I find her eyes. There are tears there. Already, they've fallen too many times tonight. But then her lips find my cheek, then my forehead; she places a light kiss just below my chin. She lingers there, a thousand words exchanged in the space of a breath. There's no word for this feeling, but I can feel fear fighting with something else. Something much, much scarier.

It takes me a minute to realize that we've fallen asleep. Marissa is still lying on my shoulder, but we've fallen over so that I'm pressed up against the edge of the love seat. The entire left side of my body feels sore, but I don't want to wake her, so I just stay there, letting myself adjust to the reality that I've been lying to myself for the better part of a year.

It's amazing what your brain can tell you in an effort to survive. I twisted everything so much in my head that I couldn't even see the person standing in front of me with her heart in her hands. If I play it all back now, I realize that it's like she was doing everything short of throwing a parade. Still—I don't know what's going on with me and Tessa. And I have no idea where Marissa and Emmanuel stand. I don't want to fuck things up even more.

"Hey," Marissa mutters next to my ear, her voice scratchy

from sleep. She rubs her eyes and leans away from me so that she can stretch. Then she shakes her head, which miraculously helps loosen out some of the kinks in her hair.

"Hey," I say, sitting upright finally and letting feeling return to my left side. "I was thinking—about you and Emmanuel." Marissa stands to do a deeper stretch. Then she turns to me with a tired frown.

"Oh. Yeah. We broke up."

My eyes widen. "Oh."

"Why do you think he called you?" she says, stifling a yawn and sitting back down. Clearly, it's because Emmanuel is the king of righteous men. Where the hell do they cultivate those? "So much for celebrating, huh?"

"Are you okay?"

She laughs a little at my surprised expression. "I broke up with my boyfriend in time for the girl I'm in love with to tell me she just wants to be friends. No, I'm not okay." She says it like a joke, but her words make my head spin. *In love with.*

"I—" I pause for words.

"Don't you dare say you're sorry again."

But I try for a joke anyway. "Sorry."

"You're the worst," she mutters, grabbing a pillow from the side of the couch and tossing it at me. She throws it so lightly that it barely does more than pat my arm. "Does this mean you're bi?" I ask as she sits back down.

Marissa rolls her eyes. "Well, I'm definitely not straight," she says. Then she takes the pillow she threw at me and places it against my shoulder.

"Why didn't you say anything?"

"I didn't think I needed to. I . . . thought it was super obvious."

I sigh. *Only if you're paying attention.*

She lays her head back down on my shoulder, like she's ready to fall asleep again. Given the past few hours, I don't blame her. "What can I do, babe?" I whisper the words, but the last one feels too heavy. Like it means so much more than it used to. Maybe she feels it, too, because she takes a moment to respond. Then she presses a little closer to the pillow, against my side, our bodies the closest they've been in months.

"Just be here with me," she breathes.

So I wrap my free arm around her shoulder and pull her closer. As close as I can without it hurting, and that's a line I'll always have to balance with us, but it's worth the patience. I don't have to be her girlfriend, but I could damn well be her friend. Sometimes, that's enough.

CHAPTER 31

When I finally get home, Dad is sitting on the stairs. There's a beat-up duffel bag next to him. Mom is in the kitchen, sitting at the table, her face, as ever, in the Bible. Dad looks up when he sees me and his eyes are red and his face is drawn, like he hasn't slept in weeks.

"Hey, baby girl," he says.

"Hey," I say. He looks at my mom, who is still reading her Bible. "What's going on?"

Dad clears his throat, looks at Mom again. Looks away. "I'm going away for a little while."

"Oh."

"I'm, uh . . . I'm sorry. About last night. You girls don't deserve that. I know that." He hangs his head, grips his hair. When he looks back at me, his eyes are even redder. "I don't mean to hurt y'all. You know?"

I don't know, not really. But he sniffs a little, and covers his face with one hand. I look at Mom again, and she's covering her face, too. I think I see her shoulders shake, but I'm not sure. I'm not really sure of anything right now. Then Mom wipes her face and stands up, coming over to us quietly.

"You go on upstairs, Aaliyah. Your dad and I have to finish up some things." She still doesn't look at me, but when I pass her to go up the stairs, she touches my shoulder. Touches, not grabs. Not even squeezes. Just a light brush. Gentle, even.

I don't know the last time Mom was gentle with me.

"Where's Trinity?" It's the only thing I can think to say.

"At her friend Maisie's house," Mom says.

I nod, and I go up the stairs, but I don't go to my room. Instead, I sit against the low wall at the top, just out of sight. I wait, and I listen. To their quiet discussion, their calm plans. Someone is crying, and this time, it's not my mother. At least, not until the front door opens, and then shuts again. Then I hear her footsteps retreat, and the scrape of her chair back in the kitchen.

I feel like I should go to her. Hold her and say that it's going to be okay, like I used to do in the before times. But I don't move. I'm still waiting. For the banging of the door, obscenities yelled through the window, a rock thrown through the glass. I wait, and I wait, and I wait. But all I hear is quiet. So much quiet.

The next thing I know, Mom's hands are on my shoulder again.

Gentle, again.

"Wake up, honey."

"Huh?"

"Go to your room."

"Okay."

Mom follows me as I wander to my bedroom, my world hazy and slow. I crawl into bed and let her pull the covers over me. As darkness returns, she waits, and I fall asleep to my mother's soft breathing, and the brush of her fingers on my forehead.

CHAPTER 32

In the olden days, there was a song I used to love at church. "Come home, come home, ye who are weary, come home." It felt a lot like a lullaby, back then. The kind of thing you drift off to, knowing you'll be safe in the waking hours.

I'm not sure I feel safe, but for the first time in a long time, I don't feel wary.

It's been three days since Dad left. I've slept pretty much the whole time. At some point, Trinity came in and lay beside me. Mom called for dinner a few times. Friends called, and so did Coach. But otherwise, it's been total slumber.

Now it's Tuesday morning, and Mom is waiting downstairs, a cup of coffee in her hands while Joel Osteen preaches from the TV.

"Hey, Mom."

"Hi, honey." She eyes my school clothes. "You feeling a little better?"

"Yeah. I have peer advisory today, so." I shrug and she nods and we stand there quietly for a moment.

"Do you want me to take you to school?" she asks finally.

"No. I'm going to take the bus."

"Okay." She puts her hands between her knees and looks around, like she's searching for a safe topic to land on. "What happened to that girl? Tessa?"

"Oh. Um. We . . . broke up. I think."

"Oh."

"Yeah."

More awkward silence.

"How's Marissa?"

God, she's batting a thousand. "She's okay."

"I haven't seen her around lately."

"Yeah. We, um . . . haven't been getting along. But we're okay."

"Was she jealous?"

I blink. "Yeah. I guess."

Mom chuckles softly to herself. "I knew that girl had a thing for you."

My eyes peel open, crusting away any sleep that had hoped to linger. Mom goes back to her coffee for a moment, and then she stands.

"Okay, well, I'm going to wake up your sister so she can get to school." She gives me a tired smile and then, after a beat of hesitation, gives me a quick kiss on the cheek. It, too, is awkward. Literally nothing about this interaction has felt natural, and yet . . . I don't hate it. I touch my cheek, feeling the slight smudge of lipstick that's left. That, at least, feels familiar. I didn't realize I missed it.

When Trinity comes downstairs, she attacks me with a hug, evidently shocked that I'm neither bedridden nor possibly sleepwalking. I hold her tightly. Mom stands off to the side, letting us have our moment. I don't know what she's thinking—if she feels awkward, maybe, that Trinity and I are clearly bonding over the departure of her true love.

But that's the thing, right? I don't even know if Mom and Dad are in love anymore.

I'm not sure if they know, either.

"How are you feeling, kid?" I'm asking into Trinity's hair.

"I'm okay," she says. "I'm glad you're up."

"Me, too," I say.

When we finally let go of each other, I make a mental note to give her some serious sisterly attention when I get home, given that I've been little more than a blanket cocoon for days. Then Mom and I give each other awkward smiles as I walk into a bright, new morning.

An hour later, Naomi, Miss Eccleston, and I are sitting in her office as usual, and this time Miss Eccleston looks happy.

"This is a great list, Aaliyah. Fantastic. So you've got four in-state schools and six out-of-state schools. Is USD still your number one choice?"

Naomi looks at me expectantly, but I shake my head. "No," I say. "I still want to go to community college . . . but I'm planning to transfer after a year or two." I sneak a glance at Naomi, but she doesn't look upset. In fact, she looks pleasantly surprised.

"That's a fine idea, Aaliyah. We can talk more about that. Now, let's talk about your grades."

When the session is over, Naomi and I start to leave together, but Miss Eccleston calls me back.

"Aaliyah," she says. "Have you considered the list we talked about last time?"

"Oh," I say. "Yeah. The, um, the safety list." I drop my backpack on her chair and pull the folded piece of paper out of the mess. "Sorry, I wrote it kind of hastily this morning."

"That's all right," she says. "It's meant for you."

"Right. So . . . I wrote music down. Music feels safe for me. And, um, my friends. And running. It's kind of a short list."

"That's okay," she says. "It's good to start somewhere. Why don't you focus on those three things for the next week, and see if you can extrapolate. Is there a way you can incorporate more of those things into your life consistently, to mitigate feelings of unease or discomfort? How can those things help you move forward to your goals in life?"

That's what I think about for the rest of the day. "Goals in life." I didn't really have that many goals this year. The main one was to survive, and not fuck up again. I didn't even really plan to "win" any of my cross-country meets; I only planned not to fail. Hell, last year, my only plan was not to off myself.

And I guess I've met that goal.

So what's next?

Funny. I've never thought that far.

When I get to Miss A's class, Tessa is still ignoring me. Marissa and Yasmin are suspended until next week, so it's just me, going through the motions until practice starts, and Naomi greets me with a warm smile. Before she can get to me, though, Coach pulls me aside. "Hey, kiddo," he says. "Everything all right?"

"Yeah," I say. "It will be."

He gives me one of his trademark pep talks about keeping my head up and then lets me join the team. On the bus ride home, Marissa video-chats me. She's still wearing pj's, and her hair is up in a wild red bun, while white acne cream dots her face.

"Hey, Mrs. Still-Doesn't-Answer-Her-Texts," she says. "Note that I am giving you the benefit of the doubt."

"Note noted, and appreciated." I lean back into my seat. "Mom kicked Dad out on Friday." It's the first time I've said it out loud. A few kids look my way, but I don't care.

"Son of a bitch," she says. The camera adjusts, and suddenly she's sitting on her bed. I can see her Brittany Howard poster on her wall beside the bed. "You okay?"

I laugh a little, which feels blasphemous but not disingenuous. "I'm fine. I guess. I'm not *not* fine." Then I take a glance at the variety of stares and whispers around me, and the full events of Friday finally come flooding back in. "Are *you* okay?"

Marissa rolls her eyes. "I'm fine. I mean, I'm not *not* fine. Are *we* okay?"

"I want us to be."

"Cool. Me, too. Can you come by after school?"

I laugh a little. "Only if I can sleep more."

"Deal," she says.

For the rest of the ride, I slip into a trance, staring at nothing and listening to the movement of the bus and the radio playing on blast. It's nothing but the Killers, and Panic! At the Disco, and I'm halfway expecting to hear an old Light Pollution song. Instead, I hear a familiar voice . . .

I always thought my heart was freezing
And I'm just cold
But I refuse to fucking suffer
Just to feel whole; now I know

It's Shamir. Of course it is.

And finally, I know what to say to Tessa. I open up my voice app and start recording. "Hey. I'll keep this short, because there's nothing I can say that would make what's happened over the last few months okay. I just want you to know that . . . I'm sorry. You deserve better. I know you know that, and I'm sorry it's taken so long for me to know that. I still have some things to figure out, but in the meantime . . . just know that you mean a lot to me, and even though I can understand if you need space, I want to work to be a better friend than I was a girlfriend. If that's okay."

When I put my phone away, I notice a couple of kids whispering and looking my way. But I don't care. I'm too tired to worry about appearances, or making people comfortable. No—not too tired. Just over it. I have to do what's right for me. To hell with what anyone else thinks.

CHAPTER 33

I made it.

Somehow, someway, I have lasted until the end of the season, and now here we are: December, and last meet of my high school cross-country career. It should feel bittersweet, but I'm too busy screaming with the team as they douse me in a bucket of ice. I came in first, again. I came in fucking *first* in regionals.

Why? Because I'm awesome.

Before I can wipe liquid sugar from my eyes, though, I'm lifted into the air by a pair of arms. "Oh my God, Curtis."

"Champion! Champion! Champion!"

He bobs me up and down as the rest of the team cheers, but Coach puts a stop to it quickly. "Curtis! Boys! You're up next. Don't lose focus now." He gives me a huge grin and two very intense thumbs-up before ushering the boys back toward the starting line.

"Good job, Aaliyah," Tessa says from beside me. She's a few feet away, hands behind her back. We haven't talked much over the past few weeks, but it's not too awkward. Sad, I guess, but not awkward. She smiles and joins the others as they start to walk back to our team tent to watch the boys run.

I guess I survived that. My first official breakup. Got to say, though: I'm not exactly a fan. My eyes don't stay glued to her too long, though, because Marissa shoves a burrito in my face seconds later, and then squeezes the very life out of me. "You did so great! Congratulations!"

"Thanks, Marissa," I gasp when she finally allows me to breathe. "Thanks for coming."

"Of course! Wouldn't miss it. It's a little weird not being on the team anymore, but the show must go on." She slings an arm around my shoulder as we walk together.

"I mean, you killed Melchior last weekend. Absolutely no one faults you for choosing that over heatstroke."

"Um, have you been beneath the lights on a stage? That shit is murder." She gives my shoulder a tight squeeze before she stops in front of me, a twinkle in her eye. In fact, she's nearly rocking back and forth with glee, and I know she's about to tell me something utterly wild.

"What?"

"I have a surprise for you."

"What's that?"

"Okay, it's not really *for* you, but I think you're going to be ecstatic."

"Okay?"

"Lonnie and I have been talking, and . . . we're gonna jam tonight. Nothing serious, the band's not back together. But, you know. We're gonna have fun."

"Oh my God." I can't help the rising fangirl that is rapidly consuming my body. "Oh my God. Does that mean I can watch you guys perform? Like, up close?"

She bites her lip and nods quickly.

"Oh my God!"

I give her the tightest hug I can imagine, feeling every bit like a huge band groupie and loving every moment of it. I'm also letting the slow seeds of a plan ferment . . .

We wait for the boys to finish their run and celebrate their good deeds accordingly. At some point, Marissa starts coordinating plans with Lonnie, and I take the time to set my plan in action. Then Marissa and I leave, driving the twenty minutes it takes to get to the north side of town. When we arrive, Emmanuel, Naomi, and Curtis are waiting outside. Marissa gasps a little and turns to look at me. "What are they doing here?"

I smile nervously and touch the back of my neck. "I . . . invited them. I figured since the whole Red Robin thing was a bust when you scored your Melchior role that we could . . . you know . . . take another stab at celebrating together. I hope that's okay."

"Aali," she breathes. It sounds happy. I hope it is. She just shakes her head at me, but the smile on her lips stays as she goes to open the Bug's door.

Outside, Emmanuelle's hands are shoved into his pockets and he looks like he'd rather be anywhere else, but as we exit the car, he manages a nod in our direction. Curtis stands beside him, his hands fidgeting with his hair and his collar, as he and Naomi exchange what I assume are pleasantries. Naomi looks calm, but I can tell by the way she's grasping her hands that she's just as nervous as he is.

Lonnie, Marissa, and I approach the group, and Emmanuel takes a deep breath.

"I'm glad you're here," I say to him.

He releases the breath with a nod. "We're a team. Right?"

"Right."

He nods again toward Marissa. "I've never seen you perform like this, so." He shrugs. "I hear you're badass." The smile she offers him is warm, even as he ducks his head and starts toward the entrance to the building, leading us on a procession inside. Then Lonnie and Marissa take the lead, guiding us to the music room, where a makeshift stage has already been arranged.

Teresa and Mychal, their bandmates, are tuning up the instruments. Lonnie goes to sit behind their drum set, drumsticks twirling in the air like dancers.

"You ready?" Mychal says the moment Marissa enters, stepping between us to put an electric guitar into Marissa's hands.

Mychal's voice is gruff, but the handoff is warm. Familiar. As Marissa straps in, Mychal jerks her head toward the two semi-broken lawn chairs and a handful of overturned crates. "That's for you guys. Aaliyah, right?"

"Yeah," I say, walking toward the crates. "And this is Curtis, Naomi, and Emmanuel."

"Cool," she says. "I'm Mychal; that's Teresa."

"Yo," Teresa yells absently in our direction. She doesn't look up from fiddling with her keyboard. Naomi sits beside me on a lawn chair, and the boys take their seats as we watch them set up.

"Ready?" Marissa asks, looking at me now. She's standing steps away, her guitar held like a precious thing beneath her fingers. Her eyes are wide and full of mischief. The sort of look that tells me we're in for a hell of a show.

"Yeah," I say.

She smiles and clears her throat. "HELLO, LAS VEGAS," she screams into the mic for her party of four. "WE ARE— NOT QUITE LIGHT POLLUTION. BUT SOMETHING TOTALLY BETTER THAN THAT." She pauses to let us laugh, and in that moment, someone unexpected slips in. The pause lasts longer than expected.

I follow her eyes to find Yasmin hovering at the entrance. Her arms are crossed, and she's watching the stage with an unreadable expression. My chest clenches. Suddenly, I feel like this is all some elaborate setup and in seconds, the stage, and the building, and all my tenuous relationships are going to crash and burn around me like leaves in a forest fire. But then Marissa glances my way. She holds my gaze for a moment.

Then she winks. And she starts again.

"LAS VEGAS. ARE YOU READY FOR SOMETHING NEW?"

"Yes!" The four of us yell out the word as Yasmin smiles, but Marissa's not satisfied. She shakes her head and does a little dance, bouncing in a circle until she faces us again.

"No, no. I said," she yells, "ARE YOU READY FOR SOME-THING NEW?"

We scream again—even Emmanuel cups his hands around his mouth. Yasmin stays where she is, but she catches my eye. She nods.

"LAS VEGAS," Marissa shouts this time, "LET'S GO!"

Lonnie taps their drumsticks against each other in the air—*onetwothree*—and the room bursts into music, loud, and full, and furious. We scream along, our throats raw. I've never heard the band sound like this. Different, yes, but also better than anything they've ever been before.

ACKNOWLEDGMENTS

Wow. Have I seriously written an entire book? Teenage me would be in awe—so thanks, you, for never giving up. And then I'll thank Anthony, Jose, and Raquel for reading countless stories of mine over the last eighteen or so years, and being with me in the trenches of junior high, high school, and beyond. You three are my heart, and I adore you.

Love and gratitude endlessly to my international spy, who inspires me day in and day out to look at this world with wonder, hope, and possibility. Without you, I don't imagine. You are the light that keeps the days warm and welcoming.

Thank you, especially, to Asha and Raquel—you know why.

Thank you, Mom. Yes you get your own line, and yes, yes, I know: "I told you so!" I always listen to you, even if you think I don't! Thank you for being my constant cheerleader.

Thank you to my sisters, for your love, support, and solidarity in being rhythmless weirdos with a deep love of Sailor Moon. And thanks Daddy for making us that way.

Gracias a Rosa por tu amor y armadura.

Thank you to Kwame, Ariel, and Margaret—the three of you changed my life, and I am so thankful to have shared part of my story with you.

And to Jesse, for everything.

Many thanks to Quressa, my fantastic agent, for seeing the possibility of this story and helping it shine; and thank you to Foyinsi for being the most incredible, astute, enthusiastic, patient, thoughtful, and kind editor I could possibly ask for. I'm so happy this story found its way to you.

Thanks, of course, to the team at Feiwel and Friends for your support and making such a gorgeous book!

And thank you Sherlock. You are the best boy.

Thank you for reading this Feiwel & Friends book. The friends who made *And Other Mistakes* possible are:

★ ★ ★

Jean Feiwel, Publisher
Liz Szabla, Associate Publisher
Rich Deas, Senior Creative Director
Holly West, Senior Editor
Anna Roberto, Senior Editor
Kat Brzozowski, Senior Editor
Dawn Ryan, Executive Managing Editor
Kim Waymer, Senior Production Manager
Emily Settle, Editor
Rachel Diebel, Editor
Foyinsi Adegbonmire, Associate Editor
Brittany Groves, Assistant Editor
Kathleen Breitenfeld, Designer
Arik Hardin, Assistant Managing Editor

★ ★ ★

Follow us on Facebook or visit us online at mackids.com.
Our books are friends for life.